Captivate

Also by Carrie Jones
Need

Captivate

Carrie Jones

BLOOMSBURY

NEW YORK BERLIN LONDON

Published by Bloomsbury U.S.A. Children's Books
175 Fifth Avenue, New York, New York 10010

Library of Congress Cataloging-in-Publication Data
Jones, Carrie.
Captivate / by Carrie Jones.— 1st U.S. ed.
p.   cm.
Summary: High school junior Zara and her friends continue to
try to contain the pixies that threaten their small Maine town, but when
a Valkyrie takes Zara's boyfriend, Nick, to Valhalla, the only way to save
him is to trust a pixie king, Astley.
ISBN 978-1-59990-342-2
[1. Supernatural—Fiction. 2. Pixies—Fiction. 3. Metamorphosis—
Fiction. 4. Valkyries (Norse mythology)—Fiction. 5. Kings, queens,
rulers, etc.—Fiction. 6. Maine—Fiction.] I. Title.
PZ7.J6817Cap 2010   [Fic]—dc22   2009031363

First U.S. Edition January 2010
Book design by Nicole Gastonguay
Typeset by Westchester Book Composition
Printed in the U.S.A. by Quebecor World Fairfield, Pennsylvania
2 4 6 8 10 9 7 5 3 1

To Don Radovich, because he is so missed, very missed, and to Emily and my own John Wayne. Thank you both so much for being beyond great.

Captivate

Pixie Tip

Pixie kings leave a glitterlike dust behind. This is supposedly
part of their souls. I'm not sure if they actually have souls,
but I remain optimistic.

There are these bizarre people who actually like physical educa-
tion class. You expect these people to grunt a lot and enjoy the
great art of sweating. You expect them to wear designer PE gear
and yell stuff like, "Dude, we are going to rock this freaking vol-
leyball court." While I don't do any of those things, I swear I am
still one of those bizarre PE-loving people.

That's because Nick is in PE. But even with the cute Nick fac-
tor, I am not super psyched about being in the freezing-cold gym
learning the rules of Ping-Pong today. I'm too busy being worried.

Coach Walsh has gathered us in a half circle around him and
already gone through his whole hand-eye coordination speech
and talked about the intricate rules of serving. I'm huddled up
next to my best friend, Issie, for warmth. My teeth chatter. Coach
Walsh is almost done with his whole speechifying bit but Nick is
still not here. I want to not worry about him. I just want him to be
safe. I squish even closer to little Issie, like she could make me feel

better. Nick could be broken and mauled somewhere out in the woods. He could be bleeding and dying. He could be . . .

I grab Issie's tiny arm and whisper, "Where is he?"

"He's just running late." She bounces on her toes and tries to be reassuring. She does not pull away. Issie is cool like that. She's okay with human contact. "He's fine. Every time any of us are late you imagine we're dead. You are no longer allowed to imagine anyone is dead."

"I'm not imagining he's dead," I whisper, but I'm totally imagining him bleeding to death on the snowy forest floor. Crows circle above him. A pixie arrow juts out of his beautiful chest. It's the same thing I imagined about Devyn last week when he forgot to check in.

"You are such a liar-liar pants-on-fire." Is kisses my cheek in her sweet friend way. "But I love you."

"I just worry about people," I whisper back. "If I'm not the one out there I feel so helpless."

Coach Walsh notices we're talking. "Girls, pay attention. And no kissing."

Everyone starts snickering. I let go of Issie's goose-bump-covered arm. My face gets hot, which means I'm in insane blush mode. Nick thinks insane blush mode is cute. I bend down and check on my ankle bracelet that Nick gave me. It's gold and thin-chained. A tiny dolphin dangles off of it. The dolphin reminds me of Charleston because they swim right off the Battery. Next to it dangles a heart, which just reminds me of love—corny but true. I'm so afraid of losing the anklet, but I can't take it off. I adore it that much.

"I'd pay for more kissing," some jerk yells. I should know his name but I still don't know everyone's yet. I haven't been here long enough and I'm not the best with names.

From his wheelchair Devyn power points at the guy, who probably outweighs him by a hundred pounds. Coach just gets this wicked twinkle in his eye, then ignores all of us and starts putting people in groups. Issie and Devyn and I clump together in the middle of the shiny gym floor. I drag the toe of my running shoe across it and straighten my shorts.

"Where is he?" I ask in a regular voice since Coach Walsh has moved away.

Devyn's eyes stay calm. He is the most mellow of us, the most analytical, and the least likely to panic, which is part of the reason Issie unofficially loves him. "He's just patrolling, Zara. I'm sure he'll be here in a sec. He probably just got held up."

I mutter, "He shouldn't go out alone."

"You can't tell him that." Devyn stretches his arms high above his head like he's stretching out his wings. Even in a wheelchair he takes up a lot of space, moves a lot, seems like he's going to fly away. "He's compelled to go out alone. It's his nature."

"I know," I murmur. Lately Devyn's been telling me a lot about what is and what isn't Nick's nature. Nick shifts into a wolf. Wolves are . . . well, they hunt but they also protect. They sleep in huddled masses. They take care of their own. They are not like humans.

Devyn stops stretching. "It's just not in the DNA."

"Goes against the whole hero-complex thing you guys have," Issie agrees. She bounces up and down, touches her toes. Her bunny T-shirt rides up a little in the back, exposing her bright orange underwear. "Isn't that a helpful hint for the guide? 'When dealing with pixies do not have a hero complex.'"

Devyn and I have started writing this guide. We call it *How to Survive a Pixie Attack*, which is a total takeoff from the zombie thing, but we figure it's important to give people some helpful tips in case we ever go public someday. Truthfully, we'll probably just post it anonymously on the Internet. A couple of months ago we didn't know pixies even existed. Now it feels like capturing pixies is all we do.

"I'll add it," Devyn says, and his attention shifts. There's movement at the door. Cold air rushes in. Winter in Maine is not fun.

Nick saunters into the gym and my heart basically stops. He's ridiculously cute in his PE shorts and dark green T-shirt; and people that good-looking seem vulnerable, almost like they can't be real.

He's real, though. He's all dark skin and dark hair and dark eyes. Okay. His eyebrows, like Devyn's nose, are a little big and if you stare at him long enough you realize that his lips are a bit lopsided. I have kissed his lips. I have felt his breath in my ear and I know without a doubt that he's real, even if he is a werewolf. The massive muscles in his legs redefine themselves as he walks toward me. He waves a late pass at the coach and yells, "Sorry I'm late. I've got a pass."

"Not a problem, buddy," Coach yells back. He and Nick are all jock bonding.

Nick pockets the note, which is probably a fake. I can smell his deodorant even though he's still far away. There are these things called pheromones, odors that guys give off to attract women. I swear his pheromones have my freaking name written on them. They hone in and attack.

"You are getting all swoony faced," Issie tells me with her sing-song voice. She pokes me in the ribs with her elbow, gently. She turns to Devyn, who is smiling like a crazy man, just hanging back in his wheelchair watching the scene. "Dev. Look at Zara. She's got her lovey-dovey look on."

As Is gazes at Devyn with her own lovey-dovey look, he says, "Yeah. Teen love. So obvious. So hormonal."

"I am not hormonal." I fake glare at him.

He just laughs. Cassidy, this girl Dev supposedly dated back in fourth grade, waves to him. He smiles and waves back. Issie stiffens and I'm about to tell her Cassidy is no competition when Nick sidles up to us. He wraps his arm around my shoulder, pulling me against his side. I instinctively lean into his solid chest. I can't help it. I breathe in his pheromones and get almost dizzy. He's all woods and clean air and warmth. He kisses the top of my head.

"People! No PDA!" Coach Walsh heads over to us. He's got four Ping-Pong paddles and a pack of balls.

Nick's fingers tighten around mine for a second and then he lets me go.

"You four," Coach barks. "Table tennis. Far table. You can handle that, Devyn?"

Devyn nods and reaches for his canes. Just a month ago Devyn couldn't really stand. Now he's walking a little bit. Doctors say it's a miracle. We know better. Devyn, like Nick, isn't quite human. He's a shifter. He can change into an animal form—an eagle—and that makes him heal faster, heal better. What would've paralyzed a normal human? He's beating it. Still, he can't hide how impatient he is with the whole thing. Sometimes his lips shake because he's so frustrated.

Is hands me a paddle and whispers, "He used to rock at Ping-Pong."

I smile. "How does someone rock at Ping-Pong?"

"Just watch," she says knowingly and gives Nick another paddle.

"It's the bird in him," Nick explains. "Crazy hand-eye coordination."

"Are you bragging about me?" Dev asks. He's got the paddle in the proper handshake position Coach Walsh drilled into us the other day.

"Yeah." Is gets all fluttery and eyelashy. "We are."

"It's not really about the hand-eye, it's about knowing where the ball is going, where you want the ball to go," Devyn explains. "It's like life. It's all about purpose and direction. You can't worry about it. You have to plan and predict and react."

I swear Issie almost swoons.

"I've been doing some research about how pixies play into Norse myths," he says. "It's interesting stuff. Very obscure, though."

"You going to inform us?" Nick serves.

Dev volleys back. "Not quite yet. Zara, I'm thinking about a chapter in the book, though, on the mythology. Is that kosher with you?"

"Yep." I twirl my paddle in my hand and flick some lint off my vintage U2 T-shirt.

Nick hits the ball again. Dev volleys. The little fluorescent orange ball flies back and forth so fast I can't really see it; just hear the *click-pop* of it on the hard table when it makes contact. I step away. So does Issie. The guys don't even notice.

"So why were you late?" I ask.

"Patrolling." Nick's wrist flicks the ball back toward Devyn. Devyn counters.

"We know that, Macho One," Issie says. She hunkers down low at the table like she's actually going to get a chance to hit a ball. "But you're late."

We are all staring at him. Nick looks away.

"I had a little encounter," Nick finally says. His forehead crinkles.

Devyn misses the ball. It skitters off the table and to the side. Issie runs to retrieve it, but it bounces and lobs under the other tables and keeps rolling across the shiny gym floor.

I push the hair out of my face so I can really examine him. He's still all there. He is not dead. I ask, "Are you okay?"

Nick meets my gaze and he lifts his arms wide like I should inspect him. "Of course."

Issie brings back the ball and hands it to Dev to serve, although it's not technically his serve because he lost the volley.

"Cassidy sent you a note," she says, her voice losing all its happy.

"Thanks." Devyn pockets it, adjusts his canes, and leans forward a little but still serves the ball perfectly in a diagonal across the table. It bounces in front of me, but I don't even really register it until Nick hits it for me. It bounces back to the other side. Issie crosses her arms in front of her chest and looks at the floor. She's terrified that Dev might like Cassidy. She is really nice and everything, but totally not made of awesome the way Issie is.

"What are you guys talking about?" she asks.

"What made me late. It was a pixie," Nick says. "I took care of it."

Nick hits the ball a little too hard and it flashes over the table and hits the wall on the opposite side of the gym near Cassidy.

"I think I'll let that one go," Is says.

"You met up with a pixie and you didn't call," I say, my voice squeaking with frustration. "You didn't call for help?"

Nick says all calm and easy, "It was too quick, baby."

"Don't 'baby' me," I say jokingly but not really. "You know

the rules. You call for help if you're going to be late. That's the rule for everyone, not just you. We're all in danger here."

"Uh-oh," Is murmurs. "Maybe I *will* go get that ball. Or else I might go all teacher on you about how men use the term 'baby' in a negative way because they can't deal with the empowering nature of birth and are jealous. Oops! I started already. Be right back."

"Is has some major conflict-avoidance issues," Devyn says, like we don't already know.

"I didn't need help," Nick says, ignoring them both. He turns to face me again. His eyes are kind but his voice doesn't lose the serious tone. "There wasn't any time."

"There is always time," I insist. "It takes two seconds to send a text."

Is returns with the ball. "Conflict all done?"

I nod but it's not totally true. Nick has to stop taking unnecessary risks and I have to make him see that, but now is not the time. We're in PE. Seriously. I bump Nick's hip with my own before we get back in our proper Ping-Pong positions. "I win this argument."

"Conflict all done," Devyn assures her.

She smiles at him. "I serve." She misses the ball. "Oops. You serve."

Devyn does. I go to hit it but Nick takes it instead.

"Sorry," he murmurs.

I roll my eyes at the irony as he and Devyn take over the game again. I try to follow where the ball is going, but I can't predict its direction, let alone make it go where I want it to. I can't stop myself from adding softly, "You're always acting so hero and you're going to get hurt."

Nick stops and looks at me. "You were in class. I had study hall," he says gently.

"Still, the protocol is that you spot one, you call for backup," Issie says. "Not to fight or anything, but that is the protocol. Wow, I love that word."

Dev came up with that term. Not that it matters. What matters is that we're rounding up any stray pixies that head into our area. We take them and put them in a large house that we've surrounded with iron. The house is in the woods and hidden by a glamour, which is like a magic spell that prevents people from seeing what's really there. I am not really cool with trapping them like that, but I don't know how else to do it. They were dangerous. They were killing boys until we stopped them. They had these needs—and those needs? They were out of control because their king was out of control. Pixie society is kind of hierarchical like that. The king and most of his local people are still trapped there, but every once in a while another pixie comes from far away.

We don't know why.

We just know we have to stop them too.

Pixie Tip

Pixies do not look like Tinker Bell. Although they occasionally wear tutus. Seriously, who doesn't?

Instead of getting real lunch in the cafeteria, Devyn and I grab some bagels and head into the library to do some research. I wave to the librarian, whose name I can never remember, which is just so wrong of me because she is super nice, and then we set up our laptops on one of the polished wood tables. The wood is so light it's almost yellow. Devyn clunks his head on it when he plugs his computer's power cord into the outlet.

"Ouch." He drops the cord.

I grab it. "Here, let me."

Little sparks of electricity flutter out and Devyn says, "Thanks."

"Not a problem."

The library is half full of people. Nobody's whispering, but yelling is against the rules. There is a bunch of girls around one girl's computer, giggling. The computer clicks. They are taking photos, I think. Some guy with dark clothes is bent over his screen. Two other guys are typing frantically away on their screens but I don't know what they're working on or playing. Dev and I are here to do research for our pixie book. It isn't easy. Most of the stuff on the Web is about Tinker Bell and this old indie rock group from Boston.

"Why are all my hits about cats and rock bands?" I ask.

"Be patient."

I try another site and scan it. "Okay, patience has shown me that this site is about a woman who is trying to get a PhD and wants to retire to Scotland and has a thing for cartoony images of women working while wearing short skirts."

Devyn's eyes light up. "Let me see that. Maybe she actually is one."

"I doubt it."

"You don't know." He pokes his head out from around his screen and pulls apart a bagel.

In the last month we've checked out about twenty blogs that have to do with pixies. None of them have been actual pixies. Most of them have been people who really like fantasy novels, which is cool, but not what we need. "I am just tired of this. I want to do something. Be more proactive."

He pauses before he sticks the bagel in his mouth. "Research is proactive."

I snort. I can't help it. "And so is patrolling."

My phone vibrates. I smile. I can't help that either.

"Nick?" Devyn asks. "It's been how long since he's seen you? Five minutes."

"Five minutes," I announce as I press the button that retrieves the message, "is a very long time."

He actually rolls his eyes. "What's it say, 'I love you, baby'?"

"Shut up. It says, 'Meet me by poetry.'" I bounce up, searching. "He's in here."

Devyn starts laughing. "You're blowing me off, aren't you?"

11

"Yep," I say, trying to remember where the poetry books are. "You're a better researcher than I am anyway."

"Not true."

I start walking toward the far back wall and then hustle back, lean over the desk, and whisper, "Look up pixie invasion. There's far too many of them right now. It's not normal."

"Good idea."

I fast-walk past the circulation desk, where the librarian is talking about source citation or something, and duck down one of the rows of Fiction Ca–Cz. Then I make a right. There are a lot of stacks in here. They reach the ceiling. Sometimes you have to use a step stool. It's an amazing library for a high school actually, and I think—but I'm not sure—that poetry books are at the very end in the far left corner.

My phone vibrates again. I check the message: You coming?

I respond: Yes, impatient one.

The library smells like old and new books, coffee, and bagels. The light shafts in through some evenly spaced windows and it's that perfect golden kind of light that makes everything seem like a big, happy glow. I step around the corner.

Nick smiles at me. He's leaning against a big gray radiator. His thick black sweater rubs against the wall. For a second I want to be the wall. Okay, it's longer than a second.

"Hey," he says.

"Hey." I smile back. "I thought you were blowing off lunch to go out patrolling with Issie."

"I lied." He squats down and picks up a small black backpack that I don't recognize. He pulls out a beach towel and starts laying it on the floor.

"Here, let me help." I grab at a bright blue towel that has a wave design on it. Our fingers meet. We get a shock but neither of us twitches away.

"Static electricity," he murmurs. His mouth moves when he says it. It moves slowly, like he's kissing me. His mouth is long lines of good. I lean forward. He holds up a finger. "One second. Sit on the towel, baby."

"Bossy." But I sit down anyway.

"You are just as bossy."

"True," I concede.

He laughs and pulls out a big Ziploc bag of something dark and round. Cookies!

I lunge forward. "Are these—?"

"Chocolate with peanut butter chips," he finishes for me.

I keep staring at his lips, but I slide open the baggie. "I love these! My mom always made these."

"I know."

"How do you know?"

"You told me once."

He sits down with me and before I can get too heart fluttery he pulls out a cookie and lifts it toward my mouth, teasing me. "Do you want it?"

I open my lips. He slides the cookie in a little bit. I chomp down. It melts on my tongue. "It is sooo good."

He laughs and leans back. He whispers, "You know we're not supposed to eat back here."

I swallow. "We are totally naughty."

"Absolutely." He bites into my cookie. "So there's this annual dance in a couple weeks."

"The Winter Ball," I interrupt. "There have been signs up everywhere."

"You want to go?"

I think about it for a half second. "Will you dress up?"

He nods.

I move forward so my hands are flat on the towel and my face is much closer to his face. Something inside my chest warms up like a nice kind of heartburn and I say, "And will we slow dance?"

He nods again. His bottom lip turns in toward his mouth for a second, just disappears and then comes back.

Stretching out my spine so my lips are nearly touching his I say, "And will you press yourself against me and we'll move really close together and then your hand will stretch out across the back of my head and your fingers will wrap into my hair and then . . ."

He doesn't nod. He just tilts his head down, moves his fingers into my hair, and his lips touch mine in a forever kiss. His lips are soft and hard all at once. His breath mixes with my breath. Everything inside of me whooshes out. It's just him and me and books and cookies.

"Is that what you want?" he asks when we finally break away.

I breathe in deep and then lift my lips to his ear. "That's what I want."

"And if I promise you that will happen you'll go to the dance with me?"

I sit back on my heels. "That and if you promise not to go patrolling alone."

For a second he freezes, then he smiles and crosses his arms in front of him. "You are a pain, a royal pain in the—"

"But that's why you love me, right?"

He tosses another cookie at me. "That and because you give me an excuse to make cookies."

I catch the cookie in my left hand. "Good reasons. And do you want to know why I love you?"

"Because I am a fantastic cookie maker?" He breaks his cookie in half and puts it in his mouth.

"That's part of it," I admit. I nibble on my own cookie. I swallow. "But not all of it."

A crumb falls onto his jeans. I brush it off for him as he says, "You're making me wait for it, aren't you?"

"Okay. I won't torment you." I cross my legs and smile at him. "I love you for the way you care about everyone, for how stubborn you are, for how you love Issie and Devyn."

He leans down and kisses my forehead and then each of my eyelids. They are tender, these kisses. They are light and true. "I love you too, Zara."

"I am so, so glad," I sigh out. And I am.

The rest of the day is pretty uneventful. Nick works at the hospital after school and Issie and Devyn are at French Club, so I go running by myself. We're allowed to run outside again because boys are no longer going missing. The school had stopped outdoor track practice for a while because Jay Dahlberg and the Beardsley boy were abducted by pixies. Nobody knew that it was pixies, they just knew boys were disappearing from the woods. Even now, only a few of us know what actually happened; everyone else thinks it was a serial killer.

Each time my foot hits the ground I hear my stepdad's laugh. But running on snow, even hard-packed Maine snow that's been flattened by snowmobiles, is just not as cool as running the streets of Charleston, my hometown, where it's warm and smells like flowers, even in the winter.

Bedford is nothing like Charleston. My mom sent me up here because I couldn't deal with my stepdad's death. It was hard to get adjusted. There are about six thousand year-round residents here and the ocean is a cold menace that roars beyond the peninsula. Everything is trees and dirt and cold, at least in winter. I've never seen it in spring. Right now the bare branches of trees look like drowning arms reaching up for help. I stare and stare at the bark and see the shapes of spirits there. The dark knots where limbs used to be remind me of screaming mouths.

Still, I zip past the trees that line the track, swerve up the hill behind Bedford Building Supply, and keep following the trail. I'm thinking about how Devyn better not like Cassidy because he and Issie are so meant to be together. I'm thinking about how everyone in the universe seems to know this except Devyn. And that's when I hear it. The sound is muffled but it's definitely human.

Mrphh . . .

Little spider feelings prickle along my skin.

"Crud."

I stop. I listen. I pull out my cell phone, punch in 9-1-1 but don't hit Send. Because, seriously? What would I say?

Hi, operator/dispatcher person. This is Zara. I'm by the railroad tracks just past BBS and I think I hear something and I've got this prickly skin feeling. It's like, um, well . . . I think it means the pixie king is nearby.

But that can't be true. Because the pixie king is trapped in a house on the other side of town, which means . . .

"I'm imagining things," I announce.

Mmrph. Mrupph.

The sound is off to the left. My head jerks up. I scan the wood for tracks. There are no tracks. No footprints at least, but something catches my eye. I squat down and touch the snow. There's dust, just a tiny bit of it. It glitters.

Okay. Not imagining things.

Pixie kings leave gold glitter in their wake. Regular pixies? Not so much.

The wind blows through the naked tree branches. One of them creaks like the pressure is just too much and it wants to break right off and plummet to the earth. I know that feeling.

Mrmph!

The sound is urgent and I know what it is. It's a voice. It's a muffled voice, which means that someone is probably in trouble. I press my speed dial for Nick. He's at work so he doesn't pick up. Cell phones aren't allowed at the hospital. Right. Duh. His voice mail comes on.

"Hey, Nick. It's me," I whisper, turning slowly in a circle, looking for predators. "I'm near BBS by the tracks, running. I think . . . I hear something. Okay. Yeah. I'm going to check it out. If I don't call again, I'm probably dead or something. Yeah. Right. Bye."

Mrmph.

I slink forward across the crunchy whiteness, cautious, looking up into the branches of the trees to make sure nothing is waiting to jump down and attack. It's paranoid, I know, but a lack of paranoia can be hazardous to your health. I start thinking about phobias. It's my thing. I chant them to make me less nervous.

Albuminurophobia, fear of kidney disease.

Philemaphobia or philematophobia, fear of kissing.

Genuphobia, fear of knees.

It's not helping. I'm in about twenty feet when I spot the source of the noise. It's a guy. He's tied up to a big spruce tree. He's blond. There's duct tape over his mouth, and barbed wire wrapped around his body. The only thing that's keeping him upright is the wire and what's left of his will, I guess. The pixies have almost killed him.

Unless *he's* the pixie. Maybe he's the one Nick had the run-in with, but Nick wouldn't just tie him up and leave him here, would he?

The answer: maybe.

My stomach falls. The guy's eyes plead with me. He looks like he's about to die. Pixie or not, I run toward him. I rip off my gloves. They flop on the ground near his feet, a puddle of blackness by his leather boots. It starts snowing down on us, big heavy water-filled flakes the size of my thumb. I work on the wire, but it's so cold that it stings my skin. I jump back. My fingers curl up, protecting themselves.

"*Mrrphh . . . Mrr . . .* " His voice is desperate and matches the look in his green eyes. Somehow I know what he wants me to do.

I uncurl my fingers and reach up. "This might hurt."

I feel bad ripping the tape off him, but I do it. I get my nail around an edge and yank. It comes off in a big sticky rush.

"Put your gloves on and then untie me." His voice is low and has a slight accent that I don't recognize. Almost Irish. Almost not. "Please. She is coming for—"

"Was it pixies? Did they do this to you? I saw the glitter. Or are you the pixie? I need to know." Guilt rushes into me. I know they are evil but to see one so hurt, if he is one—okay, he probably is one, but it doesn't matter. "I need to know if you're still in danger."

Every word he speaks seems to take incredible effort. His lips move so slowly. "What? She is . . . I am not prepared to die."

"You won't die." I grab my gloves off the snow, shoving them on again. He's a pixie, I know it, but I can't just let him die. Something in my heart hitches for him. It would be awful to be here, tied to a tree, waiting to die. "If you promise not to hurt me, I promise I won't let you die."

"I am attempting not to, but if she comes, then—"

I'm yanking at the wire when his voice breaks off.

"Watch out!" he manages to yell.

I whirl around. A glove drops. The other is barely halfway on. A woman stands in front of me. She's tiny but beautiful, with long, flowing black hair and dark skin. I think I gasp.

"Please, do not let her take me," he whispers as I back up.

"I won't." I'm not sure how I'm going to keep that promise. There's something menacing about her. And yes, it might be because she has this armored breastplate thing over her dark green velvety dress, but it might be something else, like the scary-intense look in her eyes.

"You know I have to take you with me, warrior." Her voice is strong. Her eyes flash. She steps forward. Her hands are slender and delicate but they somehow look absolutely deadly.

I put up my own somewhat wimpy arms. "Hold on a second. Time-out. Okay?"

She smirks. "Are you attempting to stop me, little one?"

"Excuse me? Did you just call me 'little one'? What are you? Like, four feet tall?" I ask. My temper comes through, turning my voice a little bitter.

The guy behind me gasps. "Do not."

The woman just smiles and takes another step forward. "It is my sacred duty to take the fallen warriors with me."

"With you where?" I scoop up the glove and step back so I can start working on his wire again. I do it like I'm so casual, like my heart isn't beating eighteen hundred beats a minute or anything, like this woman doesn't have tiny little fangs sticking out on her lip.

"Valhalla."

I search my brain. Devyn's been telling me about myths, and

I think he mentioned that word before. The data doesn't totally compute and I go, "Valhalla? As in all that Norse myth stuff? It is Norse, right? The god Odin? Is that the one?"

She rushes forward. Claws form where fingers should be. One tips into the flesh of my cheek. It cuts my skin. Her eyes stare into mine, cold and harsh. Snowflakes land on her eyelashes.

"Do you dare speak his name, human?" she says, with all this confidence and menace. "You are puny and helpless against one such as he."

The prick of her claw seems to resonate all the way through me. It feels like something fundamental inside has shifted. Dizziness threatens but I struggle to keep it down and look away from her and stare instead at the captive guy. I keep working at the wire. It's a knot. I'm good with knots, though. I don't move my cheek away. I won't show fear. "Whose name? Odin?"

Finally the knot comes undone. I yank at the wire and the pixie guy falls forward. I leap and catch him. He struggles to stay upright, leaning into my side. Both my arms wrap around his chest. The snow crunches beneath us. The trees around us sway with the wind.

The woman hisses, then sniffs the air. The world is chill and gray and without color. She looks at me accusingly. "You are not human."

I struggle to keep the guy steady. "Of course I'm human."

Her eyes narrow a little bit. "No . . . not all." Her features form into a mask of disgust. "You are a halfling."

The guy gets a little bit rigid and starts to shake. Our feet shuffle in the snow as I try to keep him upright. I lean him a little against the hard, rumpled bark of the tree.

"Whatever." I pull in a deep breath, try to ignore the claws and the fangs, and think about the knife tucked into my sock. I'd have to drop the guy to get it out. My mind is working overtime trying to figure out how to be casual about it. I keep talking. "My point is that you can't take him."

She crosses her arms over her chest. "And why not?"

A pine cone tumbles onto the snow. It looks so strange with all its rough brown edges surrounded by bland whiteness. I try to think up an answer.

The guy speaks. "Because I am not fallen. I am still alive."

"Not for long." A wicked smile creeps over her features. Her tongue leaps out to capture a snowflake. The wind whistles through the tree limbs. We are so alone out here.

"Yes, for long." I glare at her. "I am going to get him proper medical care and he will be just fine."

"Proper medical care?" She snorts. "Do you know what he is, halfling? Gaze upon him."

"Do *not* call me halfling."

"You have no strength." She gets a look on her face that would rival a haughty supermodel who just landed a five-million-dollar contract. "You can barely support his weight."

She's right. The world waits in silence. An unbearable whiteness covers us as snow falls from a cloudy sky. I sniff. My nose is running. The pixie guy moans softly. The sound is filled with sadness and pain and despair. He is vulnerable. Pixie or not, he needs me.

I steel myself. "I'm not giving him up."

She lifts an eyebrow, as if she's pondering what the heck is going on. I'd like to ponder what the heck is going on too, but I'm busy trying to just keep standing. The cold sinks into my feet, into my bones.

She says, "There is a possibility that he may live now because you have interfered."

I wait.

"What we offer him is a reward, not a punishment," she soothes. "I swear this. After his death he will fight by Odin's side in the greatest battle of all."

His words stiffen out between his teeth, hard and fierce. "I am not ready to die. I have work here. I. Can. Not. Die."

Another pine cone lets go of a tree branch and falls from the sky. It hits me in the shoulder and then tumbles the rest of the way to the ground. Tiny ridges of it break off and stick to the snow, left behind. The wind blows hard and wicked against all of us. It is hard for me to hold us up, but the woman does not sway.

"I see." Feathers sprout from her back. Menace turns her eyes red. Her hair spirals out behind her, lifting in the wind. Instead of being beautiful, it's terrifying.

I stagger away a little. The guy's arm comes up around my waist, and even though he's barely capable of standing up it's pretty obvious he's trying to protect me from her. The wind ruffles his blond hair.

"I shall not hurt the little halfling," she says. That's when I realize that the feathers on her back are wings, graceful and glistening like a swan's, but jet black.

I don't know what to think of her. I don't know what to say or do. I just stand there shivering, from cold or fear or both.

"Your mouth hangs open," she says, almost smiling. "I shall let you keep this one because he may survive now that you are here. You will have to decide if that is a good thing or not, halfling."

I start to protest.

She holds out her hand. "Also, there will be other warriors soon. Death is coming. It is on the wind. Can you feel it?"

As she says it I think I can—a low menace, a waiting storm. The snow swirls around us. She nods her head at me and lifts up. Her swan wings spread out and she soars up into the air to meet the whiteness of the sky.

I stagger sideways and fall. The guy lands on top of me. He starts laughing, a soft, crazy, exhausted laugh. "Sorry. Sorry. Wow . . . wow . . . that was close. I thought—" He interrupts himself and starts laughing again. The movement makes him wince, then moan.

I pull myself out from underneath him, worried that he's totally insane. "Are you going to be okay?"

He shakes his head. Then he nods. A trembling hand, square and scratched, reaches up to rub where his hair touches his forehead. His eyes meet my eyes. His lips move. "Thank you."

Then he passes out.

Great.

Pixie Tip

Pixies are not good. They are evil. Not bad-hair-day evil, but scary-movie-that-still-freaks-you-out-when-you-go-to-bed evil. Actually? Way worse.

The wind blows hard and awful. Seconds stretch into two or three minutes. I have to do something intelligent, something that doesn't involve just staring at a guy who is passed out on the snow. He's youngish, probably just a couple years older than me—if that's how pixies age. I have no idea. He's not wearing a coat, just a dark Irish sweater and jeans. He must be freezing.

I look up into the white sky searching for the woman. Snowflakes drop into my eyes, instantly melting. She's vanished. Blinking the water away, I check the guy for major wounds, big bleeding ones. I find a whopper: a massive bite mark on his stomach. The flesh is jagged and torn. It oozes blood that's a deep bluish red, maybe because it's mixed with the dark fibers of his sweater, or maybe that's how pixies bleed or something. I don't know.

Another second flips by and his eyes start to flicker open.

There's nothing to wrap the wound with except my outer coat so I whip it off and wrap it around his stomach. I tie the arms and try to apply pressure. The smell of blood is coppery and metallic.

Flipping open my phone, I press my grandmother's cell number. She's good with the massive-wound thing. She's not just an EMT, she's a weretiger. Weird, I know. The phone rings once. His hand clamps over mine and the phone disconnects.

"What are you doing?" I say, anger rippling through me. "I'm calling for help."

"No. No help." His lips are parched. "Have to hide. Until I heal."

"You're speaking in sentence fragments," I explain, "and that means you are not in a position to make this decision."

He shakes his head. "Please. No one else can know I am here. Kill me—while I'm weak."

The phone starts ringing. It's Gram calling back. I start to run my hand in my hair but forget it's all bloody. "I don't think that's a good idea."

"Please."

"I can't let you die."

He coughs out a bitter laugh. "If I was about to die Thruth would have taken me."

"Thruth?"

"The Valkyrie."

My phone stops ringing.

"Oh. Yeah." I swallow hard. "I have no idea what a Valkyrie is."

He raises one eyebrow and sniffs. "You are pixie, are you not?"

"No . . .," I start to say, pressing my hand against his wound. He moans, but still manages to give me a look. "Okay. I am half pixie. Does that hurt?"

"Some." He cringes more like it's a lot. "You are half pixie. It is true—"

He loses his sentence to a moan and I suddenly feel really badly for him. "I'm sorry. I'm so sorry I'm snapping. I don't want to be mean. I'm not a mean person. But we need to get you out of here. You're hurt. I need to get you fixed up. I need to bring you to the hospital or something."

He groans. "Not the hospital. My room."

"You should go to a hospital," I insist.

"They cannot treat me." He pulls himself into a standing position. Snow covers his dark jeans. "I need you for balance. Is that all right?"

"It's okay," I say as he drapes his arm over my shoulder. I get my arm around his waist. He is much lighter than Nick, which is a very good thing. We start a sort of quasi shuffle through the woods. He coughs like a seal and stumbles a bit. My heart kind of breaks for him. "Don't worry. My car's not too far."

He nods and murmurs something. Beads of sweat drip down his forehead. The wind picks up a little bit. The snow keeps trundling down, covering us, sticking in our hair, erasing our footprints. It's a long haul, but I get him to the parking lot, which, thankfully, is nearly empty. He seems to be regaining a bit of strength.

"I have to take you to a hospital," I insist.

"It will kill me."

I lurch backward. "I know you aren't human. Are you a normal one, though, or a king?"

He shakes his head. "No more questions, please."

"Are you a king?" I ask again.

"I said—"

"I know what you said, but that doesn't mean I have to do what you say." I swallow hard. "We have a place to put pixies."

His eyes whip up and meet mine. "The rumor is true?"

"What rumor?"

"Someone has been trapping us."

I don't answer. Cold fills my nose, crystallizing it. I hit the key fob and unlock my Subaru. It beeps.

"That is barbaric," he snarls.

I don't completely disagree. We hobble closer to my car, Yoko, which is parked next to a big black truck, the standard motor vehicle of Bedford High School's male population. I try to explain. "They were killing people. They were torturing guys."

"Because their king was weak." He shakes his head and coughs. "If I were not injured I would force you to bring me to them now."

I state the obvious. "Well, you *are* injured."

His eyebrows lower and his pupils focus on me for a second. Then he scans my face. "Your skin is tinting blue."

"It's cold," I sputter.

He smirks and I resist the urge to scream. I have no idea what to do with him now. I mean, he's hurt, but he's a pixie. He's a hurt pixie, possibly a king. This is so not good. This is beyond bad, really. I blurt out, "I'm going to take you there to the house."

"You must not." His voices goes panicky and high. His face contorts in pain and he steadies himself. His hand clutches my wrist. "I cannot go there in this state."

I twist my wrist away and open the passenger side door of my car. "I can't let you kill people."

He grabs my arm, higher this time. "I do not kill people. Just enemies. I am under control. I swear it. Not all pixies—not all of us—are like the ones here. You cannot judge all of us by your experience with a few. It is unfair."

That hits home. Something inside me weirds up again. The world dizzies out. I must be getting the flu. I force myself to focus. "Who bit you?"

"What?" His eyes scan me, searching.

"Who. Bit. You?"

His mouth hardens. "A wolf."

I was right but the rightness of my assumption does not make me feel any less sick. The pixie guy watches my face looking for a reaction. I try really hard to make my face calm. "A wolf, huh?"

"You know him." It is a statement, not a question. His grip on my arm tightens and it's pretty strong even though he's wounded.

"Yeah, right. I know a wolf. We hang and get pizza and I brush out his fur. Of course I don't *know* a wolf," I snark. "Get in the car."

He cringes when he gets in the passenger seat. I'm not sure if it's because it hurts or because the car is made out of steel and iron. Pixies are no good with steel and iron. For a second I ponder the point of the seat belt. It would go right over his wound. I bypass the idea and start to shut the door. "Watch your feet."

He does.

After I shut his door, I head around to the other side of Yoko and check my watch. I should be able to get him to the pixie house and be back before Issie gets done with French, but something inside me hitches. I don't know if he deserves to be there. I don't know if he's ever done anything wrong. What's his crime, really? All I know is that he was born a pixie. Am I condemning an entire race just because of what happened here? Are they really not all super creepy and insane bad guys?

I open my door.

Nick would not have any doubts, obviously. There wouldn't be a wound across this guy's stomach if he had any doubts. Nick's a little more black-and-white when he looks at stuff like good and evil. Me? I'm into the gray areas. That's not a bad thing. It's just different.

I sit down and buckle myself in. I glance over at the pixie guy. He's leaning back in the seat. His mouth's a little open. His eyes are closed. He must hurt so much.

"I'm sorry you're hurt," I start to say. I must be getting dehydrated, because I'm dizzy. I put the key in the ignition to start Yoko up, turning and looking over my right shoulder so I can back out of the spot. "I mean, it's not cool that you're hurt, especially if you really are—"

Something flashes in the corner of my eye and a hand locks on my shoulder. The world suddenly goes dark.

Pixie Tip

Despite folklore, pixies do *not* prefer to be naked. Fortunately they wear clothes. This prevents a lot of indecent exposure charges and frostbite.

When I wake up I'm alone in the car and Issie is banging on the window. The hair that's not tucked underneath her rainbow-striped hat flies all around in the wind.

"Zara!" Is yells. Her little fist thumps hard against the glass. "Zara! Unlock the door!"

I unlock the door.

"Devyn! Hurry up!" Is yanks the door open and leans in. She's almost crawling on top of me. "Oh my gosh, are you okay? Are you okay? I thought you were dead!"

"I'm not dead," I manage to say, wiping a hand across my eyes. "I feel dead though. Groggy."

"This is not a good place to sleep! Oh my gosh, I totally don't want to disempower you or your choices but this is dangerous, Zara. Your car is halfway out of the space, but the engine is off," Is rushes out. Her eyes are frantic bunny big.

"He must have shut the engine off," I say, still trying to get a grip on what's happened.

"Your skin looks funny. Bluish almost. Wait. He? Who is *he*? Nick?" She gets close to my nose. Cold air rushes in the open door as she stares into my eyes.

I've been slumped across the front seat and there's an embarrassing drool spot on the dark gray upholstery. I pull myself up into a sitting position. "Oh, that damn pixie guy."

Is gasps. "What did you say?"

He must have knocked me out somehow. I don't know how. I touch my shoulder, but there's nothing there. No pain spots. No blood. There's a smear of blood on the passenger door handle, but that's it. That's the only sign someone was here.

Devyn appears with Cassidy standing behind him. Her mittened hand rests on his wheelchair like she owns it. His face staggers into worry. "Zara? What's happened?"

I give him big eyes and glance at Cassidy's concerned face. Her braids swing in the wind. "Nothing. I—I just fell asleep, and, uh—"

"She hit the parking brake. The car rolled." Issie covers for me.

Cassidy's eyes narrow. She's good-looking and dark. She's a lot taller than Is, a lot more glamorous too, and, it seems, a lot more savvy. "We aren't on an incline."

"Oh, you know gravity!" Issie blunders. "It's always pulling on you, right?"

She elbows Devyn in the shoulder so hard that his wheelchair skitters to the side. Cassidy catches it. He makes eye contact with her and says, "Thanks."

Things seem to go all slow-motion then and I don't know if it's because I'm a little woozy or if it's because of Issie. She gazes at Devyn. Devyn's still looking at Cassidy. Cassidy's smiling down at him adoringly. Crap.

31

"Are you sure nothing happened to you, Zara?" Devyn asks, once he's managed to look back at us. It's obvious that each of his words carries a double meaning. There's no way I can tell him the truth, though, not with Cassidy right here.

So I use the code we've developed. "I've been tinked."

"What's tinked?" Cassidy asks. She tugs at the end of her coat sleeve.

For a second none of us say anything. "Tinked" is the code word for "Tinker Bell," which is the code name for "surprise pixie interaction."

Devyn lies authoritatively with that professorial voice of his. "Tired. Fried. Frazzled. A state of extreme exhaustion."

Cassidy smiles at him. "Oh. I am always tinked after Mr. Burns's tests. You too, Zara? That man is evil. I thought bio was supposed to be fun."

I nod a little too aggressively, because the world gets woozy again. Issie leans forward. "You almost look blue, Zara. You're more pale than normal."

"Yeah," I manage to say, "that test killed me."

For a second everyone is silent and awkward. Cassidy takes charge, scratches at her jeans. Then she says, "Well, Devyn, you ready to go?"

"I'm—uh—" He fidgets with the folder in his lap. It's the book we're working on. "Yeah. Cassidy's driving me home."

"Sheesh, dude. You make it sound like an apology." Cassidy stretches her long arms above her head. She fixes her long purple scarf and gives Issie a weird, probing look. Then she itches at the skin the scarf just touched and jokes, "Is driving home with me so awful?"

"No," he bumbles. "I didn't mean—I didn't mean that."

He is not looking at Issie. Her face is one ball of crushed. For a second I forget about the pixie guy. Issie's hurt wipes out everything else.

"Call me later, Zara," he yells as he and Cassidy head toward her car.

Issie slams into the passenger seat of my car. "Are you okay to drive?"

"Yep."

"Then drive," she orders. "As fast as legally possible so we can get away from here."

I turn Yoko on, steer back into the travel lane of the parking lot, and drive over something that crinkle crushes with a horrible noise as the tire moves over it. I poke open the door and peek. It's an abandoned Coke can, flattened now. I shut the door and as soon as the car is positioned forward I reach over and brush the hair out of Issie's face.

"Is, you want to . . . ?" I start.

"No. We are not going to talk about it. My lack of a love—whatever—is not important. What's important is that you were passed out in the car. So talk. Talk now." She pulls her arms in front of her chest.

"But—"

"Seriously, Zara, just tell me what happened."

I do.

Right after I've dropped Issie off Devyn calls, demanding to know what's going on.

"It's hard to explain on the phone," I tell him. "Can I just come over?"

Then it dawns on me. I've never been over Devyn's house. I

don't even know where he lives. There's a big silence and then he goes, "No."

I pull Yoko into my driveway, stare up at the cute wood-shingled Cape where my grandma Betty and I live. It looks so sweet, so normal; not like a place that's been ransacked by a pixie king. Devyn's been here a hundred times working on our pixie book, hanging out, researching. Something hardens in my gut. What is up with him? Hanging out with Cassidy, blowing off Is, never having me over. I can't hold back the harshness in my voice. "Why? Is Cassidy there?"

"No."

Now it's my turn for silence. I put Yoko in park but don't shut her off. I want the benefit of the heater. Half of me wants to ask him what's going on with Cassidy. All of a sudden she is with him all the time like some sort of major character in our lives. I want to lay into him about how he's meant to be with Issie, how every time Issie sees him with Cassidy her heart breaks a little bit. Instead I say, "Why not?"

"It's just not a good time right now," he says. "I'm sorry, Zara."

I feel dismissed. I tell him everything that's happened as quickly as I can. When I'm done, I rest my head on the steering wheel. It smells like ketchup for some reason.

"That is fascinating." He pauses. "It implies a mythology behind weres and shifters, you know? It means I was right to start to explore those Norse myths."

"Yeah. Can you use those mad research skills of yours and really focus in on Valhalla and Valkyries? I can't believe there's this whole other type of fae that we didn't even know about, Devyn. It freaks me out." I lift my head up from the steering wheel. Outside, everything is white and cold and barren. The wind moves the tops of trees, scratching them against the sky. "Can you tell Nick? About what happened?"

"Yes, Zara, I'll tell him that you let a pixie go." He sighs so loudly I can hear it through the phone.

"Thanks."

"He knows you're soft, Zara. Don't worry. He won't be mad for long."

"You think?" I open the door, scan the area for signs of pixies.

"I know. I'll take care of it. Wow. Valkyries and Valhalla. I can't even imagine what this means . . ." He hangs up mumbling and doesn't even say good-bye.

I close the car door behind me and rush up the walkway to the front porch. I take the steps two at a time and shove my key in the door. I don't look behind me. I never do. I'm always too afraid of what I might see out there, what kind of dangers are hiding behind the trunks of trees, waiting.

After an hour of doing homework I start googling "Valkyrie" on the Internet. The first thing that comes up is some 2008 movie about Hitler starring Tom Cruise. There's about a page of that and some links to female bodybuilders before I get a hit on Norse mythology. I know Dev's probably doing the same thing at his house, but whatever . . . I can't not try to learn stuff. Basically, all I get is that Valkyries brought slain warriors to Valhalla, the hall of Odin, who is the head god guy. Yeah, I've got mad research skills. I can't figure out if it's an actual place on Earth like say, Norway, or more like heaven.

The door to the house opens. I don't look up from the screen. "Hey, Betty!"

"Nope. Not Betty," Nick's voice says. He shuts the door behind him and steps into the living room. He yanks off his coat and puts it on the post at the end of the stairs.

I put my laptop on the coffee table next to some old Stephen King books my stepdad used to read and jump up toward him, talking as I walk. "You cannot be mad at me, okay. I wasn't a hundred percent sure he was a pixie. He was dying and I couldn't let that happen and when that Valkyrie woman came I just—I don't know. I couldn't let her take him."

Nick's hands catch the back of my head. He smells like the forest. His eyes stare into mine. I look down and he says, "I am not mad at you, Zara."

"Good!"

"I'm just frustrated. I never should've left him there, but I ran out of time. Now he's loose again and that sucks, but you—I know how you are. You aren't someone who can just let something die." His mouth moves in closer and he whispers, "I'm not mad. It's part of why I like you so much."

His lips lose their straight line and soften. I lean. Our lips meet and he is all gentle and tender. His hand moves through my hair. "You are complicated, though."

We sit on the couch and kiss some more. I happy sigh and squash myself against him. "We'll have to go looking for him now. I'm sorry."

"I know." He flops down and puts his head on my lap. His long legs hang off the side, over the armrest. He smiles and closes his eyes. I run my fingers across his forehead and the delicate skin on his eyelids. He grabs my hand and kisses it, then lets it go.

"You're so good to me," he murmurs and then—just like that—he's asleep. Guys.

I manage to get my laptop and put it on the couch next to me. I keep looking up things about Valkyries until I hear a tapping on the window. It's a robin. There's a piece of paper dangling from its beak. It hits the window again and drops the paper before it flies away.

I slip away from Nick as gently as I can and tiptoe across the room to open the front door. The paper is on the bench on the porch. It's tiny and all rolled up. I look around. There's no sign of the robin. In fact, there's no movement anywhere. I unroll the paper. The writing is minuscule and almost calligraphic:

Your wolf is in danger. If you want to know why you're going to have to set me free. Two days. Do not bring the weres.

I tuck the note into my pocket and shuffle back inside. Nick moans in his sleep. I touch his eyelids. I have no choice if Nick's in danger. Of course I don't. I have no choice at all. I've been summoned by a pixie via a bird. A bird? Panic fills me. If he can summon me via a bird, can he summon someone else? Maybe get rescued?

"This is not good," I murmur. "Not good at all."

Pixie Tip

Pixes are ruled by kings—and by needs. Exercise extreme caution. Turns out they can use birds.

Two days later, Is and I are frantically driving away on crazy, tree-lined paths.

"I'm not sure this is smart," Is says.

"Can we ever be sure things are smart?" I say, all philosophical. "We have to be confident, Is. We have to trust ourselves to do the right thing."

"Uh-huh," she says not very convincingly.

The note freaked me out. I didn't tell Nick even though I wanted to. Instead, I planned—I recruited Issie's help.

From the back of the station wagon comes a tired male voice. "As much as I enjoy the prattling insecurity of teenage American females, I was hoping for some relief back here. Could you untie me now? Or must we continue with this mock-kidnapping charade? It was my idea for you to release me."

"No! No untying!" I yell. Then I put my hand over my mouth. "That sounded mean, didn't it?"

Issie nods. "It's okay, though. You're not good at the tough stuff. That's why we have Nick."

"I need to be good at it. We can't depend on Nick for everything," I say.

The voice comes back. "I'm also not altogether comfortable being tied up with iron wire in a motor vehicle made of steel."

"That's a big hint," Issie yells back. "And we are so not taking it, Mr. Pixie."

I clutch the steering wheel with my right hand, flick on the directional to signal I'm going out on the road even though there's no sign of cars anywhere, just woods, woods, and more woods. The pixie house is hidden pretty deep in there. I explain to Is, "It's just not cool to kidnap people."

"They aren't people. They're pixies. And technically we aren't kidnapping him because we've already imprisoned him. This time he agreed to be tied up and dumped in the back of the car. Right?" Issie logics out. "This is a mutual agreement and not a kidnapping at all."

"Right. Right," I say, but I'm still thinking about what that other pixie had said. I'm still wondering about making a massive generalization based on just my own anecdotal evidence. But that guy was a different guy and this pixie, the pixie we've hauled out of the house and put in the back of Yoko, this pixie I know has done some evil bad things. I know it. I will not feel guilty.

I lean toward Is and whisper, "I feel guilty."

She fake punches me. "Not allowed."

"Tell me how you controlled the bird," I yell toward the pixie.

"I talk to him. Some of us are capable of that," he answers.

"Then why didn't you have him get you rescued for good, have someone take down the iron around the house?" I ask.

"Zara!" Issie frantically whispers. "Don't give him any ideas."

As I curse myself, he explains that most people wouldn't realize that a bird could even have a note. The paper is so tiny. It would be ignored. It turns out he sent the bird about five times before I finally saw it. Then there's the fact that it is Maine in winter. There aren't a ton of birds here anyway.

I pull out onto the road, trying to let things process. The bird thing is not my priority even. For most of my life I thought the world was normal, round, safe, populated by people (good and bad) and animals (wild and tame), but then it turns out that's not the way the world is. Reality isn't round, it's flat. There are edges where you can fall off and this October when I moved to Maine, I fell off one. That's when I learned about pixies and shapeshifting weres. That's when I learned about need and pain and how unsafe, how unround the world can really be.

"We've trapped them," I say, convincing myself all over again. "So people would be safe. That's the right thing to do."

"We had no choice," Issie says, biting her nails. "No choice at all."

"And talking to him now? Just because he summoned us?"

"We have no choice about that either."

It's a solution, yes. But lately I've started to wonder if it's the right one.

I park the car behind Hannaford's, the Maine grocery store chain. Big, elevated cement docks for loading produce stick out of the back of the building. Tire tracks mar the snow. Ugly green Dumpster covers rattle in the breeze. The wood creeps in behind us.

Issie gulps as I turn off Yoko. "Maybe we should've just gone to your house."

"No. Nick or my grandma would have smelled him there. You know their noses."

"Like they aren't going to smell him in your car?"

"Good point. Okay. Good point." I run my hands over my face. "But they never actually get in my car, do they?"

"That's because nobody would voluntarily ride in your car because you're such a bad winter driver. No offense."

"You volunteered."

She half smiles. "I'm a little nuts. Plus, I love you. Plus, I am a worse driver than you."

I pull on the knit hat that my mom ordered me from American Eagle. There are no outlet stores up here. No malls. It's crazy. The big place to hang out is actually the grocery store.

"Let's just do this," I say.

"Yeah."

Neither of us moves.

"Girls . . . ," comes the voice from the back of the car.

"Do not talk!" I yell. "If you talk I will just haul you back to that house and put you inside, got it?"

"You plan to do that no matter what I do," he says.

Issie's hand twitches on the door handle. "He has a point."

The wind blows loose snow across the back lot in random patterns. It has no path. It doesn't know where it's going. It just moves and settles, moves and settles.

"Okay. I'm going." I push open my door and hustle around to the back of the car. Issie does the same. We stand there together, staring at the back of my Subaru. It's covered with road filth. Sand and slush obscure the license plate.

"We don't have to do this," Issie whispers. Her hand grabs my coat sleeve.

I take in a deep breath. "He said that Nick was in danger."

"He could be lying."

"He might not be."

"True. But I'm not in a super trusting mode since he is Mr. Evil Pixie Man."

"He let us tie him up," I argue.

"True." Issie lets go of my arm. "But maybe he thought we sucked at knots."

I reach forward and squeeze the handle-latch thing that's underneath the middle part of the door. I don't know what to call that. Luckily, the word doesn't matter. The action does. The back of the Subaru slowly lifts open.

There's a blanket there, an old red quilted blanket. Issie and I sewed iron into the batting last night, filled it up with tiny bars. Then we wrapped iron wire around his feet and hands.

"You think that's enough to hold him?" Issie asks.

"He didn't escape when we were driving."

"True. I kept thinking he was going to jump up and strangle us."

"Me too!"

"Seriously? You were acting so brave." Issie hugs her arms around her chest, hopping to stay warm in the cold. The wind blows again. The Dumpsters rattle. The snow swirls.

My stomach falls into some faraway place. "I'm going to have to reach in there and fold the blanket back."

Issie stops hopping. "Uh-huh."

I reach out and tug the edge of the blanket, folding it back just enough to show his strained white face. Little lines of blue seem to trace right under the surface of his skin, making him look less human than usual. He used to be so handsome with his thick black hair, his features angular and masculine, the eyes that focused so intensely on everything, but now . . . Now his face is as pale as winter feet. Now his eyes hunch into his face. Now blue lines tattoo their meaning underneath the surface of him, declaring his foreignness. He looks like he's about to die, and that is basically my fault.

His chapped lips twist up into a half smile. I almost want to reach out and touch him, soothe him somehow, but I don't. I can't. I know what he is.

"Princess," he whispers.

I nod. "Dad."

Pixie Tip

If you have to fight pixies, remember to use weapons with some sort of iron. As in the metal. Not the thing you use to dewrinkle clothes.

A lot of people suffer from vitricophobia, which is a fear of your stepfather, but neither Devyn (whose parents are psychiatrists and shape shifters) nor I can find the name for fear of your biological father. And I would say in my case this fear is not irrational, since my biological father is a pixie. It is rational to be afraid of pixies.

"Dadophobia," I say.

My father's eyes flash.

"What?" Issie whispers. She's sort of half hiding behind me.

"Dadophobia. It's a word I just created."

"Zara, sweetie, I don't think this is the time to—"

He cuts her off. "You don't have to be afraid of me, Zara."

I don't respond.

"I'm not your enemy."

Issie's not taking that. "Dude, you tried to kidnap her to bait her mom into coming to you. Then you tried to turn her mom into a pixie. Come on. I mean, no offense, but you are not Daddy of the Year stuff here." Issie steps a little forward. "Plus, you didn't even show up on the scene for what? Sixteen years? That's lame. Seriously. That is *very* deadbeat dad stuff right there."

His hand shoots out from beneath the blanket and he grabs her wrist. "That wasn't my fault."

She squeaks in pain.

I bang forward, try to pry his fingers loose. That's when I notice the iron wire hanging loosely off his wrist. I growl. "You let go of her or I swear—"

"Fine." His voice is calm. "I'm letting go."

Each of his fingers leaves her wrist, one by one. Issie snatches it back to her chest and starts rubbing at it. "He's really strong."

A truck backfires and Issie and I jump. He doesn't move his hands or legs, but he winces like he's in pain.

"Does the iron in the car bother you?" I ask, not bothering to hide the hope in my voice.

He ignores the question. There are scorch marks on his fingertips. But he used those same fingers to grab Issie's lower arm. He's tough. He may be weak, but he's tough.

"It wasn't my fault that I wasn't there . . . when you were a child . . . ," he says, almost wheezing. "Your mother left with you. She hid you away."

I point at him. "Because *you're* an insane pixie king who drains guys of blood and tortures them."

"Only when I'm without a queen," he protests. "Only after years without a queen. And only because my people were restless. You know that. That was the only way to maintain order. And now . . . now . . . it's chaos. You have no idea how horrible things have become."

Somehow I know he's thinking about the big house where we trapped them all a few months ago. I think about how they'd strapped Jay Dahlberg to a bed. Fear made him crazy. There'd been bite marks in all his limbs where they took his blood. The pixies stood around him, around me, like we were on an altar.

"I know you think I'm a monster, Zara. I know your mother thinks so too, but if I was I never would have let her go the first time. I never would have let you live your lives." He swallows. "But the need became too great. I was losing control. And now . . ."

"And now?"

"Not all pixies are like me. Not all kings are like me."

"What do you mean?" Hope surges in my heart. Maybe that pixie was right.

"I mean that most have no mercy, no thoughts about human death or torture, no remorse. It isn't a last resort for them. It's a daily occurrence."

The pixie I pulled off the tree? He said the opposite. I meet my father's eyes. We have the same shape eyes; they tilt up just a tiny bit at the edges. "What are you saying?"

"They are coming."

"Coming where?"

"Coming here."

Issie looks at me with frightened eyes. The wind seems to mold itself into something solid for a moment. Then it lets go, drifts and swirls and batters against us.

"They're already coming," I tell him. "Some have already been here. We've put them in the house with you."

He sighs. "None of them have been kings. They've all been scouts. You know the difference, Zara. Your skin reacts to those of us who are kings or who have the potential to be."

"The spider feeling," Issie gasps.

"Why? Why does my skin do that?"

"It's because you're looking for a mate. You respond to power," he says.

"I have a mate!" I cringe at the word and correct myself. "A boyfriend. We haven't actually mated."

He scoffs, "He's an animal."

I whirl on him. "He's a man. He's a hero kind of man. He is *not* an animal."

"Not that there's anything wrong with animals," Issie says, getting all huffy. "I don't get why they're always on the bottom of the hierarchy. Like you go to jail for less than a year if you kill a dog but you kill a person and you're in jail forever, and birds . . . Anyone can just kill birds unless they're on the protected species list."

I ignore Is, who *always* rambles when she's nervous, and keep trying to move forward. I ask him, "Why are they coming?"

"Because they know I am missing. They know I must be weak. Everyone wants more people to rule, more territory."

I put my hands into my pockets. "We'll just stop them. That's all."

He shakes his head. "One of them will find the house. They'll hire humans to take down the bars you've made. They'll release us, and my people . . . my people are hungry. They'll go with him and it'll be chaos. Without a queen, I can't control them. You know that, Zara. That's why all this happened."

I hear what he's saying, but this isn't why I brought him out here. "What? What does this have to do with Nick? I mean, with Nick more than anyone else?"

"Your were." He snarls on the word a little. "Your beau—"

"Beau?" Issie interrupts.

"Boyfriend. It's an old-fashioned word for boyfriend," I explain impatiently.

My father's eyes are angry. "Your beau is also the self-proclaimed protector of the town and of you."

"Whatever." The whole "Nick protecting me" thing drives me insane. I can protect myself.

His lips move for a second like he's trying to figure out the words ahead of time and then he says, "When the other pixie or pixies come, their king . . . he's not going to be worried about Nick or his welfare. And Nick is the biggest stumbling block to you, so he will be directly in the line of fire, if you will. The pixie king will not care about one were's death. He's just going to be going after the prizes."

"'Es? Did you say *prizes*, as in plural?" Issie asks. She asks it slowly as if it takes forty-two lifetimes to get the question out of her mouth and into the frozen air.

"Yes. Plural. Prizes." He shifts beneath the blanket. His eyes are hollow, pained.

"And those are?" I ask.

"My pixies, my territory, and you."

The wind gusts again, pushing Issie and me toward him. I brace my hands on the car. My hair flies all crazy in my face. Issie's does too. When we can stand up straight again, we do. I try to tuck my hair into my coat collar.

"You're angry," my father says.

"Really? How can you tell?" I'm being sarcastic. I don't care.

"The flames coming out of your eyes are probably the tipoff," Issie says.

I fluster. "I just don't like people thinking of me as a prize. That's sexist."

"Sexist and disgusting," Issie adds. "And totally representative of the male dogma that has persisted in keeping us sisters all subjugated."

"Exactly."

His eyes drape down. "It's my fault, Zara. Your blood is half mine."

"I am human." My stomach knots. The taste of Tic Tac mintiness in my mouth somehow makes me want to throw up.

"Not all pixies torture. Only the bad ones, the neglected, who don't have a leader, or those who have a leader who is cruel or weak, or without a queen. Some of us are on the side of good. Some on the side of evil. Some, like me, are in between due to circumstances and fate." My father doesn't blink. "Zara's human. But she smells different than humans. The weres sense it. The pixies sense it. And if she turned—"

"I will never turn!" I shout.

"—she would be powerful, a powerful queen."

I sort of stare at this pixie man who is my biological father. He's all hunkered down on the gray carpeting in the back of my car. He looks almost human and almost innocent. He's not.

An old McDonald's quarter-pounder-with-cheese wrapper whips into my ankle and sticks there. I reach down and grab it, even though it's vile and gross. I can't just let it blow around forever, littering the world.

"Can I sit up?" my father asks.

"No," Issie says at the same time as I say, "Yes."

She stares at me. The wind twists her hair around her face. She doesn't even notice.

I try to explain. "Issie . . . he asked. He could have sat up a million years ago. Think of how he grabbed your wrist."

"That *is* what I'm thinking about." Her mouth becomes a tight line and then she loosens it to add, "I think it's a ploy."

"It is not a ploy," he says. His voice is infinitely weary. "My ploys are much more interesting."

"You can sit up," I say. He scoots backward and slowly brings his body up. His breath comes out in a cold puff, mingling with the air and then dissipating. I reach in and wrap the blanket around his legs. "Just in case."

He half smiles. A dimple appears at the left side of his mouth. "For a moment I thought you were being maternal."

"Daughterly would be more appropriate," I say.

We stare each other down. His eyes are mesmerizing, really. They pull at you. It is creepy.

"You survived before because I let you," he says.

My head snaps up so hard something cracks in my neck. "What?"

He is calm, propped up against the seat. "I let you survive. I let your boyfriend survive. I was out of my mind with need, out of my mind wanting your mother, and still I let you, my daughter, survive. I saw that you were trapping us there and I let her escape through the wires while I pretended to be distracted by you. That has to give you some assurance that I am not against you."

"Then how come you're not out of your mind now?" Issie asks, hands on her hips. "Huh? How come you aren't lunging at me, trying to pixie kiss me or something?"

"You are not meant to be my queen," he says matter-of-factly.

"Geesh. Nice." Issie blows air out of her mouth.

"Don't be insulted," I say. "It's a good thing."

My father stares into her eyes. "And you are not a young man. You are not someone I can bleed."

Creepy tension charges the air. I shudder. Something in my coat starts vibrating and then I hear it: Nick and my song.

"Crap."

Issie gives me big eyes. "Is that him?"

I pull the phone out of my pocket. "Just a text."

My father ignores us and continues. "I know you think that I am a monster, Zara. And maybe I am. However, I know that if my needs are not taken care of, then the others, my people, they are worse, much worse."

"So what am I supposed to do?" I ask.

"Set me free."

"I can't do that." My eyes meet his eyes.

His eyes are fierce and sad and tired. "I have to feed. That is the only way I can be strong enough to battle. I shall feed and then I shall protect you and your wolf and my right to rule."

"I can't let you just go torture some poor boy, even if it is to protect us."

"Then I need a queen." His body stiffens almost as if he is going to strike.

My hands become fists. "Nope. No. I mean if you could find some weird woman who actually wants to be a pixie queen, fine. But you are so not taking Mom. She's not even here, you know."

"Zara . . . there aren't many possibilities." The skin by his eye twitches.

"Those are not options. Torturing boys and turning my mom are not options."

"I'm the only one powerful enough to stop another king. I'm the—"

Issie slams the trunk shut, cutting off his words. "We need to take him back, don't you think? We need to just let this settle and think it over."

I make myself nod and just stare at the back of the car and my father's face. He slowly closes his eyes, giving up maybe.

Is studies me. "You're shaking."

"It's cold out," I say.

"That's not why you're shaking." Issie wraps her arm around my shoulders, hugs me to her. "I can't believe I get to be the tough one."

The wind bumps us against the car. Dirt gets on our jeans, our jackets.

"Eww . . . ," Issie says. "Dirt."

"Very tough, Issie."

She laughs and pulls open the passenger door. "Thanks."

But I am not done with him yet. Once I've started the car I yell back, "What do you know about Valhalla?"

"It is the mythological hall of Odin," he answers.

"Odin?" Issie asks, turning up the heat.

"Norse god." I pull the car out of the parking lot. "So it isn't real?"

"Of course not," he scoffs. "I wish you would rethink your assumptions about me, Zara and release me. I assure—"

"What about Valkyries?" I interrupt, stopping at one of our town's two stoplights. Mr. Burns, one of my teachers, pulls up next to me and waves. Issie and I plaster grins on our faces and wave back.

"Valkyries?" This time my father laughs. "Myths."

Issie starts to speak, but I put a finger over my lips to keep her from saying anything. The light turns green.

"I don't know why we bothered with him," I tell Issie.

She turns up the radio. "Me either."

When we drop him off, he tries to run. I'm forced to tackle him and drag him back within the steel perimeter of the house. This earns massive respect from Issie, who said I was Super Bowl–worthy. After tromping back to the car we drive away fast. We're both shaking but neither of us talks. Back at Issie's house I shift Yoko into reverse but keep my foot on the brake, ready to leave. Waiting for direction, I guess.

"It's not like I totally believe him, but I am super worried about Nick," I say. "I'm worried that I won't be able to keep him safe."

Is cocks her head. "Zara, honey, it isn't all up to you. We're all part of it, okay? You're not alone."

"Right." I grab the steering wheel a little tighter. The roads are getting slippery. "I know that, but even though I know I can count on you guys, I still feel like it's up to me somehow, like everything is my fault or my credit."

"You are just as bad as Nick." She smiles to take the edge off her words. "The fate of the world does not depend on you, Zara White."

"Promise?" I ask as cold air rushes in through the passenger door.

Issie gets out and grabs the top of the door so she can slam it shut. "Promise."

I back out of there and wonder if promises ever mean anything at all.

Once I leave Is, I check for reception and call my mom while I drive. She's still in Charleston but she's moving up here. She's already quit her job and everything, but when you are a CEO-type person you have it in your contract that you have to give a certain amount of notice between the day you resign and the day you actually get to leave. If you mess with that, the company you work for can impose "financial penalties" or sue you. Right now, thinking about what my father just said, I'm glad that she's still down there. But I miss her hugs and her power suits and her mom smell.

The phone rings and goes to voice mail. She's probably at a meeting about physician recruitment or something heinously boring like that. I babble out a message and click the phone off. I tell myself it's okay. Driving isn't easy, so I shouldn't be messing with the phone. Poor Yoko; her tires try to grip the icy road. I try to steer and not vault into one of the towering snowbanks that hunker at the side of the road, waiting. It's all about trying, right? That's all we can do in life: try to do the right thing, try to survive high school, try to navigate treacherous icy roads, just try.

Devyn's always quoting Yoda from one of the original *Star Wars* movies. Yoda talks in a total stoner voice and is supposed to be all philosophically centered with the good force stuff. I think of him as a kind of Tibetan monk crossed with the dude who hangs out at 7-Eleven even though he's thirty. To finish the picture add in a green cat. So anyway, Yoda says, "Do or do not. There is no try." I hate that. Sometimes you can't just do. Sometimes all you can handle is trying.

I crank up the radio. Listen to Bono sing about loss and need and hope. It's vintage U2, not their newer stuff.

On the side of the road shadows form in the woods. They look like people. But I'm imagining things, right?

Right.

The winter fog creeps around the tree trunks, shrouding them and whatever else might be hiding at the side of the road. It's gray. It's dangerous.

"I'm not looking at you, fog," I announce, and I turn up the radio volume to twenty-two, which basically ensures that my eardrums will stop working by the time I'm twenty-three.

My skin starts to feel like thousands of spiders are crawling on it, doing an Irish step dance. Maybe it's residual from being with my father for so long, or maybe we didn't secure him well enough in the house. Maybe he got out.

"Crap."

I flip open my phone. Press the speed-dial number two. It rings and rings.

"Issie?"

"Zara?" Her voice is muffled and I'm not sure why. It almost sounds like she's been crying. "You okay?"

"I'm fine. Are *you* okay?"

"Yep. Okey-dokie-Pinocchi . . ."

I smush the phone between my shoulder and my head and put both hands on the wheel. "I have the feeling."

"The pixie feeling?"

"Yeah."

Keep driving. Going forward. Moving.

"The 'pixie king is near you so your skin feels like spiders are crawling on it' feeling?"

"Yeah."

"Uh-oh." She mumbles something away from the phone and adds, "She's got the wiggly feeling."

"Would you hate me if I asked you to come over?"

"We'll be right there. Devyn's here. Call Nick right now!"

I click off the phone again and think for a second. I don't want

Nick in danger. Putting the phone away, I turn up the radio again and then round a curve. I'm barely through it when I slam on the brakes.

There's a blond man standing in the middle of the road, waiting. Oh please, do not let him be waiting for me.

Definition
Pixie-led: *to be lost, to be confused, to be led astray*

Yoko skids out of control. She slides left, then skitters right, rushing toward a tree. The tree trunk is massive and thicker than my
car. If I hit it? It won't be good. It'll be broken-bone bad. I'm
going to hit it.

"No!" My voice is screaming the word but I don't really hear it.
I'm pressing harder on the brakes. The brakes are screaming too.

"Nick!" I yell his name without thinking about it. The car
smashes into something huge and hard. The tree? My head whips
back and forward or forward and back. I don't know. The airbag
smashes into my face and chest. I can't see. I can't breathe. The
world is plastic and pain. Wires burn. The smell of acid hits my
nose. I push at the airbag. My entire chest aches.

"Get out! Get out!" A guy's voice yells at me.

The door wrenches free. Cold air rushes in. It smells worse
now. More burning. Hands are reaching for me as I scream and
flail, stuck. "Nick?"

"I am attempting to help you," the man says. He is not Nick. Of course. Of course he's not Nick. Focus, I need to focus.

I try to pull in a big breath. "I can't move."

"Your seat belt."

Seat belt? What's a seat belt? My brain can't quite compute. "Unclick it."

Click? Seat belt? Right. Hands reach across my waist. Fingers push at my seat belt. His fingers. The guy in the road. Not Nick. The pixie. The young one, who was injured.

"I am unable to get it," he says. "Damn, I despise iron. I should have taken my pills."

I try to reach around too and free myself, but my arm's not quite working. It's the same arm this pixie Ian broke when he kidnapped me and tried to turn me. It feels broken or sprained again, judging by the pain spiraling up into my shoulder.

The pixie's voice gets urgent and higher pitched. "Fire!"

"Yoko? Yoko's on fire?"

"The car is on fire. Please, just stay still so I can help you."

I don't move even though everything inside of me is shrieking, *Get out, get out, run!* Something is ripping. The seat belt? How can he rip the seat belt? Hands are yanking me out of the car, into the cold. But there's heat pressing at my back. Pain shifts from my arm to my chest. My nose burns from the smell of hot metal and rubber and chemicals burning.

He groans and falls backward into the snow. I tumble on top of him. There are all these pinging noises coming from the direction of the car. I manage to turn my head enough to look but my neck is all stiff and crazy slow. Yoko is a jumbled mass of steel. Her door is wide open. Flames shoot out of the hood. The smoke is heavy and dark, toxic and unworldly looking. Glass breaks and falls onto the road.

"It might explode," I say, sounding like I'm asleep or I've lost forty IQ points or something. "Cars can explode."

He nods and stands up. "Are you capable of walking?"

"I—I don't know. I— That's a good question."

He bends and pulls me up into his arms. He drapes me over his shoulder and starts walking fast down the snowbank. His feet are barely touching the ground.

"You're hurt," I gasp. "Your stomach. You'll hurt yourself more."

More glass shatters.

"You are suddenly caring about a pixie?" He laughs. It's a harsh, awful sound full of pain. I don't know if the pain is mental or physical, I just wish I could fix it somehow, make it better. He smirks. "What is your boyfriend going to say about that?"

He falls to the ground in a sitting position. I slide off his shoulder, coughing. My hip hits the hard, packed-down snow. We're a football field away from Yoko. She's smashed into a huge tree. Her hood is crunched in and wrapped around the trunk. I struggle into a sitting position. My neck doesn't feel like it wants to support my head. "We have to get the fire out. My car—"

She explodes. The sound blasts my ears. Before I know what he's doing, the pixie guy grabs me and pulls me to him. His hands wrap around my head and he twists so his back is facing the car, like he's protecting us from the impact, which is really nice of him, but I don't know why he's taking care of me, why—

"Oh man. Oh . . ." I can't even begin to breathe. His jacket is in my mouth. It tastes like wool, bitter and nasty. I struggle to get enough room to look. Orange and black flames leap out of Yoko's body. The first things I think of? My cell phone. My cell phone is in there. And my iPod. And my homework. And my laptop. My head throbs. Is this normal? Is it normal to think?

"This is why I hate technology!" he half mutters, half shouts. "It is ridiculously dangerous."

Suddenly my head clears and I am furious-angry. "What? This is *not* technology's fault. This is your fault," I yell at him. "*You* were in the road. That's why I swerved in the first place. *You* made me crash."

He scoffs. His nose actually twitches.

"Why were you in the road?" I demand, trying to keep my arm stable. "Were you trying to kill me?"

He doesn't answer. A little blood is seeping through the gray T-shirt that's under his open jacket.

I scuttle backward and cringe from the pain. I stop moving and try to control my anger. "You knocked me out before—in my car—you escaped . . ."

He plucks a piece of ripped-up seat belt off his leg. I don't know how it got there.

"You lost consciousness. I availed myself of the opportunity to leave." He smiles. It's a wicked smile. Kind but not kind. Handsome but dangerous. Feral almost. I can see why Nick nearly killed him. Nick . . . My father's warning echoes in my ear. Still, I need to call someone—the fire department at least.

"Do you have a cell phone?" I ask.

He gently touches my cheek. Gently? "I do, but I cannot let you use it. Then they will have my number."

I try not to shrink away. "Please. I'm hurt . . ."

He seems to think about it and then nods. He does something. "I am blocking the number. I have called 9-1-1." He then speaks into the phone. "There has been a one-car accident on Route 3 about a mile past the Bedford Convenience Store. The car is on fire. One person injured. It's not life threatening.

"There. Done." He clicks the phone off and stares at me. "You still look faint. Can you manage sitting up?"

"Thank you." I fall back into the snow as he starts to put his arm around to support me. It gets stuck under my body, really awkwardly. "Sorry."

"I apologize," he says at the same time. I didn't know pixies could actually say they were sorry. He pulls his arm out slowly so it doesn't hurt me too much.

He seems to listen to the woods. "I am going to have to go in a second, little one. Are you going to be all right by yourself?"

"Little one?" Anger wells up in me again.

"I do not know your name." He squints down at me. His eyes are a beautiful deep green like the tops of pine trees, but it's a glamour. It's not what he really looks like. His eyes are silver like all pixie eyes. The glamour makes him look human. It's part of the magic. "I should know your name now that we have both rescued each other."

I don't give it to him. I don't want him to do what my father did and start whispering it at me when I'm in the woods, trying to get me confused. Instead I ask again, "Why were you in the road?"

"I was waiting for you."

I nod like it makes sense. It doesn't make sense. "I don't feel right."

"You are in shock." He lightly presses his fingers against my arm. "You are hurt. You are also turning a bit blue."

"It's cold."

He lifts an eyebrow and shifts position, cringing again as he moves. "I do not believe that is why."

"Are you hurt?" I ask. "Your stomach—"

"Is already healing. I am not at a hundred percent yet, but I appreciate you asking and thank you for saving me that day."

The snow shocks the skin on my bare palm. I study him. He looks so normal. I try to focus on his face, that wind-ruffled blond hair, his eyes. Try to see the pixie under the good looks. "Why were you waiting for me on the road?"

"I want you to lead me to them."

"To who? The other pixies?"

"Yes."

"That's not going to happen," I say. I take a big breath and my ribs sting with pain.

He puts his hand behind my head. "No deep breaths. I believe you have bruised your ribs."

We are so close. His face is inches away. I swallow hard. "You have to promise not to hurt my friends. Hurt me if you have to, but leave my friends alone."

"I shall never hurt you." His eyes stare into mine for a minute. "I hate to leave you, but you will be all right."

He sounds so sincere, as if he really wants to help. "Tell me about the Valkyrie," I press. My chest burns.

"I shall sometime."

"No. Now."

He slips his hand out from the back of my head and then stands up and pats my shoulder like a mom would. He only does this a couple times before he says, "Your wolf is almost here."

I cough and then manage, "My wolf? How do you know that?"

"His scent is all over you." He flinches as if the scent is bad, like cooking broccoli or something. For a second he almost looks sweet and young, like I can see the little boy he used to be. It makes me want to comfort him—almost.

I struggle toward him. One hand goes back into the biting snow for balance. "What do you mean *my* wolf?" My father warned me about this. "He's not mine. I don't own him. People don't own each other."

But he's already gone, the jerk, just melded into the fog. I'm alone on the snowbank. Yoko is a burning mess. There are sirens in the distance.

He's put it all together already, I bet. Pixies are like that: cunning and smart. They aren't perfectly evil, just evil enough. Figures.

"Zara!" Nick's voice brings me back to reality. It's a struggle. My eyes open. He stands over me and blocks out the scene. "Oh . . . oh, baby."

"I'm okay," I manage. I reach out my good hand so I can touch him. He looks so warm. I want his warmth. "I killed Yoko."

"Are you cold? You're a little blue." He reaches down and scoops me against his sweatshirt. I scream from the pain. He loosens his hold right away. "Baby?"

"My arm," I gasp. "And my chest."

"I'm so sorry. I'm so sorry I hurt you." His face is full of shock and worry. There is a piece of pixie dust on it. "I just wanted to hold you."

"It wasn't you."

He gently leans me back on the ground. He whips off his coat, tucks it under my legs, and then plops himself on the snow so I can rest on him. Sirens get closer. The trees sway in the wind. He smells like warmth and Old Spice and a little bit of antiseptic from the hospital.

"I'm so sorry, baby." He rocks back and forth. "What happened? Did you hit black ice?"

"There was a pixie. The same one—the one I let go."

He stiffens. "What happened? What did he do to you?" His voice turns positively icy. "Did he kiss you?"

"Nothing. He was . . . He was in the middle of the road. I stopped fast and skidded. There was a tree." I try to sit up. "I can sit up. It's just a little achy."

"Stay there." Nick surveys me for damage. "Can I open your jacket?"

"Yeah."

He shifts me around so that I'm pretty much lying across his lap. He unzips my jacket and pulls my running shirt and my Under Armour down from my neck a bit and says, "You're bruising. Are those sirens for you? Did you call 9-1-1?"

"He did. My phone's in there." I gesture toward Yoko. "So is my laptop and my iPod and—"

"He called? The pixie?" Nick interrupts.

"He saved me. He pulled me out of the car before it caught fire."

Nick snarls. His back goes rigid and his head whips up. "He did not save you. He made you wreck. He probably only left you because you were too injured to kiss and turn."

"That's not true. He wants to know where the pixies are. I think he wants to let them out."

Nick groans. "This is all my fault."

I pull myself in closer to him and wrap my good arm around his neck, even though he's trembling with rage. It pulses through him. I don't want to argue. I'm too tired to argue. "It's not your fault. And it's fine."

Nick draws in a ragged breath and I can tell that a tiny bit of tension leaves him. His big hand rests on my neck and he starts kissing my face with these tiny, gentle pecks. At the same time his fingers reach up and stroke my cheek. It feels so good. I feel so safe all of a sudden. But it can't last, can it? Of course it can't.

A fire truck peels in next to my car. I notice it doesn't skid. I am the one who skids in crazy directions because I am the one who does reckless things and then doesn't fess up. Firefighters jump out of the truck, hauling hoses. One of them starts down the road toward us.

"Nick, even though I let him go and now all this happened," I start to explain, "I still don't regret letting him go. He would have died."

"And that would be a bad thing?" Nick snaps. He tilts his head back for a second and closes his eyes before he speaks again, and this time his voice is much milder. "You are too kind for your own good, Zara. You've got to learn to not be nice." He kisses my forehead to take the sting of his words away. "Especially to pixies. Deal?"

I nod, but I can't promise it. I can't say, "Deal." Instead, I say, "I'll stop being nice when you stop taking chances."

He shakes his head but we both know that I mean it and we both know that neither of us is going to back down, at least not anytime soon.

Grandma Betty slams out of the ambulance and power strides across the snow, speaking into her radio and hauling her EMT bag. Only a flicker in her eye betrays any emotion. She is all business. There are no hugs from her right now. She leans toward me, hovers over my face, and checks my eyes. "Pupils look good."

I open my mouth to speak.

She silences me with a finger. The wrinkles at the corners of her eyes crease even deeper. "Tell me your name."

"Zara."

"What state are you in?"

"Maine. Or consciousness?"

"Funny. Nice sarcasm, miss. Although you have learned from the best." She starts to smile and then gets professional again. "Were you thrown?"

I don't understand.

"From the vehicle," she explains. "Were you thrown?"

"No."

Her eyes narrow the way they do when she's trying to figure things out. The wind whips her gray hair straight above her head. "How'd you get all the way over here, then?"

"I—I—"

I must take too long, because she interrupts me. "Did you move her, Nick?"

Nick shakes his head gently, I guess so he doesn't hurt me too much. "I wasn't here when it happened. She was tinked."

Betty nods really quickly and switches gears. "Where's it hurt?"

"My arm. The one I broke. My chest. My head and neck. It's not too bad, though," I explain as Betty directs the other EMT, this tall guy, Keith, who has movie-star hair and a very bad chin. They get a gurney-bed thing out.

"We're going to move her," Betty tells Nick.

"Excuse me. I am not 'her.' And I'm right here. And I can walk," I complain, struggling to get up.

"No." Betty slaps a big, ugly neck collar on me.

"I didn't break my neck," I insist as they lift me up.

"I'm not taking any chances," she states. Her boots clomp down in the snow, hard and no-nonsense.

Nick gives me a sympathetic glance. He almost looks like he's going to laugh. I twitch my nose at him, which makes him smile.

"Can I go in the ambulance with her?" he asks.

Betty thinks about it for a second.

"I can walk," I say again. "People are staring at me."

"Firefighters are not people. Firefighters are professionals, and it is their job to stare. Yes, you can come, Nick," Betty says just as Issie and Devyn pull up. Issie flies out of the car and rushes toward us.

"Oh man, Zara! Did the pixies do this?" Is blurts out.

Keith's head whips up and his mouth drops open. He stares at her. "Pixies?"

"The rock group," Betty covers. "Zara listens to music far too loud. The Pixies are one of those old alternative groups from the 1980s."

"Very retro," Is says, trying to cover up. "Very old-school. But hip. Yeah. Zara's hip. Oh man, Zara, did you break your hip?"

Nick's hand lands on Issie's shoulder. "Is, take a deep breath."

"Deep breath?"

"Inhale and exhale," Nick says calmly.

Some firefighters start yelling. There's a heavy knocking sound by Yoko's remains and then the clanking of metal hitting metal, the whirling of water through hoses. Nick shifts his weight and keeps talking to Issie like nothing else is happening. "And maybe take a step back so they can get Zara in the ambulance."

"She's going in the ambulance!" Issie exclaims. She reaches out and grabs my hand. "We'll follow you the whole way. We'll be right behind you. Do *not* worry. Okay? No worrying."

"Breathe, Issie. I'm okay." I smile and squeeze her hand for a second before I let go. "No hips broken. No massive concussions."

"Thank God for small miracles," Betty mutters as they lift me into the back. She slides in next to me. Everything is tight space and instruments, drawers full of medicine and needles, just enough supplies to keep people alive and stabilized until they get to a hospital. Nick hauls himself inside too. He bends his head so he can fit.

The moment Keith gets into the driver's seat Betty mumbles so only I can hear, "You are going to tell me exactly what happened, right?"

I try to nod but it's hard with the silly neck brace thing. "I'm sorry about the car, Gram."

"The car, my dear, is the least of my worries," she says. Then she does a very un-Betty thing. She leans over and kisses my cheek. Her lips are soft and dry. "You are going to be the death of me."

She chuckles. I'm on my back, staring up at their faces. The light is so fluorescent bright that I can make out their pores, Nick's individual eyebrow hairs. So many people have been in this ambulance dying. Some of them Betty has saved. She is a hero. So is Nick, taking down so many pixies all by himself and never complaining, just trying to keep everyone safe. A hero can be anyone, but I have two right here, and they love me. Tears seep out of my eyes.

Nick leans down and kisses my eyelids. "Loving you, Zara, is a full-time job. It's a great job, don't get me wrong. It's the best job in the universe. But it is not easy, because you tend to . . ."

"Get hurt?" Betty suggests. "Find trouble? Pass out? Break arms?"

"All of the above." Nick laughs.

My hand finds Nick's wrist and I grab onto its thickness. "You know, I'm the patient here. Where's the bedside manner? Where's the sympathy?"

"Zara, sympathy is just a good excuse to buy greeting cards and make sorry eyes and secretly gloat over how glad you are that you aren't the person whose crap is hanging out there for the world to see," Betty says.

A check at the hospital reveals:

- one sprained wrist,
- a couple of minorly bruised but unbroken ribs, and
- one small neck strain that does not require a neck brace.

Gram changes into her civilian gear at the hospital, putting on a flannel shirt and L. L. Bean cords, and then drives us home in her truck. I'm in the middle seat leaning against Nick.

I push my thigh against his. "Well, thank God."

"Thank God what?" he asks. His hand slowly rubs up and down the place where my shoulder meets my arm. It makes me good shiver.

"That I don't have a neck brace. It's hard to rock a neck brace, especially if we're still going to that dance."

He leans in and kisses my nose. "If anyone could do it, you could."

I tilt my head so our lips meet.

"Hormonal ones, I am right here. Me. The old lady otherwise known as your grandmother," Betty says.

"Sorry. He's just irresistible," I say, settling back against him.

"Well, try to resist the irresistible," Betty says knowingly as the truck bumps over a pothole. "Sorry! Didn't mean to jostle you."

"Wait," Nick says. "What did that mean?"

"She said to resist the irresistible," I explain.

"But that means me."

Betty starts laughing again. "You have a high opinion of yourself, don't you, Mr. Colt?"

He starts stuttering. "But Zara said and then . . . and you said . . ."

"I didn't just mean you, Nick," she says, her voice softening for a second. Then it hardens up and I know what's coming. We told her about the pixie guy I freed. The voice hardening means Official Grandmother Lecture Time. "For Zara the irresistible isn't just you, it's justice. It's being noble. It's being the martyr. It's about ending pain for others and forgetting about herself or the big picture."

"That's harsh, Betty," Nick defends me.

"Harsh? I'll tell you what's harsh. Her little do-gooderness set a pixie free, possibly a king, judging from how quickly he healed, and she almost died because of it." She takes a corner and even though she's mad at me she takes it slow so I don't bounce around too much. "You get that, don't you, Zara? You could've died today."

My bruised ribs hammer home her point. We pull into our driveway. All the windows in the Cape are dark. The sky is dark. Everything is dark. The woods are just pieces of shadow. You can't tell what's back there. You can't tell who might be watching.

Pixie Tip

A pixie's true skin color is blue. Cookie Monster, Grover, and other lovable Muppets are also blue. Do not confuse the two. Muppets don't kill you. Usually.

"Wake up. Zara! Honey! Wake the hell up." Betty shakes me.

I swat at her, hit her flannel pajama top. The soft plushness of it is so different from Betty's hardness. The lights are on in my room. Huh? My eyelids flutter, but I manage to open them, sit up. My voice is a frantic mess. "What? What is it? Pixies?"

She holds my arms up by the shoulders, but her grip loosens. "You were having another nightmare."

I flop back onto the pillows. My chest aches from all the movement. "Again?"

I've had one every night since the accident. That makes a week's worth of nightmares.

"You remember it?" Her hand touches my forehead, soothes away some hair.

"Yeah."

"You want to tell me?"

"Gram, nobody likes to hear about other people's dreams. It's like watching PowerPoint presentations of somebody else's vacation in St. Croix or something. You hear about the beach but you aren't really experiencing the beach, so it's just not that interesting."

Her eyes close a little bit as she examines me. Her hands work at soothing out her pj top, which features frolicking lions and lollipops. Then she stills herself. She is so solid and good and crusty, the best kind of grandmother. "I'm sorry I woke you up," I finish.

"Not a big deal, sweetie. I'm up all the time." She leans over and kisses my forehead. She straightens up and walks stiffly across the hardwood floor to the open door of my bedroom and hesitates by the light switch. "You want me to shut this off?"

My pulse speeds up. It hits against my skin, like blood is trying to beat its way out of my veins. "No. Light is good."

The door clicks shut and I stare up at the Amnesty International poster that hangs over my bed. There's an image of a candle wrapped in barbed wire, a flame that still burns.

There were flames in my dream. They flickered around my feet and I was running through them, running up the stairs of a house, running toward someone. Every single part of me needed to get up those stairs, deeper into that fire. The hallway was just like the one in the big pixie mansion that we've trapped my father and the rest of them in. I thought for a second that's who I was looking for, but I suddenly realized that it wasn't him. Nick called my name from the bottom of the stairs, but I ignored him, rushing deeper and deeper into the flames where the blond pixie was waiting for me.

Then Nick screamed. I turned around and he was surrounded by pixies, feeding pixies ripping at his clothes, his flesh. I hesitated and that's the worst part of the dream—me hesitating. The flames were so tempting, the pull to go farther into the house so great. But then I ignored my need and started to head back toward him. And when I did? Bam. Something grabbed me from behind. I shrieked. And Betty woke me up.

That's it. End of dream.

Man, I hate dreams. How is it they can make you feel guilty when they aren't even real?

Worry keeps me from sleeping. I get out of bed to use Gram's laptop, which she's letting me borrow until we go up to Bangor and buy a replacement. I open up my e-mail to read Amnesty's current Urgent Action paper. It's about Fidelis Chiramba, Gandhi Mudzingwa, and Kisimusi Dhlamini, who are in a jail in Zimbabwe just for being political activists, though they all have major medical issues. They weren't even allowed to appear for a trial. It drives me nuts. I shoot off an e-mail to the Zimbabwe government and consider getting ready for school.

Instead I work on the pixie handbook for a bit. I'm working on the chapter "Saving Yourself from Pixies." Even that gets old, though. So I mosey up and open the shades. The sky is bright blue, a brand-new day. I wonder how those captured monks I've read about feel, what their sky looks like, if they can even see it, if their candle of hope shudders against shrill scenes.

The woods just beyond the driveway sway with the wind, and for a second it seems as if something is moving between the trunks, a man. I shiver. It reminds me of my father always vanishing before he finally told me who he was, what he wanted.

"He's locked up," I announce to the window. My breath fogs it up. I use my fingertips to wipe the fog away. "And I refuse to let the other pixie guy be out there."

I try to make it sound tougher. "Absolutely refuse."

The woods sway some more and for a second I sway with them, dizzy, confused. I shake my head, imagine Nick's broad face, the line of his chin, his mischief-twinkling eyes. I turn away from the woods and go take a shower.

It's when I'm getting dressed that I get an idea. My stepdad wrote in the margin of an old Stephen King novel a long time ago, tipping us off about pixies. Maybe he did that again. Just because Betty and my mom don't know anything about Valhalla or Valkyries doesn't mean he didn't. I race into his old bedroom and eye the ratty-looking paperbacks in his bookcase. They are almost all Stephen King. The top shelf starts with King's first book, *Carrie,* and goes on chronologically to this short story collection, *Nightmares and Dreamscapes,* which was published in 1993. Stephen King wrote a lot of books after that, but they aren't here. They are probably at our house in Charleston. I thumb through them all, flipping through the pages, looking for my dad's writing in the margins; little notes about things, signs that he existed. Sometimes just seeing a page earmarked makes my stomach hitch up. Losing people you love affects you. It is buried inside of you and becomes this big, deep hole of ache. It doesn't magically go away, even when you stop officially mourning. I do not want that hole to get any bigger. I do not want to lose anyone else.

I thumb through the books pretty quickly and find nothing. I slide the last paperback into its place. There are other books here and I should go through them too, but I can't be late for school. I pull out an H. P. Lovecraft collection of short stories. On the cover is this monster hiding in the far back of this horrifying cavern that looks straight from hell. The cavern is beneath a tombstone.

"Creepy," I mutter.

I find a couple phrases in the margin. The first one is: "Leave Risk Sixty."

The second is longer: "A Baa Ebbed Fly Tight Vigor Trolls."

Total gibberish. I tuck the book under my arm and bring it downstairs with me and say to the room, "Great. Thanks, Dad."

Downstairs, Betty's left a note on the fridge:

> Early shift. Take your pain medicine. Do not sell it at school. JUST KIDDING! Sort of. ☺

I drop my spoon onto the floor. "Crud."

It clanks. I pick it up and stand, woozy. I have to steady myself by placing a hand on the fridge. I throw the spoon into the sink. Metal hits metal. All my organs seem to shudder inside me. I am instantly cold as I peek out the window. There's nothing out there, just shadows. I try to uncurl my fear and pour some Cocoa Puffs. The crunch of chocolate balls is strangely tasteless in my mouth. I check to make sure my ankle bracelet is still safely fastened. It is.

"There is nothing to worry about," I announce.

The refrigerator hums in happy oblivion. That's the only answer I get.

Pixie Tip

Pixie eyes turn up a tiny bit at the ends.

Nick has driven me to school for the last week, which is nice because it means we get to spend more time together and I get to make sure that he has not been murdered by any evil pixie kings. Truth is, though, neither of us are all that good in the morning and we both kind of spend the whole car ride grunting and stretching and yawning.

He parks his MINI and grabs my bags for me. Sometimes having a slightly sprained wrist is good. It's healing well, though. The splint is off and it's just wrapped now.

"Do you have to take *all* your books home every single night?" he asks, hauling my new book bag over his shoulder since the last one died a fiery death.

"Yep." I smile at him.

He leans lower so he can whisper in my ear. "You are lucky you're so cute, baby."

I wave to Paul and Callie, who are going out and are both in our art class. They have matching Mohawks died green, which is really sweet in a retro way. Jill and Stephanie are holding hands and looking very much like morning people. They are so in love. Lovebirds are all around us, basically, but none of them have to worry about their other half being murdered by pixies because of who they are . . . or aren't.

I walk closer to Nick, put my good arm around his waist. We reach the glass doors at the front of the high school. He opens it for me. Suddenly there is heater-warmed air and lots of noise. He keeps holding the door so that Paul and Callie and Jill and Stephanie can get through too.

"We are *so* late," Jill says. She gives me a thumbs-up. "Love your jeans. Nice."

"Thanks," I say as I see Issie zipping up the ramp to the second floor toward Devyn. Her gauzy blouse sways with the movement.

"Issie! Devyn!" I yell.

Devyn turns around and waves, smiling. He's wheelchair free—just the metal braces that connect to his forearms! Cassidy's standing next to him.

Nick's hand death-locks around my forearm. "He doesn't have his wheelchair! Zara, he doesn't have his wheelchair at all!"

He lets go of me and vaults over the railing of the ramp. Nick's arms wrap around Devyn and he swings him around in a big circle with the force of his hug. People scatter out of the way. One of Devyn's braces falls off his arm and hits the ramp. Issie leaps over it as she runs up. She lunges right into the group hug. She's screaming, she's so happy.

We knew this was coming, but to see it . . . to actually see him without his chair? The feeling is heart-stopping good. I pick up the brace as I trot up the ramp.

"No wonder you didn't want a ride today," Issie's saying. She keeps patting him on the back. "No wonder! Did you drive yourself?"

"Nope. Cassidy drove me."

"Right!" Cassidy interrupts, fiddling with her sparkly pink barrette.

"She—she drove you?" Issie sputters.

"Yeah, Is. I wanted to surprise you all." Devyn smiles at me. "What do you think, Zare?"

Handing him his brace I say, "I think this is one of the most beautiful things I've ever seen in my entire life."

And it is.

"Now I can finally start doing the things I want to do," Devyn says.

That stops me. "Like what?"

Devyn just smiles. Cassidy clears her throat and gives him her own little hug. "I am so psyched for you, Dev."

Issie's backed up against the wall. Her hand is on her throat. She looks away.

"Thanks," Devyn says.

They pull apart and Cassidy starts scratching at the back of her neck. "I knew this would happen."

The way she says it stops me short. It's almost eerie, but she whirls off before I can say anything.

"We are all late," she says over her shoulder, still scratching. "Congratulations, Devyn! Let me know if you need a ride home."

We all head toward our first period. For a tiny bit Nick doesn't talk about protecting and pixies and pain. For a tiny bit his shoulders relax and he smiles, and it is that very moment that I realize how hard all of this is for him.

Tears spring to my eyes and I'm not sure why. I think it's just that I don't want Devyn to ever get hurt again. I don't want any of us to ever get hurt again.

Spanish class used to be my least favorite part of the day. It's not because the entire room reeks of our teacher's lilac perfume and my nose always goes instantly stuffy. It's because of this girl Megan. Megan used to sit diagonally in front of me and every so often turn and glare. Then she'd whisper something to her friend Brittney, and they would witch cackle. Even though she's not here anymore, it still feels like she is.

I breathe out, suck on the edge of my pen, and make a list.

ILLEGAL THINGS WE'VE DONE AND WHY
1. Betty killed Ian because he tried to turn me pixie by kissing me.
2. Megan disappeared, so Mrs. Nix forged her transfer papers, which is okay because she was not just a mean jerk, she was a pixie.
3. We trapped all the pixies in a house because they would have kept killing.

Okay, it's not *that* long a list and I feel a tiny bit better even if the crimes do include murder, forgery, and mass kidnapping. I fold the list up and tuck it into the back of *The House of the Spirits*. I start translating again, but I am really thinking about how my grandmother has killed, how I have trapped, how there is a history of violence that exists and I don't know how to deal with it. I'm in Amnesty International. I mean, I care about human rights. But what about pixie rights? They are kind of human. And what do you do when the world has no clue that they exist?

I'm getting nowhere with the book so I pull out a new piece

of paper and start working on the pixie handbook, scrawling in an entry that I'll type into Devyn's or Gram's laptop later.

TOP TEN THINGS TO REMEMBER WHEN
DEALING WITH PIXIES

10. Think pixies are like Tinker Bell? You think wrong.
9. Pixies do not hang out with Peter Pan.
8. Pixies do not sleep in glass jars nor do they carry magic wands.
7. Pixies hate iron and steel.
6. Pixies will call you by name and try to get you lost in the woods.
5. Pixies are great fighters; they use claws and teeth.
4. Pixies can look like humans. They are not human.
3. Pixies may go to your school or work with you. We have no idea.
2. Pixies have needs.
1. Never let a pixie kiss you. Ever.

"*¿Zara? ¿Atiende usted?*" My Spanish teacher eyes me. She's right at my desk, smiling sweetly. Her dark brown hair is up in a high ponytail. She arches an eyebrow.

"Yes . . . yes. I mean, *sí*," I try to correct myself. I hit my head with my hand and the book flops closed. Brittney giggles.

"*Usted no traduce el libro.*" She taps her finger on my half-empty page for emphasis. "*Usted está mirando por la ventana.*"

I wasn't translating. I was looking out the window. Guilty as charged. I try to think of something to say and can only come up with sorry. "*Lo siento. Lo siento.*"

I am sorry, only I'm not just sorry about not paying attention.

I'm sorry that pixies exist and that my existence puts my friends in danger. I am sorry about everything.

The moment the class ends everyone jumps up and escapes into the hall, a bunch of cattle in the wild west running from one pen to another. We bump and jostle and finally each get our own personal space as we try to get to our next class. Someone grabs my good elbow. I yank it away screaming.

"Baby? What's up?" His face is a worried ball of cute.

"It's okay. I'm sorry. I'm edgy," I say, trying to calm down.

"Are you scared about the . . ." He doesn't say the last word because there are people around. He jams his hands into the pockets of his cargo pants. "We haven't found him yet, but I will. I swear."

The bell rings. "We're late," I say, trying to look away, but I can't. His eyes are so brown beautiful. I brush a piece of dog fur off his deep blue shirt. He's got a sort of half jock, half skater look today. I like it.

He shrugs a little. "Mrs. Nix will give us a note."

He tugs my hand and pulls me into the stairwell. We sit on the landing by the top stair. Callie bullets by us. She smiles. "Lovey lovebirds."

We smile back as she scampers down the stairs. Her Mohawk waves from our heating system's way-too-powerful forced hot air. There's a big puddle of slush on the floor just to the left of my feet.

"So, are you worried about the pixie?" he asks again.

I shrug so I don't have to answer.

"Zara? Are you worried?"

"A little." My voice is a quiet breath in the stairwell.

He moans a little bit, a half growling, half sighing kind of noise. "What are you not telling me?"

"Nothing."

"Zare? We work better when we're a team."

"We're a good team."

"Yeah, we are."

For a moment neither of us says anything. I close my eyes against the flickering fluorescent lights, against the ugly gray staleness of the stairwell. I would like to take Nick around Charleston, show him the Battery, watch the dolphins frolic in the river, laugh at the tourists coming off the cruise ships wearing their matching outfits and fanny packs, buying as many sweetgrass baskets as they can scarf up.

Cassidy rushes by, her long legs taking the stairs two at a time. She stops abruptly when she sees us. She doesn't look at me, only Nick, and her mouth drops open. She gasps and staggers down a step, grabbing the railing for balance.

I jump up, ready to lunge around and catch her. Nick leaps up right behind me.

"You okay?" I ask.

She closes her eyes for one long second. When she opens them they are filled with sadness. "Yep. All good. Just startled. Yeah."

She scurries off still muttering in sentence fragments.

I sit back down, pat the stair next to me so Nick will sit too. "That was weird. I hope she's okay. She was staring at you."

"I have that effect on the ladies," he says all lounge lizardy. "I make them stagger and run away."

"Oh really?" I turn and try to raise my eyebrows at him. His fingertips move from my ear to my chin, following the line of my jaw. Something inside me aches with need and want and all those things, all those human, hormonal-normal things. He smiles and leans in, kissing me. I kiss him back, hard and long and good. When he finally breaks away his eyes are soft and passion filled, darker than their normal rich brown.

"You are too much," he says.

My hand flattens out against his chest. His heart beats beneath it. One beat. Another. A steady rhythm of life, of comfort.

"I don't ever want to lose you," I manage to say, and then I duck my head.

He gently lifts my head back up so I can face him.

"You won't ever lose me." His voice is husky.

"Swear?" I whisper, but even that one whispered word is a gulp that threatens to yank me into a dark hole of loss and despair and—

Nick's fingers stroke my skin. "I swear."

The school cafeteria is an octagon-shaped room with the lunch counter and kitchen on three sides, the doors in and out a fourth side. The rest of the walls are windows and an emergency fire exit. The white of the snow combined with the fluorescent lights make it ridiculously bright in here, which is not a good thing.

Is and I get bagels in the lunch line. They come on paper plates with plastic knives.

"Not environmentally friendly." Issie makes a little tsking noise and slides her ID payment card through the machine.

Giselle Brown, who is behind me, says, "I have been protesting about that forever."

She shakes her head and her dreadlocks fly all around. She's got an old tie-dye Grateful Dead T-shirt on. She is one of the few people who always come to my Amnesty International meetings on Wednesdays and therefore I love her even if she does occasionally swear at the dictators when she writes. Whatever. We can't all be perfect. And if you're going to swear at someone a dictator is a good choice.

Giselle leans toward Issie and says, "What's up with Devyn and Cassidy?"

Issie freezes. "What do you mean?"

"She's all over him. I thought you two were a thing," Giselle explains.

The paper plate Issie is holding shakes. "No. No. We're not. We're just friends."

"Oh. I won't hate her on your behalf then." She smiles at me and then scrunches her nose. "It smells like butt in here."

The lunch lady looks up from her supervisory duties and bats her eyelashes. "That's not butt, that's cabbage."

Giselle jerks backward, fumbling. She drops her banana. I grab it before it hits the floor. "Oh! Oh! I didn't mean that meanly. I am so sorry. I am really, really—"

The lunch lady points a white Bic pen at Giselle. Her hair net wiggles to the left a little bit. "Hush up. I think it smells like butt too."

I slide my card through and head to the table with Issie. It's a small four-seater with a puke pink top. Nick and Dev are already chowing down on pizza. I scoot into the seat next to Nick.

"Hey, baby," he says and kisses me. His breath smells like pepperoni. "What's up?"

"Nothing." I open up my bagel with one hand.

"Giselle just told the lunch lady that it smells like butt," Issie says just as Giselle walks behind her.

"I didn't mean it meanly!" she insists, still shaking her head.

She plunks herself down at a table with Callie and some other kids who are into art and theater.

Nick spreads cream cheese on my bagel for me because it's hard to do with one hand. You need to hold the bagel and everything.

"You are the nicest boyfriend ever," I tell him and kiss his cheek.

"Gag," Devyn says.

"You're just jealous," Nick teases him and points his plastic knife at Devyn. "Which is ridiculous because you are *the star* of the school now that the wheelchair is totally gone. Everyone is talking about you."

"Star of the school?" Devyn asks. He takes a swig of Gatorade.

"All the girls." Nick gestures to the girls giggling behind them. "They like miracles. It's sexy. Remember how much play Jay Dahlberg got when he came back from being abducted?" He does not add *by pixies* because he does not have to.

"Really?" Devyn does this cheesy and really fake eyebrow wiggle thing so he looks like some sleazy porn dog.

Issie makes a gasping squeal noise and drops her water bottle. The cap wasn't on and it splurts everywhere, all over the table and our plates. "Oops! Oops! Sorry."

She tries to wipe up the wetness with her sleeve. Nick gives her napkins while I jump up and grab some more. Water's dripping off the table onto the floor.

"I am such a klutz," Is says, frantically dabbing at things. "I am so sorry . . ."

Devyn grabs her hand in his. "Issie, sweetheart, it's okay."

She freezes. Their eyes meet. Their hands are still touching. She whispers the word, "Sweetheart?"

It's like all the air and all the noise has gushed out of the cafeteria. Nick and I and everyone else are just silent witnesses to the movie that is Devyn and Issie.

Nick starts smiling super big and I know that I am probably smiling the same way. Issie's mouth, however, has dropped into a stunned O. Devyn lets go of her hand and reaches over and closes her mouth by gently touching the bottom of her chin.

"Kiss her!" Callie yells. "Kiss her!"

A couple people start chanting it.

"Kiss her! Kiss her! Kiss her! Kiss her!"

Issie's face turns bright red. She squeals for real and stands up. She flies out of the cafeteria so fast that for a second I think she must be the one with the pixie blood.

Devyn's face, unlike Issie's, drains completely of color. People start murmuring and sighing, obviously disappointed. Nick grabs the disgusting clump of soggy napkins off the table and says, "You've got to do it, man. She's totally in love with you."

Devyn shakes his head. His eyes are hard. "I can't."

It takes me a second to respond. "You better not like Cassidy, Devyn, because I swear I will kill you."

"Cassidy?" His voice is numb.

"Dude. Everyone's talking about it," Nick says.

"I don't like Cassidy," he says.

"Then stop flirting with her." I stand up.

"Flirt?" Devyn looks at Nick, probably for help.

"Yeah. Flirt. You're always with her. She's giving you rides to school. You're always talking about her and messaging her," I protest.

"I don't have the vaguest idea how to flirt. I'm a nerd. We have no social skills."

I can't believe him. "Well, you are flirting up a freaking storm, Devyn."

"Zara, take it down a notch," Nick says. "You sound jealous."

"Do *not* tell me to take it down a notch," I say, and we glare at each other. "You can be so patronizing sometimes."

He looks away first.

"I'm just trying to figure Cassidy out." Devyn wipes at his hair, ignoring us.

"Why? Why is she so fascinating? She's always itching," I ask. "And you have Issie. She is right here and she loves you. You know she loves you. I'm going to check on Issie," I announce. I point at Devyn. "You better stop being an idiot and kiss her soon, or at least tell her you love her or I swear, Devyn, I will be the one who breaks your back and shoots you with an arrow next time."

"Cassidy needs me —," he starts to say.

I stomp out of there but not before I hear Nick cracking up and Devyn saying in this high confused voice, "I thought she was a pacifist?"

"Not when it comes to her friends. So do you like this Cassidy woman or not?" Nick says, and that's all I hear because I'm too busy slamming out the cafeteria door.

I find Issie in the bathroom that's in the hall off of the cafeteria. There are these big sniffing noises coming from behind the bathroom stall that has the words 2KOOL4SKOOL scratched on it and then traced in what looks like black Sharpie pen. That has to be the most ridiculous graffiti ever.

I pull in a big breath and knock on the stall door.

"Is?"

She sniffs.

"Issie?"

After a second her voice comes out small and tired. "I'm not here."

"Oh." I back up so I can stare at the bathroom door. No feet. "Then I should probably freak out because the toilet is talking back to me, huh? A little too many pain meds for Zara today."

"No . . ." Her voice sulks out from the cracks between the door and the metal frame. Her feet pound down on the floor. Her shiny red shoes flop on the edges, the soles face each other.

"Were you standing on the toilet?" I ask.

She opens the door slowly exposing a very sad, very blotchy Issie-has-been-crying face.

I grab her with my arm and sort of hug her sideways. "Oh sweetie."

"He wouldn't kiss me," she sobs.

"Issie!" I keep my hand on her shoulder but step away so I can peer into her teary face. "Do you want your first kiss to be in the high school cafeteria with a hundred horny masticating peers watching and cheering you on?"

"Masticating?"

"It means chewing."

She rubs at her nose with the back of her fingers. "I just want— I actually want to *have* a first kiss, you know?"

I nod fiercely, remembering how it felt back in our pre-kiss days. Nick wasn't even my first kiss, though. Poor Is. "I know."

"And I guess I don't care if there is an audience because it would mean he actually likes me and he thinks I'm kissable." She peers up at me. Her nose is running. Her eyes are red. "Am I not kissable? I'm not kissable, am I? Is Cassidy more kissable than me?"

"Issie, you are totally kissable. If I were a guy or gay or bi or something I would absolutely kiss you."

She sniffs in. "Really?"

"I swear." I get a brown paper towel and fold it a couple times so it's a square and then hold it under some cold water. I use it to dab at Issie's blotchy face.

For a second she's calm and then she goes, "Then why doesn't he like me?"

"Issie!" I resist the urge to shake her. "You don't know he doesn't."

"He doesn't." She stumbles away toward the mirrors. "Oh, man . . . look at me. I'm a mess. Look at my lips!" She pokes at them. "They are too thin! They hardly even count as lips. Cassidy has much better lips, and he doesn't like me, Zara. Do you remember when you called me right before the accident?"

I remember. She'd sounded like she was crying. I never even asked her about that. Wow, what is wrong with me? How can I be such an awful friend?

"I was crying," she continues, sniffing, "because I just told Devyn that I *liked* him, liked him and you know what he said?" She doesn't give me a chance to answer. "He said that he 'didn't currently know what to do with that information.' I'd finally told him that I liked him and he just totally blew me off like I was nothing."

I try to take it in. I can't understand it. "Did he tell you why?"

"No. Because you called and I—I—we just haven't talked about it again."

"That makes no sense. He is probably being macho or valiant or ultra-nerdy or something." I grab another paper towel and wipe at her cheeks, trying to get all the wet tears off. "He called you *'sweetheart,'* Issie. No guy calls a girl sweetheart unless he likes her."

After much convincing I finally get Is to head back to the table. The entire walk into the cafeteria she refuses to look up and just sort of slides into her seat.

"Hey." Her voice is barely recognizable, it is so low and whisper soft.

"Hey," Dev says back in an equally quiet voice.

"So . . ." Nick searches for something to say. "Do you think all high school cafeterias serve bagels?"

"Why, yes," I banter in a forced good mood that's totally fake. "I think they must because not only are they carbs and therefore qualify as food, they come out of plastic freezer bags and when not defrosted can pass as lethal weapons."

"I'll have to remember that next time," Nick says. "Instead of tying a pixie up to a tree when I don't have time to bring him back to the house, I can just knock him unconscious for hours with the power of a frozen everything bagel."

"Yes, you should," I counter. "Instead of continuing our lessons with crossbows and swords and knives you should switch to bagels and L. L. Bean boots."

We both give each other desperate eyes. Issie and Devyn just appear miserable. The blond pixie guy randomly pops into my head, and I remember how he held me when Yoko exploded. I push the thought away with a curse.

After just a couple minutes of horrible forced conversation, Nick and Dev go into "we are males, we protect our females" mode, and I mean, it's outdated and macho, but there is something a tiny bit cute about how they hunker down, elbows on the table, backs curled over, hands turning to fists, turning to pointed fingers as they anger out their concerns and worries.

Devyn says, "I checked the house this morning. There was nothing. No dust anywhere."

"There's been no sign of any new pixies either," Nick says.

"Maybe they've stopped coming," I say.

"Or maybe they're getting smarter." Nick cracks a knuckle.

I pick a raisin out of my bagel. "Well, it could actually be a good thing."

"You can't keep lying to yourself that you're safe," Nick says. "It's not good for you, baby. You almost died last week."

"No, I didn't. I just got hurt—not fatally hurt," I counter. "And what about you? You're always out there hunting alone. That's not safe either."

Issie kicks me under the table. I get up.

"It's okay, Zara," Issie says, trying to soothe me. She puts her hands on top of the ugly cafeteria table. Her fingers splay out, white and delicate. I stare at them for a second, pale against the mauve tabletop, hanging out there by the paper plates holding half-eaten bagels, the plastic knives, the water bottle, empty cream cheese containers. I stare and I stare and I stare and I get this weird feeling, almost spider-legs-like when pixies are near, but something else too, something more, something different. My legs wobble.

"I feel—I feel—ah—" I can't get the words out.

Someone grabs me by the waist and pulls me back into a sitting position. Big hands. Steady hands. Nick hands. "Zara? What? What is it, baby?"

"Some . . . uh . . . some . . . thing . . . ," I manage. "Spidery. I have a spidery feeling."

I lift my head up, stare out the big window that shows a field, the edge of forest. It's the same window through which I once saw my pixie father stand and point at me, back before I knew he was my father. The world sways. There's nothing there now.

I'm sitting sideways on the chair and Nick's squatting on the floor in front of me. His hands are on my knees and he looks into my eyes. It's his worried face, soft and caring. Then he shifts into commander mode. "Devyn," he barks. "You smell anything?"

Devyn breathes in deeply. "No. There's too many smells in here. I can't isolate them."

A low growl comes out of Nick's throat. "Me either."

He stands up and surveys the cafeteria. His body shudders. His hand catches mine. "I don't see him."

"Nick?"

His body shudders again. People are noticing, staring.

"Oh crap," Devyn says, totally out of character. "He's turning."

I stand up, haul Nick toward the bathroom, fast-walking through the cafeteria. "Do. Not. Turn," I insist. "You cannot turn here. Nobody is in danger. Do. Not. Turn."

Issie flies out of her chair and Devyn starts after us but I'm so fast he can't keep up.

Once we get out of the cafeteria Nick stops, leans against the wall, and shudders. His voice is a plea that matches his eyes. "Zara . . ."

I put my hands on either side of his face. "You aren't going to turn. It's okay. Everyone is safe. No pixies. Look at me. Nod, sweetie. Listen: I. Am. Safe."

Issie and Devyn catch up to us. Nick is still shuddering like he's freezing cold, trying to control himself. I keep my hands on his face and say, "I think he's got it under control."

Some freshman carrying a huge pink Lillian Vernon shoulder bag walks by and stares. "He okay? You want me to get the nurse?"

Issie reassures the sweet freshman that all is okay and sort of steers her away while Devyn and I try to get Nick calm.

"That just doesn't happen," Devyn says. "There's got to be a reason."

"He changes when people are in danger," I state the obvious. "Someone was in danger. That's the reason."

"Right, but what's the danger?" Devyn asks.

Nick swallows hard and moves his lips. It looks hard. It looks like he's dying of thirst, but he says, "That blond pixie. He was here. He was in the cafeteria. I know it."

"But you didn't see him," Issie insists.

Nick's hands reach up to touch mine. He looks at me, not Issie, and says, "I don't have to see him. I just know."

Pixie Tip

Pixies are like cats. They are not named Muffin or Mr. Cocoa Puffs, but they like to scare their prey before they kill. They think it's fun.

We decide that we need to leave school and regroup, plan what to do next. Things aren't right. We know that. There haven't been any new pixies scouting out the area after a steady stream for weeks. Plus, if the blond pixie was in the cafeteria, that's upped the stakes a bit.

I stare at the inside of my locker for a second and announce, "Patrolling isn't good enough anymore. We've got to figure out what's going on with the Valkyrie thing, and maybe hunt down the pixie king before he hunts us down."

"None of it makes sense." Devyn pulls out his coat from his locker.

"Hey. Where you guys going?" Cassidy asks. She appears out of thin air, I swear. Cassidy half smiles and then she eyes me. Her pupils get a little bigger. Her skirt hem touches my jeans because she's so close. "Zara? Are you okay?"

I nod vigorously, the way I always do when I lie. "Yeah. Why?"

My fingers yank up the zipper of my coat. I realize they are shaking. The bell rings, but still Cassidy stands there. "Because it almost looks like you're turning blue."

"What?" My question echoes in the hall. Nick, Is, and Dev all stare at me. Their faces are paler than normal. Nick's mouth is a hard, straight line. He yanks me away from Cassidy and starts pulling me down the hall in a hardcore power walk.

"What? What?" I keep saying it, but nobody's answering.

Devyn goes, "Yeah, Nick's taking her to the nurse. No fears, Cassidy. No fears. Yep. Call you later."

Nick's hauling me down the hall and I say, "Hold on. What's going on?"

He chews on his lip. Then he reaches out and pulls up my coat sleeve and my shirt sleeve underneath it, exposing my naked arm.

"Don't let her faint!" Issie yells.

"I'm not going to faint." My voice is flat as I stare at my skin. It's like all my veins are suddenly visible just beneath the surface layer of skin. And all those veins carry a blood that's light, light blue, tinting all of my skin, coloring it into sky.

"It's beautiful," Issie, who has caught up to us, whispers.

"It's weird." I yank my shirt down. "Is it happening to my face, too?"

Nick nods. His eyes are shaded. I can't read them.

"Oh wow, I look—I look—" I can't get the words out. My body slumps to the ground, my back pressing against the too-hot monster radiators that line the wall beneath the windows.

"You look fine," Issie soothes. She squats down next to me and rubs my shoulder that's not touching the radiator. "You're still pretty. Really."

"Pretty isn't what I'm worried about: I don't look human." I shake my head as her hand moves in tiny circles, like a mother's hand. "I look like a pixie."

We all stay there for a minute.

"Is it getting worse?" I ask.

Issie shakes her head, but Devyn is all about honesty over feelings and he says, "It was. The progression seems to have stopped. And it's only your skin, not your eyes and teeth."

"Progression?" I hide my head in my hands. Somebody gentles against me, lifts me up, but I won't look.

"Come on," says Nick's gruff voice. "Let's get to the office, get a pass, and get out of here."

Our school secretary, Mrs. Nix, is one of my grandmother's friends. She is roundish with thinning hair and this massive, happy smile. She is the old-fashioned kind of school secretary who bakes cookies and brings them in on a big printed plate and leaves them on the counter for kids to take. She has thick ankles and wears embossed sweatshirts with pictures of white puffy kittens. She wears sensible flats and puts rubber things over them for when she walks across the parking lot to her Chevy sedan.

She is also a shifter, specifically a bear. There is nothing bear-like about her now, though. She squeals and steps backward when she sees my face. Nick's arm moves protectively around my shoulder and she steps forward. One step. Another. She makes it around the big counter and reaches out her hand. Her fingertips gently touch my arm.

"Oh, Zara, honey," she whispers. "What's happened to you?"

I shake my head. "I don't know."

I sort of slump forward and Nick lets go of me so Mrs. Nix can gather me into a big hug. She smells like roses.

"You come sit down over here." She hustles me into a plastic yellow chair. "Nick, get the cookies."

Nick half smiles as he gets the cookie plate. He passes them around.

I chew. "It's really good. Um, am I still blue?"

"Not quite so bad," Mrs. Nix says. "Nick, be a love and go get my pocketbook."

Nick goes into a back room and comes out with Mrs. Nix's purse. The phone rings. She tells Dev to answer it and put whoever it is on hold while she paws through the contents of her big fabric bag.

"There!" She snatches out a compact. "Foundation. Issie, help me put this on her face."

"It's too dark," Nick says.

"Well, it'll have to do until you get to a pharmacy, won't it? Unless you have some makeup hiding in that leather jacket of yours, Mr. Colt," she says.

"Whoa. Snappy," Dev whispers.

Her big brown eyes peer into mine, gentle but obviously worried. "None have kissed you, right?"

"Pixies?" I whisper. The thought overwhelms me.

She nods.

"No." I shake my head and look to Issie for confirmation. "None." *But I was unconscious for a bit in my car . . .* "I would notice if they did, right?"

"Most definitely. You'd be out of it for a good long while. If you even survived . . ." Mrs. Nix's voice trails off and the office is suddenly far too silent. She finally breaks it and says, "Well, that's a relief."

Issie spreads some more concealer over my chin. Her fingers move in quick, soft strokes. "It's looking better."

"She looks orange," Dev says, leaning in, taking another cookie, and peering closer.

"Devyn!" Issie glares at him.

"It's better than blue," he says.

"True," Issie agrees. "Now she just looks like that picture of my mom from the eighties. She would put on all this base and not rub it in. There'd be a big white line on her chin."

We all exchange a look because Issie totally does that too.

Mrs. Nix leans back to inspect my face. She wipes her hands against each other. "Much better."

I force myself to look at Nick. He nods. "Beautiful," he whispers. He is such a liar.

Mrs. Nix turns to us, eyes flashing. "You want to be dismissed?" She doesn't even wait for an answer, just writes us all notes and files them away quick as a flash. She meets my eyes when she's done and says, "Do. Not. Worry."

"But—"

"I mean it, Zara. Do. Not. Worry. I'm sure this is a random fluke and it does not mean what you think it means."

I swallow hard and lean against the counter. "You don't think I'm—"

She holds up her hand to stop my words. "No. I do not think you are turning into a pixie."

"You swear? Because I don't think I could handle that. I wouldn't be me. I'd be all evil and my teeth would look like sharks' teeth and what if I had those needs?"

Her hand goes up straight like she's taking an oath. Nick's hip brushes against mine. I lean into him. Her mouth forms the words. "I promise that you are a hundred percent human, Zara. I have no doubts."

. . .

We all ride together in Issie's car. Nick drives. His MINI is too small for all of us plus Devyn's gear.

Is and I sit huddled in the back together, and Nick pops open the far end to shove Dev's braces in. He slams behind the wheel, angry and distressed. "This is crazy, Zara. I feel like we're missing pieces of the puzzle."

"Tell him," Issie mouths.

I don't want to, but I do. "Um. Nick . . ."

He pulls the car out of the parking space. Issie squeezes my hand tighter.

"Nick?" I try again.

"You're going to be okay, baby. I swear. We're going to take you to Betty, figure this out."

I swallow. "That's not it."

Dev turns around in his seat to stare at us. "What is it, then?"

"Um . . ."

"Zara?" Nick's voice is almost a warning.

I scrunch down a little more in my seat. "The other day Issie and I . . . we, um . . . we, um . . . we kind of took my father out of the house—"

"We put him right back in, though," Issie interrupts.

"Yeah. And we wrapped him up really well in this blanket we sewed iron inside," I add.

Is interrupts again. "And the car. He hated the car because of the steel and iron in it. Wait. Zara, you don't have a headache or anything, do you?"

I manage to tear my glance away from the back of Nick's head to look at Is. "No. Why? Oh. Because I'm in the car and I'm blue, right?"

"Zara!" Nick's voice is a roar. Dev grabs the steering wheel. He's nervous like that. "I've got it, Devyn."

Nick yanks the car over to the side of the road, which is a completely disrespectful way to handle Issie's car. She is a sensitive car and her tires or the rods or something in her squeals in protest. He slams on the brakes and turns around to look at me. His eyes are darker than I've ever seen.

"Simmer down, man," Dev says.

Nick pays no attention. "What were you two thinking?"

Issie clutches my hand harder. "We were thinking that—"

This time I'm the one who interrupts. "You know what, Mr. I'm the Boss of Everybody?" Dev snorts. I ignore him and rant on. "Payback sucks. Issie and I can go rogue sometimes too."

I let go of Issie's hand so I can point at him. He stays turned around as cars zip by us. He grabs my finger in his giant hand. Something in his jaw twitches. I gulp but I don't look away. Then something in his eyes shifts. His grip is a tiny bit lighter.

"You're right," he says finally.

Issie lets out this massive sigh and flops back against the car seat. She mumbles something that sounds like "I hate conflict."

Nick's eyes flick in her direction for just a second before focusing on me again. His voice is still flinty and hard, and his shoulders slump a little, like he's disappointed in us, in me. "But it was incredibly dangerous."

I nod. "I know, but we all do dangerous things. Our lives are dangerous."

"And we had to find things out," Issie blurts.

Dev's voice is soft and tired. "Find out what, Issie?"

"What the danger is," she says.

"And did you?" Nick asks.

"Yeah," I say softly. "We did."

. . .

Nick pulls back onto the road and Is and I explain as we drive to the ambulance headquarters. We tell them what my father said, about how other pixies will come because he is so weak and they will claim this territory, which actually extends throughout New England and eastern Canada. The other pixie king will attack his headquarters, here in our town, and he will not care about humans. He will claim me as a prize, supposedly, because I am half pixie and the king's daughter.

"Which puts you in danger," I finally say as we pull into the parking lot for the ambulances. Betty's big truck is sitting as far away from the front door as she can park it. She likes to walk.

"How does that put *me* in danger?" Nick asks. It's the first question he's asked the entire time. Devyn, however, has been Mr. Nonstop Wondering Question Guy.

"Because . . ." I don't know how to say it, struggle for the words. "Because you and I are a thing and you're a threat."

"You better believe I'm a threat," Nick growls. The entire car seems to shake with his energy. Little hairs on my arm lift and vibrate.

"He's going macho again," Dev says, totally nonchalantly, while he unlocks the door.

"He's always going macho," Is adds. "It must be the wolf thing."

"I am not *going* macho. I *am always* macho," Nick says, and for a moment the tension ratchets down, but then his face muscles become rigid again. "I can't believe he used you like that. He totally manipulated you, scaring you just to get some kind of sick joy ride. I thought my parents were bad, but crap, your freaking father, Zara."

Nick slams open his door and gets Dev's braces. As Is and I get out I whisper, "What did Nick mean about his parents?"

Issie's face opens up. She whispers back, "He hasn't told you?"

"Told me what?" I am hissing almost. Pebbles crunch beneath our feet. One rolls into an icy mud puddle.

"I'll tell you after." She nods her head toward the guys. Dev is standing, waiting for his braces. An eighteen-wheeler carrying Poland Spring water trundles down the road. About a year ago three people from Myanmar gave some water to monks who were walking in the street protesting rights abuses. The government said that giving water was an act of supporting terrorism. For a second I wish I could magically transport that entire truck to those monks. For a second I wish I could magically explain to the government of Myanmar about pixies and show them what terror really is.

"Zara? You there?" Is pokes my arm.

"Yeah. Sorry. Am I still blue?"

She eyes me. "A little, but you can't really tell from the makeup. I think it's getting better."

My fingers touch the edge of her dirty car, make marks on it, just light little lines. I lift my fingers away, examine the dirt. "Are you lying because you're my best friend and you don't want to scare me?"

Is makes a smiley face out of my lines. "Yeah."

We head into the building and once inside the square front office, Josie the dispatcher stands up from her old, monstrous metal desk and smiles. The blue and yellow beads at the end of her cornrows sway. "Well, look who's here. Are we all legally skipping school or should I call in one of those deputies to bring you all up on truancy charges?"

"Legal. We have a note," Nick says. He bounces on his toes; too much energy inside him has nowhere to go.

"I should have known. Working the system, right?" Josie nods her head toward the coffeemaker. "You all want something to drink? Or just Betty?"

"I'll have some water," Devyn says, hitching across the ugly linoleum floor that looks like it came out of some 1970s discount department store. He grabs a cup and puts it under the big blue jug of water.

Josie presses a button and says, "Betty, you've got visitors, a whole troupe of them."

My grandmother's voice crackles on the intercom. "Who is it?"

"Zara, her handsome boy toy"—Josie wiggles her eyebrows and Nick starts blushing beside me while Is cracks up—"and friends."

"Tell them to come on back," she orders.

"Thanks, Josie," I say. I give her a kiss on her cheek. "You smell like coconut."

"My moisturizer," she says. "How about your boy toy gives me a kiss?"

Nick does.

"Boy toy," Dev mocks as we walk the narrow corridor to the back room.

"You're just jealous," Nick grunts.

Dev sort of laughs through his nose in an absolutely geeky boy way. "Right, boy toy. Are you a Mr. Potato Head or a Wolverine action figure? No! Wait! A Transformer."

"Shut up." Nick and I make eye contact. He smiles. I break free from Is so she and Dev can be a little closer, and also so I can open the door to the break room where the EMTs hang out when they aren't on a call. Nick beats me to it. He hauls open the door and holds it there for all of us to go through.

"Thanks," I say, inhaling the scent of him as I walk by.

"Anytime." His free hand touches the small of my back really lightly. It makes me shiver. It's the good kind of shiver.

He notices. "You okay?"

"Yeah." I tilt my head up at him.

Is and Dev are already in the room. Nick takes my arm and gently pulls me back into the hallway with him. We're alone. He whispers down, "You don't need to be brave with me, Zare. That's the point of a relationship, right? You tell each other things. You let each other see things that you don't let the rest of the world see."

I swallow hard. "I just don't want . . . I don't want you to worry. I'm sorry I went off with my father."

His hand cups my cheek. His thumb grazes my skin, slow and light and strong all at once. "I know. And I'm sorry I get so macho."

I press my lips together.

He nods fast and hard like he's trying to hold back some big emotion. "Come on, let's go in and have Betty check you out."

The ugly yellowy lights in the room make Betty and Mike, the EMT with her, look a little jaundiced, like they have some sort of liver disease. Mike is sitting on the dilapidated brown sofa watching CNN, absentmindedly picking at the edges of some duct tape that is wrapped around the sofa arm holding it together. The TV drones on about sex scandals and politicians. There is a box of Dunkin' Donuts on the middle of the table at the left of the room. Betty is doing what she does best. She is walking on the treadmill with a copy of *The Economist* splayed out in front of her. She used to be an insurance company president. She retired before they started making eight hundred million dollars a year. This is unfortunate. I'm sure if she was still a CEO I'd already have a new car and a new laptop.

"Well, Devyn! Look at you walking again. That's a blessing for sore eyes." Her gray hair bounces with every forceful stride and she smiles at us. "I have thirty seconds left before I hit five hundred calories. You should see my pulse rate."

"Steady?" Nick asks.

"As a rock." She smiles and presses a button. The incline of the treadmill lowers. She adjusts her uniform shirt, tucking the white ends more neatly into the awful blue polyester-blend pants she has to wear. "Cutting school?"

I try to smile but I can't quite make it work.

Nick stands next to me. His arm wraps around my waist. "Zara is feeling a little blue."

He puts some extra stress on the words "feeling" and "blue."

Betty takes a swig from her water bottle. She squints at us.

"Really blue," Issie emphasizes before looking over at Mike, slightly panicked.

Betty hops off the treadmill. She puts her big hands on my shoulders and leans down a little to stare into my eyes. "Blue, huh? Depressed?"

I sniff. Her deodorant is working overtime. It is nice and everything, but a little too baby fresh for me.

"Mike," she says in a louder voice.

"Yeah." He turns his head to sort of half look at us. He gives a wave.

Dev and Is wave back.

"You okay with keeping Josie company for a minute while I talk to my granddaughter here?" Betty asks. But when Betty asks things like this, it's more of a telling. Believe me, I know. She's uses the same tone about bringing my laundry downstairs. There's no choice when she talks like this. It's a command.

"Absolutely. I need more coffee anyway." Mike stands up and stretches. He is pretty tall like Nick, only super skinny, all scarecrow limbs. Mike points a finger at me in a pretend gun sort of shape and leaves. The door swings behind him.

The moment he is gone, Betty leaps into action.

"Devyn, get me the kit by the coats," she orders.

Dev grabs the alarm red box that looks like something you lug fishing lures in, only it has medical symbols on it. It's kind of cool how he can do this with his braces.

"Take your coat off, Zara." Betty unlocks the kit and slams it open.

Nick helps me shrug off my coat.

"Roll up your sleeves," Betty insists.

I pull them up.

"You're blue," she says. She stops for a second. Her eyes meet my eyes.

"I know."

"It was worse before," Nick says.

Betty pulls out a needle and a vial that you store blood in. Her voice is stunned. "I've never seen anything like this."

Issie grabs my hand. "Do you want to squeeze?"

"Sure," I say, grabbing her tiny hand back. "Why are you taking my blood?"

Betty plunges the needle into the underside of my elbow. "To see if you've turned."

I shudder.

"Stay still," she says as the vial fills up.

"You can tell by my blood?" I ask, watching. "Wouldn't I feel different? Evil or something?"

"Tell me when it's over," Issie says. She's the one changing colors now. She's all pale and looking like she's going to faint. "I can't stand it. I hate blood and needles. Even the word 'need-le.' Urck."

I let go of her hand. "It's okay. It doesn't hurt. Much."

"You're always trying to be so brave, Zara. You don't have to be." Betty eases out the needle. "Nick, put some gauze on that. Light pressure."

She caps the vial and turns back to us. "I'm going to send this out for some tests."

"Send it where?" I ask.

"My parents," Dev answers. "They're kind of experts."

I don't get it. "I thought your parents were psychiatrists."

"They are. But, um, they have some side fields that they work on."

"Like what?"

"Cryptozoology. Medical research on blood differences in weres, pixies, others."

I swallow. "Others?"

He nods. "Since I was attacked, my parents have become a little . . . um . . . zealous."

"They're brilliant people," Issie interrupts.

"Yeah, but they've gone a little crazy about this. They've converted the entire basement into a lab. They're online 24-7 researching and they didn't even know pixies existed until this fall."

I pull my sleeves down. "And why has *nobody* told me this before?"

Everyone looks at Devyn, who is sitting in a metal folding chair with this amazingly introspective look on his face. "Because they're protecting me."

I resist the urge to ask why and wait for him to tell me instead.

He sits up taller and says, "My parents aren't exactly the most normal people and my home is a sty."

"Beyond a sty, really," Issie says. "You know the opposite of anal retentive? That's them. No offense, Dev."

He slowly stretches his legs out in front of them. "I don't bring anyone back to the house except Is and Nick. I never have."

"And it took him years to let me come over," Nick says.

"He beat me up first." Devyn smiles. "It was seventh grade. We'd been friends since kindergarten."

I swallow hard. I understand but I still feel left out of the loop. It makes me feel all new kid and not trusted, like I'm not one of the pack. Part of me wants to pout about it but I buck up and say, "How's my skin, Gram?"

She leans over and peers into my eyes. Her strong hands rest on my shoulders. "Nobody is going to panic about this. You will get some good cover-up. You said it's already fading?"

"It's faded a lot," Nick answers.

"When did it start?" she asks, letting go of my shoulders.

I settle back against Nick's chest. It is solid good.

"Can *you* tell her?" I ask.

He wraps an arm around me and tells her about the weird feeling I had. He tells her how Issie and I broke my dad out of the house (and put him back) and what he said about the other pixie.

She listens to it all before she says anything and when she does, she shakes her head.

"This is bad." She whirls on me and Issie. "I can't believe you two did that. You cannot trust pixies."

"So you can't trust me?" I ask.

"You're not a pixie. You're human." She snaps her medical kit shut.

"Right. So that's why my skin is blue." My stomach threatens to knock a hole through my skin and leave my body in protest.

"Zara . . ." Nick's voice is a warning.

"She's just sad," Is says. "That's why she's being all snippy. Or else it's the pain meds."

"They are mood altering," Devyn agrees.

"I am not snippy. I'm mad because nobody is listening to me." My hands ball into fists. "What? Just because you don't want to believe it, Nick, doesn't mean it isn't true. I remember how you acted when you found out who my father is. I remember you running away, okay? I know how you totally hate pixies and if I'm a pixie that obviously means that you—"

His arms reach out to me, but his hands are fists. "Zara—"

"Just. Don't. Say. Anything." I stare at all of them, take a step back. "Nobody say anything. This is not your problem. This is my problem. Mine. I'm the freak here. Me."

Betty starts laughing. "Zara, think about who you're saying this to."

"You're weres. Except Is. Weres are not pixies. They aren't all evil, okay?" I yell. I grab the doorknob on the emergency exit door and turn it. It's locked. I turn the little lock mechanism in the middle of the knob. My fingers fumble and shake, but I finally manage to do it.

"Where are you going, honey?" Issie asks. She moves a step closer to me.

"Don't." I yank open the door. Cold rushes in. "I'm just going, okay? I'm just going."

I rush out the door, slam it shut behind me, and race across the parking lot into the muddy edge where it meets the woods. Before the door closes I hear my grandmother say, "Just let her go. She needs to be alone. She's always been that way ever since she—"

I run away, stumble through the mud, slosh it up into the cuffs of my jeans, and head out to the woods. I run away, but the truth is, I don't have anywhere to go.

Pixie Tip

Pixies will whisper your name and try to get you lost—usually in the woods. Do not listen. You will not come back. In general, it's always best to avoid contact with disembodied voices.

I have the emotional maturity of a two-year-old. I know this! I know, but it doesn't make me stop trying to escape my grandmother and friends and the pity in their eyes and in Nick's eyes . . . the eyes I suddenly can't read.

So I run as best as I can through the sloshy snow and mud. My feet take me far enough into the woods that I don't hear cars anymore. I don't hear anything. No wind blows through the high branches of the spruce and pine trees. Their thin, pale brown trunks don't creak with the weight of snow and ice. No birds sing. No squirrels chitter and squeak and make all those noises that squirrels make.

Nothing.

No noise.

Nothing.

That is not normal. I sniff in and smell. It's just wet wood and old pine needles. Olfactophobia is the fear of odors. Odor fears get more specific, though. Bromidrosiphobia is the fear of personal odor. You know, body odor. Luckily, I don't have that. There is no name that I know of for the fear of a lack of odor. There is no name that I know of for the fear of lack of sound. The fear of sound itself is acousticophobia.

Why are there no names for the fear of the absence of things? Why is there no name for the absence of humanity? Because that is my fear, right here, right now. I am worried that I am losing my humanity.

I've seen what happens then. Jay Dahlberg was tortured and bled and bitten when I found him in an upstairs bedroom at my father's pixie mansion home. Jay doesn't remember any of it. I do. I remember his body shaking as I tried to help him down the long flight of marble stairs. I remember the smell of his fear permeating everything.

Pixies did that.

I can't be one of them.

I can't.

I force the images out of my head and stand here, leaning against a tree for about a half an hour, just trying to understand why I ran away, but the truth is there's not much to understand: I don't want to face that I'm turning blue.

My footprints show the way back to the parking lot, to the ambulance, to reality. I walk, staring at those dark footprints indented in the snow. Then it happens: spiders creeping on my skin where no spiders are. And something else: an ache. I fold over in half. My hand presses into my stomach.

"Even your moans are lovely," says a voice. It is male, deep, husky but with melody, like a country singer. I recognize it. "I should not be surprised."

The feelings intensify. The snow impressions blur. I use a tree trunk to help me stand up straight. My throat closes, almost trapping my words. "Oh wow, not you again."

"You sound panicked."

Trees surround me. Half-gone snow. Everything dull and white and gray brown, gray green. No place for a voice. I say as toughly as I can, "I wouldn't be panicked if you weren't hiding."

"What form would you prefer?"

What form? It takes me a second. Pixie or human? That's what he means. I sway toward the tree. My hand slips down the rough edges of the trunk. "Human."

"Human it is." Hands grab me, steady me. I jerk back, but they are surprisingly gentle. He doesn't smile as I turn to see his face. He just stands there, letting me inspect him. He's tall with a wide forehead and dark blond hair that's cut short. His green eyes are deeply set beneath that forehead. His lips are wide and rugged like the rest of him. His hands have huge knuckles like he's a boxer or arthritic or hits walls. He looks like he did when he pulled me out of the car, but stronger, taller somehow. He must be completely healed. He looks my age and he looks good, like the guy in high school that everyone, even the teachers, fall in love with.

I shake him off, step back, press into the tree. "You're the other king, aren't you?"

"*The* king, really, since your father is not doing so well currently."

"You figured that out?" I manage to say. I look for weapons. A tree branch? Could I break off a tree branch? But do I need a weapon? He saved me before. I stall for time, try to think. "You figured out who I am?"

He sighs, rubs his hands over his hair, and changes the topic.

"It is so cold here in Maine. Your poor father is stuck with this territory. He must have annoyed someone."

He makes a face like the entire state is distasteful.

"You could always leave," I suggest.

I look both ways. It would take me about three minutes to run back to the parking lot, but what then? He'd catch me.

"I would catch you," he says.

"Reading thoughts?"

"Guessing."

My teeth chatter.

"See?" he says. "You despise it here as well. I have done my research. You are a southern girl, correct? Charleston. Mint juleps. Lazy, hot days on the veranda. Now you are stuck here eating bagels with all those people."

"I choose to be here."

He lifts an eyebrow. It's a slow, calculated lift. His voice matches it. "I do not believe that. You are here because you have to be. Just as I am."

I meet his eyes. They are deep and almost mesmerizing. Did I say deep before? Yeah, right. That's not it. They have a pull to them, like currents, like Velcro or something, totally captivating, like when you see a convertible flipped over on the highway and there are body bags and you don't want to look but you look because you can't look, because you can't *not* look, because you are just riveted and . . .

Stop. Just stop.

"Are you going to let me go back?" I ask and nod my head toward the ambulances and the station.

"Of course. I am not the kind of pixie who makes people lose their way or traps them."

"Mm-hmm. Right. No calling people's names out in the woods?"

"That is archaic. Did they really do that?" His voice loses its mesmerizing quality and creeps into curiosity. He seems so young compared to my dad, too young to be a king.

I start walking. The snow invades my sneakers. My feet are already soaked, frozen, cold. He walks just behind me. His breath hits my hair because he is so close. If I stopped fast he'd slam into me.

"No kidnapping either, right?" I say. "Because I am not into being kidnapped."

"No kidnapping." He lifts his hand. He still looks amused. "Pixie honor."

I snort. "Pixie honor. Right. I've been kidnapped before, you know. I know all about pixie honor."

He grabs me by the shoulder and whirls me around, suddenly, alarmingly fierce. I flinch. His mouth moves hard and fast with his words. "I know you have not had good experiences with us, princess, but your father was weak. His people were barely controlled. That is not how we are meant to rule."

"Really?" I yank myself away. "Sorry. I've found you all aren't the most trustworthy."

He eyes me. His voice deepens and almost sounds concerned. "You are turning blue. It was faint when I first saw you and I was not sure, but it is much deeper now."

The wind suddenly blows. I sway again, almost crumple. "I'm so dizzy."

His arms are around me. "I shall carry you back."

"No," I protest, but he doesn't listen. He lifts me up into his arms. "I said no."

"You are not going to make it." He pulls me against him as if I weigh nothing.

The world rocks back and forth, uncontrolled, unplanned. "What's—"

"Happening to you?" he finishes. "I am not positive. But I think you're reacting to me. My presence sets off your pixie blood, calls it up. There are not that many halves like you, Zara. It is just not allowed, and there are none who are descended from a king. There is not a lot of precedence for what is occurring."

"I didn't turn blue when I was near my father." I flinch.

"That is because he is your father. It would be like—um— being attracted to him, that way." He says this awkwardly with none of his earlier assurance. "I think something in my blood calls out to yours. We attract each other."

I shake my head. "I'm not attracted to you. I love Nick."

"Nick," he mutters. "The wolf's name is Nick."

"Do *not* hurt him." I groan from the movement. "I will *kill* you if you hurt him."

He stops walking for a moment. "I shall only do what I have to do, Zara." He's silent for a moment. I let him think. Then he says, "What is important right now is you, your skin. Your eyes are unfocused."

"Am I turning?" I whisper. "Am I turning into one of you?"

He strides through the woods, turning sideways when the trees are too close. He is graceful and strong. "No. I do not believe so. You have to be kissed. And you still smell very human and nice. I am not certain, though. I shall try to find out."

My mind flashes to when Ian tried to kiss me. He'd kidnapped me, tried to turn me, so he could defeat my father, take his power.

"You won't kiss me," I say, pounding on his chest for emphasis. "You promise. Promise you won't kiss me."

His mouth goes up to that same smile, half mischief, no teeth, crinkling his face into something almost happy, something not so sad. "I cannot promise that, but I promise that I will not kiss you unless you want me to."

"That will never happen," I say, pointing at him. "And no hurting Nick."

"Right." He laughs and I turn my head away, looking at my hands. My hands are almost totally blue. They spread across the dark wool material of his jacket. They clench into balls and shake.

That's the last thing I see: my blue skin, shaking.

I wake up in Issie's car. He's opened the back door, laid me down on the rear seat. My hand touches one of Issie's old French tests, folded over, muddy, like it's been stepped on and discarded.

The pixie guy shudders. He's standing just outside the door. He puts his hand gently on my arm. "Do not attempt to get up yet. You fainted. I believe I am a little much for you to handle in your present human state." He winks like a total jerk, like some kind of pixie player. "I was not about to bring you inside, because I am not in the mood for a bloodbath. You should go in a minute when you are not quite so azure."

He reaches out and touches my face, just one fingertip against my cheek. I shiver.

"I hate cars too. We all do," he says.

"That's not why I shivered," I insist, sitting up, swinging my legs out and trying not to shake. "I suppose I should thank you for bringing me here and not turning me or eating me or anything."

His broad face droops a little bit. His jaw clenches. "That is not how I play."

"Play?" My hand drags across the upholstery in the back of the car, hits the old test paper, rips it a little more.

"I do not play at all, really. Not like that. We are not all like that."

"Like what?" I ask.

"Like your father."

"You keep saying that."

"Because you keep not believing me."

His face shifts again and I can glimpse the blue tint beneath his skin. I grab the test, try to smooth it into something not so crumpled and worn looking. I fold it into squares, deliberately matching the edges of paper up before I fold, just to have something to do with my hands. Finally, I say, "I don't understand what you mean."

His hands twitch next to my knees. He makes me think of one of those old-time boxers, all power underneath skin and words. "If I had wanted to kill you, you would be dead already."

My head whips up and my fingers grab his wrists. The test falls out of the car and into an icy mud puddle. "You don't hurt anyone. Got it? Not even my father. You don't hurt him."

"I am not who you should be worried about."

I shake my head. "What? What do you mean? Of course you're who I should worry about."

He moves just a little bit and my fingers fall off of his wrists. He stands up and just walks away, shoulders straight, but different than before. There's something humble about them almost. I don't know. I don't understand anything.

"Hey! Do you have a name?" I call after him. My voice is weak but it stops him.

He turns around. This time he gives a full smile, revealing perfect teeth, white and even. His whole face transforms into something beautiful, the same way Nick's face changes. "Astley."

I touch my feet to the ground, repeat it. "Astley?"

He lifts his shoulders and smiles. "We do not have the opportunity to choose our own names, unfortunately."

"What does it mean? Does it mean something?"

"Star." He turns and disappears into the woods like he was never there at all.

"Wait! Can you tell me about Valkyries?" I yell after him.

There's no answer. I collapse onto the car upholstery and watch my skin gradually turn back to pale again, almost like nothing happened. Almost.

"I will never kiss you," I whisper. "I will never kiss anyone except Nick."

Of course, nobody hears.

Pixie Tip
Pixies do not just eat pollen and honey. Not by a long shot.

I have had friends back in Charleston who were totally anupta-phobic. You know, they are terrified, absolutely one hundred percent terrified, of not being part of a "couple." They are so frightened of singledom that they will go out with anyone with a pulse or anything breathing just to make sure that they aren't single and alone. I didn't get it. I wanted to slap them in a non-violent way and tell them that going out with the soccer player who sniffs glue with his mother and is also completely laying down with the band girl who picks elbow scabs is not better than being alone, especially when his breath always, always smells like blue cheese salad dressing.

I've never been like that. But now that I've met Nick, I can kind of understand the fear. The thought that you might never kiss someone again, that you might never be wrapped up in solid arms and breathe in the smell of soap and strength and trees, that you might never hear the words "I love you" and have someone really, truly mean it.

I get up out of Issie's car. My feet find sturdy places to stand but I still wobble a tiny bit. I steady myself and dirt gets on my fingertips. Issie's car needs a bath. I need a bath. I soldier myself up and slip back toward the station. The door flies open just as I'm about to grab for the handle.

Nick looks at me. I can't figure out his facial expression at all and I hate that. His pupils seem to shift a little—become more oval—like a wolf's. His voice is gruff. "You okay?"

"Yes, thank you." I swallow hard. "I'm sorry I was a drama queen."

"It's okay. You—you—you've got a lot to deal with."

He reaches out his hand but Issie pushes past him, sidles up to me, and says in her singsong, love-everybody voice, "She's embarrassed. It's okay to be embarrassed, Zara, but your emotions are normal, perfectly normal. It's okay to be upset by this, honestly, but you have to affirm yourself for the positive traits you have, not the heebie-jeebie pixie stuff."

I just stare at her.

"Psych 101," she says. "You should have taken it. It's such an easy A."

She jostles me around, and Dev comes out too and explains, "Betty had a call."

It's the first time I've noticed that the ambulance is missing.

"Oh," I manage. "Okay."

Issie pivots me toward the car. "We're going to go to your house. No fussing. We still love you. Right, Nick?"

Nick reaches out to put his arm around me again and stops. His voice is like a big piece of hurt. "Zara?"

I swallow.

His nostrils twitch. Dev gets closer. "Crap."

"What? What is it?" Issie asks.

"She smells," Nick says. He's frozen, not sure whether to come closer or back away.

Issie still doesn't get it.

"Duh. We all smell. It's called pheromones or perfume." She sniffs at my hair. "Zara smells exactly like the Body Shop Honey Almond Conditioner with a little mango body butter lotion mixed in. Am I right?"

I barely manage to nod.

"Issie, she smells like a pixie," Dev explains.

"Oh!" Issie says. She clutches me even closer, though, which is why I love Issie. "Oh. Does that mean she's turning?"

Nick doesn't even look at her. Those brown eyes of his just stare into me. "She smells like the guy in the woods."

"Zara! What is wrong with you?" Devyn asks. "Are you hanging out with pixies?"

His words hit me in the gut like bullets, like a torturer's fist. But he's not a torturer. He's just Dev, and I am the one who is holding back information. It's me. Not him.

"No," I say, "and how come you never smelled Ian or Megan? They were pixies."

Nick glares at me.

"What? I'm just wondering."

"Because I didn't know what to smell for then," Nick explains. He pulls in a breath. It's obvious he's trying to calm himself down. "Now I know. It smells like Dove soap."

"The problem," Devyn says, "is that a lot of non-pixies use Dove soap. The smell isn't a sure bet. It's ridiculous, actually. Dove soap . . ."

I gently extract myself from Issie and open the passenger-side doors of the car. "Why don't we get out of the cold and then I'll tell you what happened, okay?"

Dev's and Nick's eyes meet. I wish I knew what they were thinking, but finally Nick nods and at least his hand trusts me enough to brush the hair out of my face. "Okay."

Nick speeds so fast that the trees just blur by us and I tell them what happened with me and Astley.

"Astley? That means 'star,'" Devyn announces from the front seat.

"How do you know that?" Issie leans forward, then thinks better of it and comes back.

"He's a genius. Devyn, my man, you are a genius," Nick says. He reaches over and ruffles Dev's hair. It is the first hint that Nick might not explode.

"I'm not a genius. I just retain things, mostly useless things," Dev says, but he's smiling and not bothering to fix his hair.

"So, what do you think this all means?" Nick asks as he yanks the car around a hairpin corner. Is and I sway in the backseat.

"Me? I don't know," Dev says.

"Well, he's the king Zara's father talked about," Issie says, trying not to slam into me by hanging on to the seat back. "Gold dust. Spidery feelings . . ."

"What I'm wondering is why was he so insistent that he wasn't like Zara's father?" Devyn asks. His words come out slowly. "You know? Why he's so . . . Does it seem to you like he was trying to say something but not saying it? Did you tell us everything, Zara?"

He turns so our eyes meet. I am annoyed. "Of course I told you everything."

"Okay, okay! But you and Is weren't exactly forthcoming about the little excursion with your dad," he replies somewhat snidely. Issie seems to fold into herself.

Nick snorts. "Forthcoming?"

"Shut up." Dev punches Nick in the arm. "I aced my Critical Reading SATs. It is nothing to feel humiliated about."

"Be proud, Linguistic Acuity Man," Is fake cheers. Her words fall into emptiness.

"Linguistic Acuity Man?" I echo, trying to make it better.

"Oh, Is . . ." Devyn turns to look at her.

"It can be your superhero name," I say.

We drive along in awkward silence. The tension from Issie is pretty thick. I know it's hard for her to be in the car with Devyn because she wants him to invite her to the dance and she feels weird about the whole Cassidy situation. We drive past trees and logging trucks. We drive up hills and around curves and then Nick slams on the brakes. My head pounds into the head rest.

"What is it?" Issie yells.

"Holy—" Nick jumps out of the car. He's looking up at the sky.

We bail out of the car too. I crane my head up. There is something funny flying up high. It looks like two figures pushed together, with giant wings.

"It's the Valkyrie," I whisper. "She's got someone."

We stand there staring for a second and then I bark out, "Devyn? Can you change?"

He nods. "I think so."

"Well, try. Follow her. See where she goes," I order.

Devyn ducks down low. Issie comes to my side of the car and Devyn starts throwing his clothes over it. It doesn't take long and he's a bird. He takes off, super large eagle wings flapping hard and strong into the cold white sky. The clouds are high and stormy looking.

"Stay safe!" Issie yells. "Do not get hurt, Linguistic Acuity Man!"

He just soars up and away. Issie leans against me and I hustle her into the car. Nick grabs Devyn's clothes and comes inside too. We blast the heater and wait. None of us talk about anything; not about pixies or dances, not about love or science tests or blue skin.

Luckily, it's not long before Devyn's back. He turns human by the side of the car, gets dressed, and shudders from the cold. Putting his hands in front of the heat duct, he tells us what he saw: a woman with swan wings. She held a female pixie in her arms.

"I lost her. She went into the clouds and then she was just gone." He runs a shaking hand over his head. "I can't believe I lost her."

Devyn and Nick theorize that it's a good thing the Valkyrie is here because if she's taking pixies, then there are fewer pixies for us to deal with. They think she might be why we haven't seen so many in the last week. But me? I've seen her up close, and I am not so sure.

Pixie Tip

Pixies are stronger at night. Stay inside. Nighttime is not the right time for pixie hunting.

"Easily the freakiest thing I've ever seen," Issie says.

We're back at my house and I am showing them the book I found upstairs and what my dad wrote in it.

"Leave Risk Sixty? Baa Ebbed Fly Tight Vigor Trolls? Those aren't the best clues," Nick says playfully. "Sorry, baby."

I poke him right above his belt loop and hand the book to Devyn. "I think they are anagrams."

Devyn takes it. "You're probably right. Let me think. The only one I can get off the top of my head is A Evil Sexy Skirt, which isn't grammatically correct. It should be: An Evil Sexy Skirt."

"There's an anagram server on the Net," Issie says, opening up Betty's laptop. "Let's see what we get."

She gets to the site and types in: "Leave Risk Sixty." There are 14,683 results. We all crowd around the laptop as she starts reading them aloud. "Relatives Xi Sky. Relative Xis Sky. Relative Six Sky. Relaxes Skit Ivy. Relaxes Kits Ivy. Leaver Ski Sixty. Reveal Ski Sixty . . ."

"This isn't working," Nick growls. He starts to back away, but I touch him on the arm and he breathes out slowly. It's almost like gentling a horse.

Devyn agrees. "There are too many results. And it doesn't show them all, only the first hundred. There's no way to access the others."

"We're not giving up. It might not have anything to do with anything, but it could be important," I say. "Leave Risk Sixty. That has all the letters of Valkyrie in it, doesn't it? Issie, open up a blank document."

She does. I make her write it:

Leave Risk Sixty

Then we cross off the letters in "Valkyrie."

~~Leave Risk~~ Sixty.

"So that leaves—oh, *exist*," Devyn says. His lips do this weird sort of half raspberry noise. "'Valkyries exist.' That's not that helpful."

"Crud." My hope seems to fizzle out.

Nick squeezes my hand. "No. There's still the other one. Don't give up."

We don't give up, but we don't get anywhere either. Eventually Devyn goes home to research and give his parents my blood. Nick goes out patrolling with Is for backup. Instead of curling up with a mirror and turning all fetal, I write letters to the Georgia Board of Pardons and Parole, e-mail the information forward, wish I could do more for human rights. In the back of my head are these worries thundering about, static, insistent: what the blood test will mean, why the pixie guy in the woods was nice to me, what Nick will do if I am pixie now because, let's face it, weres are pretty bigoted against pixies, and seeing what I've seen, I can't really blame them.

"Do not think," I order myself. "You have thought this *over* and *over* again. It is self-indulgent. Just research."

So this is what I'm doing, scrunched up with Gram's laptop googling "how not to turn pixie," when my grandmother struts through the door, all in uniform, all tall and brave and fearless—all unlike me.

"Hey," she says, kicking the door shut behind her. "You still moody, still . . . what's the word? Emo?"

"Emo is a derogatory word." I close the laptop, running my hand across the cold, blank surface.

She laughs. "Why? Because it's short for emotional? There's nothing wrong with being emotional. There's a lot of good emotions out there, you know."

The phone rings. Gram grabs it. "Hello?"

I wait. Images of Astley flash into my head. I force them out by thinking of Charleston, dolphins breaking the surface of the water, warm air, flowers.

"No. I just got home, Josie. What's up?" Gram asks.

I plug in the power cord to recharge the laptop and then find my grandmother, who has wandered into the kitchen, still talking on the phone.

"I'm going to take a shower," I whisper. "I've got a date tonight with a pixie-hating werewolf. I have to smell human."

She makes a fake, exaggerated sniff and then an overacting mimic of grossness.

"Nice," I bounce back. "You're such a *nice* grandmother."

She waves me upstairs. Dismissed.

My cell phone rings when I'm in the shower and since I'm a total slave to technology, I answer it.

"Zare?"

"Hey, Nick."

"What are you doing?"

My good arm drips water onto the little pink rug that's right in front of the toilet. It deepens the color. "Um . . ."

"Are you taking a shower?"

"Yeah."

He doesn't say anything. I don't say anything. His breath is so loud that I can hear it over the water. I'm naked. He knows I'm naked. This is freaking me out. I eye the towels and finally say, "I'm not blue anymore."

"Is that because you're red?"

"Huh? How do you know I'm red?"

"Because you're blushing." He laughs.

The water splashes hot against my ankle, which is still under the stream of it. He doesn't say anything. I don't say anything. I am wasting water. I don't care. Bad Zara. Bad pseudo-environmentalist, pseudo-human Zara.

"You aren't actually standing in the shower with the cell phone, are you, because that's dangerous." He coughs.

I press my lips together for a second and ruin the mood. "You don't trust me at all, do you?"

"I do," he answers too quickly.

"Yep. Uh-huh. Right."

Even though the shower's making so much noise I can still hear his breath rush out, exasperated.

The drain sucks the water down.

"You know," he says. "I really, awesomely, amazingly love you."

"You say the perfect boyfriend things." I step out of the shower, grab a towel.

He laughs. "I say the perfect boyfriend things, but what about what I do? I mean, you are always complaining about the whole macho alpha dog thing."

"Well, yeah, there is that and your whole secret love of Snausages."

"You promised to never mention that!" he says all mock upset.

"No, I promised to never mention the whole fire hydrant thing."

"Zara!" He cracks up.

"Or the barking at the vacuum cleaner."

"Do not go there," he warns, but he's still laughing hard.

"Despite your vile nature we still have a date tonight. And you are also still going to that dance with me."

I imagine him clutching his warm stomach as he laughs. I close my eyes. "You think you can get Dev to ask Issie, too?"

"I'll try."

"Cool."

Nick picks me up later. He doesn't even knock on the door, just comes right in like he lives here or something, which he practically does.

"I'm kidnapping your granddaughter," he shouts to Betty. She's in the kitchen cleaning up dinner dishes. I am off dishwashing duties because of the whole injured arm thing. Score!

"Good. Keep her awhile. She's on my computer so damn much her fingers are curling into a perpetual typing shape." She steps into the living room, smiles, wipes her hands on a bright yellow dish towel. "You two have fun. Don't be back too late."

I rush across the room and kiss her cheek. She pats mine and says, "You are a sweetie."

Nick runs across the living room and does the same thing, giving her an overly exaggerated smack. Then he grabs her up in this big wolf hug and twirls her around.

"And you are just fresh," she laughs, swatting him with the dish towel. "Now scoot."

We hop in Nick's MINI Cooper, which smells faintly like dog. I try to pull on my buckle and my hand is so cold that I can't quite get it locked. Plus, the whole hurt wrist thing makes it awkward. Nick reaches over and does it for me. His fingers touch my fingers. All of my internal organs swirl and melt and tingle. His lips are beautiful. I am staring . . . I am staring at his lips. I should kiss him. I lean up and in. His lips open a little bit. The whole world is gone. It's just his mouth and my mouth. His hand goes to the small of my back. It's strong there, solid. I move my body toward him.

"Where are your mittens?" he murmurs. His breath hits my lips.

I murmur back, "Forgot them."

"You want me to go get them?"

I shake my head but he leaps out of the MINI anyway. "One sec."

"Nick!"

"No frostbitten fingers for my girlfriend."

He grins and runs to the house, jumps up the stairs, and disappears. I settle in, rest my back against the cold upholstery of the Cooper and close my eyes for a second. It's been a hard couple of weeks. I kidnapped my dad; I accidentally saved a pixie; my car blew up; my skin changed color; not to mention that I had a Spanish test and an art project due and I have nothing to wear to the dance except T-shirts and it's semiformal. I blow on my hands and shudder because . . . the feeling? The spider crawling feeling? I've got it again. It's like hundreds of arachnids have gone creepy-crawly all over me.

Something screams. It's not quite animal, not quite human. It is definitely not a good noise. It is a pain noise. It's not terribly close. I grab the handle of the door, clutch the cold metal in my fingers, listen . . . Nothing.

"Astley?" I whisper into the dark.

There's no answer. The door to the house opens and Nick barrels back to the MINI. I expect things to jump out of the dark and bite him. I expect fear and blood and fight.

Nothing happens.

He slams shut the door, smiles, and hands me my baby blue fluffy mittens, my favorites. "There. All better."

He leans over and kisses my nose, presses the start button, and cranks up the heater. The engine's not warmed up enough yet so it's really just blowing out medium-cold air. It's just recycled cold air wandering back and forth from engine to cab to us to outside, wandering . . .

"Zara? You okay?" he asks.

I push my hands into my mittens, feel the warmth, try to make myself into somebody normal, not some half-breed thing. "Yeah."

He cocks his head a little bit, looks at me. "You sure?"

"I'm sure."

"No spidery feelings?"

"A little one maybe." I grab his hand in my mittened one. "I thought I heard a scream."

He bolts up and out of the car again. This time I scurry out after him. He cocks his head, listening.

"I don't hear anything," he says finally.

The woods are so dark. A fog creeps in, hiding everything in mist, hiding secrets. I tug on his arm. "I probably imagined it. Let's get in the car."

We climb back in and we both take a breath. Nick leans over again and whispers into my ear. "I love you."

I say it back and it is the biggest truth I know. "I love you, too."

He smiles super broad. "Really?"

"Really."

Pixie Tip

Pixies do not need an invitation to show up in public places like bowling alleys or cafeterias. Being in public doesn't make you safe.

We hold hands the entire car ride and for a tiny bit I don't think about being blue or pixies or women flying with people into the sky. I just think of my hand touching his hand. I think about how saying that you love someone can make your heart feel like some sort of brownie sundae, warm, gooey, sweet, and good. He brings me up the hill to Eastward Lanes and parks.

"A bowling alley?" I say.

He nods.

"You're bringing me *bowling?*"

He nods again and a goofy smile spreads across his face. "You are such a diva sometimes."

"I am not a diva. My wrist is sprained and I have a monster bruise all over my chest." I let go of his hand.

"Yep. You just think you're too good for a Downeast Maine bowling date."

"I do *not* think I'm too good for a bowling date, in Maine or anywhere else, thank you very much," I say, yanking the door open. Cold air blasts in. I jump out, shut the door, and meet him at the front of the MINI. "I just think a bowling date is a little . . . um . . ."

He presses the key fob button. "I can make it romantic."

I snort and grab his hand. Our fingers clasp each other's again and I feel grounded, connected, better. That's only part of the truth. Everything still feels dangerous—like we could be attacked any moment, like some warrior woman might swoop out of the pitch-black sky and take us away.

We stride across the parking lot. I try not to step on the icy patches, sort of zigzag around them, even though I know if I start to fall Nick will catch me. There is a flashing neon bowling pin on the bowling alley sign. It is incredibly tacky in kind of a cool retro way. He hustles me toward the glass front doors and grabs the metal handle. I touch his arm. "Nick?"

"Yeah."

"I've never actually, um, bowled before."

"So?"

"So, well, I'm probably going to suck. Plus, you know . . . slightly sprained wrist." I hold it up to prove my point.

He leans down and kisses the top of my head. "I'll help. It'll be fun."

"I hate sucking at things."

"It's good for you. Keeps you humble."

"Yeah right, says He Who Sucks at Nothing."

He yanks open the big metal door. "Not true."

I say as I step inside, "Totally true. Name one thing you actually suck at—"

"Being calm. Not being patronizing."

"Well, at least you're self-aware, right?" Laughing, I step inside the bowling alley. Issie and Devyn and a ton of people from school are already there. Issie's renting shoes at a long counter. Cassidy is already bowling. A disco ball hangs from the ceiling. Shifting lights flash across the entire alley and they are playing retro eighties music.

"What do you think?" Nick whispers.

"I love it!"

The love doesn't last very long because, okay, let's face it. Bowling is evil.

"I am developing a bowling phobia," I tell Issie before I go up for my next turn. If there is a name for the fear of a painful bowel movement (defecaloesiophobia) there should be a word for the fear of bowling. Bowling is definitely phobia worthy.

I hold the ball in my one hand. Luckily, it's candlepin, which is some weird kind of mini bowling ball that they have in New England. It's lighter and stuff. I try to think about form and alignment and the physics of it, which Dev went on and on about during my crash course. It doesn't help. The annoying brown bowling ball veers totally off to the left and clanks into the gutter every time.

"Why is it not doing what it's supposed to?" I yell as I turn around. Nick cracks up, all doubled over. Dev's hand covers his mouth and his shoulders shake because he's trying not to become hysterical.

Issie straight-arm points at them. "No laughing."

"It's not staying in the lane," I say. I check to make sure the latch on my anklet is secure. It's so delicate. I'm terrified of losing it.

"You have to roll it straight," Nick says. He stands up and grabs a ball out of the ball return bin thingy that's between all the lanes.

Bowling balls crash into pins in other lanes. Cassidy squeals, "I rock!"

"Awesome job, Cassidy!" Devyn yells.

Issie starts trying to tie her shoes better, fumbling around with the laces.

"Okay. First, when you throw the ball with your right hand you want your left foot to be the one in front. Opposite way if you're doing it leftie," Nick says. He puts the ball in my hand. Our fingers touch. Something electric passes between them. I sniff. He smells good, like trees and mint and cake.

"Uh-huh."

More pins fall down. More balls thunder down the wooden lanes. He takes my good arm and swings it back in slow motion. "You want to keep your wrist and palm rigid, don't bend it."

"But the ball is heavy. How do I not bend it?"

Nick's fingers steadily brush against my skin. Warmth shivers up my tendons and ligaments. I try not to sway.

"They're candlepin, Zara," Dev says. He's got a ball balanced on his lap, patiently awaiting his turn, but obviously thinking I'm a complete fool. "They aren't even big balls."

Issie starts snorting. "Big balls."

I snort too.

Dev groans. "You guys are not mature."

"Okay, let's just try it. I'll help you," Nick says. He's still right behind me, swinging my arm for me. I am so focused on the heat of him that I almost turn around and hug him. Then I remember. I release. I release really, really late. The ball lobs through the air and plunks in the middle of the lane. It smacks. People stare.

"No throwing! You'll damage the floors!" the bowling atten-
dant person yells from behind the counter.

I hide my face behind my hands and run back to Issie. "Did I
hit anything, at least?"

"No, sweetie. Sorry."

"I think it's her follow-through," Nick says to Dev. "She has
no follow-through."

"She's not meant for bowling," Dev agrees. "The trajectory is
all off."

I slump down and cross my arms over my chest. "Nice. Totally
nice thing to say to me when I'm still trying to recover. Injured.
Remember?"

Dev blushes. "Sorry, Zara."

I punch him in the arm. "Just kidding."

"You know what I like about the Norse gods?" he asks randomly. "I like that Odin was their head guy and it wasn't because
he was the hottest or strongest. It was because he was the wisest
with the best magic."

"And this has to do with bowling, how?" I ask as Issie gets a
fantastic gutter ball.

"Because in the big scheme of things it's not always the phys-
ically gifted who rule," Devyn says. "Being in the chair helped me
understand that. I'd give up my legs over my mind any day. Don't
get me wrong. I'm glad to have them back."

Devyn's right. So what if I am a horrible bowler. Besides, I
can't feel too sad about having ten gutter balls in a row, since Issie
is even worse.

"Eleven!" she squeals. "That's eleven zeros in a row."

"This is so normal," I whisper to Nick. "It's so wonderful
normal."

. . .

About halfway through the night, I head off to the girls' bathroom alone, which is very brave of me, apparently.

Cassidy is in there washing her hands at the sink across from two blue stalls. "Zara? Hey!"

"Hi, Cassidy." I try to be nice because there's really no reason to hate her. It's just that she's a threat to the love that should be Is and Devyn.

She squints at me a couple of times, shuts the water off, and says, "Nick doing okay?"

"Yeah. Why?" I ask as she starts wagging her hands in the air to dry them.

She stumbles around for the words. "Yeah . . . he just . . . he looked a little off at school today. Something happen at lunch?"

"He's okay," I say.

"You guys are honestly just the cutest couple."

I cock my head. I have to pee but I don't move. I wait for her to say more.

"You are!" she says, scratching at her neck. "You are lucky! Don't look at me that way. I know you had to move up here from Charleston and everything, but it's like . . . oh, I don't know. You and Issie are like this." She makes her first two fingers stick together.

I nod and try to say pretty pointedly, "She's my best friend."

"Plus, with Dev, it's like you're a gang of four." She keeps talking. "I get jealous of it, you know? And you have Nick and he so obviously is into you. He's always watching you and smiling at you. He's like a bodyguard."

I grab the handle of the stall door and stare out the tiny black window that's way up on the wall at the opposite side of the room. It's just a rectangle of darkness. A bodyguard. Is that why he loves me? Because I'm someone he can protect?

"And you're smart but not nerdy. And you are such a great runner." Cassidy finishes her lip gloss, smacks her lips, and tosses the tube back in her purse, which looks like it's a Kate Spade knockoff. "I don't know. Maybe I'm just talking crap, but it's like your life has already started and the rest of us are just waiting . . . you know? Waiting to get out of here or something? To find someone? Something? To be something."

I have no idea if she's talking about liking Devyn or just in general. I guess I take too long to answer, because she smiles at herself, shaking her head. "I'm obviously an idiot. I need a life."

I touch her arm with my free hand. "You have a life, Cassidy."

"Yeah, right." She snorts. "I feel like I spend half my time hiding who I really am."

"I can relate to that."

"Really?" She stretches her long arms up above her head. She reminds me of a cat waking up. "Devyn's one of the few people who really 'get' me, you know? But it's lonely."

"What's lonely?"

"Not having people really understand you."

"Well, you could tell them, maybe? Just be open." For a second I wonder if she's a pixie, but Devyn and Nick would be able to smell that. Then I wonder if she's maybe gay? I don't know. I wish I were some kind of feel-good talk-show host so I'd know what to say. "Is it something serious? Something you need help with?"

"Oh, Zara, you are so sweet. I totally don't need any help. I'm fine." She looks at my hand, still holding the stall door. "Oh wow. You still haven't gone pee. I'm so sorry. Take care of Nick, okay?"

She rushes out the door before I can answer. So I do what I've come into the bathroom to do and then I go wash my hands. I turn the water on and bang on the soap dispenser to try to make it work. I push it again. A little drizzle of neon pink liquid soap leaks out. "Beautiful."

The soap smells like vomit. It makes my skin feel creepy, almost spidery creepy. I rub it on anyway and put my hand under the water. That's when I look up and see myself in the mirror. I'm blue. I'm blue again. I am so blue that I match the bathroom stall doors.

My butt hits those doors because I guess I've backed up. I don't know. I rush forward again, yank some brown paper towels out of the dispenser, shove them under the faucet and wet them. I scrub them across my face.

"It's not going to work," a voice above me says.

I scream, bang my hip against the sink, and pivot, my hands in fists. Astley is hanging by his hands through the now-open window.

"Go away!" I order. He drops onto the floor. His shoes barely make a noise even though he looks heavy. He's almost as big as Nick now. His muscles are bulkier, too. It's like he keeps growing. "Randomly showing up is not cool. It's creepy."

He eyes me. "You're blue again."

"Obviously."

He swallows. I can actually see him swallow. He takes a step toward me. "I've only just arrived and you're already blue."

I turn away from him, stare at the monster in the mirror. "I wish I weren't."

"If you were pixie you wouldn't be. You could hide it."

"I'm not pixie," I snarl. I lean forward. My forehead touches the gross mirror. It's cold. I don't care. I stare at the sink; white porcelain, cracked in places, ugly.

His fingers graze my shoulder and I jump. "Zara?"

"What?"

"Are you always so nervous?"

"No. Yes. I don't know." My hand rubs at my face wildly.

He grabs it. "You need to calm down."

"How can I calm down? I'm blue. And my boyfriend hates pixies."

"All pixies?"

"Can you blame him?"

"Yes, I can. We aren't all bad." His eyes are dark, deep.

"Right." I somehow want to believe him though.

"Really. We aren't, Zara. And I think somewhere, deep down, you know that."

He lets go of my hand.

I try to unwrap the scared anger that seems to be enveloping me. I take a big breath and ask, "Why are you here?"

"Didn't we go through this?" He sighs.

"No. I mean right now. Why are you here in the girls' bathroom with me?"

He pulls his lips in toward his mouth before he speaks. "I wanted to warn you."

"Warn me?"

"Dangerous things are happening. You need to be careful. You should stay in groups. Try to stay inside. Warn your friends, too. Your grandmother."

"Warn them about what?"

"Another king has arrived."

Pixie Tip

Pixies have sharklike teeth. Unfortunately, unlike sharks they can breathe out of the water.

"What other king?" I spin away from the mirror to face him. The spinning movement continues even after I stop. My voice creeps up high into hysteria but I can't stop it. "How many of you are there? Man! It's like a freaking pixie infestation."

He grabs my arms.

I yank away. "Don't. Touch. Me."

He cringes and his hands stay up in the air grabbing nothing. "You looked like you were going to fall. I was trying to help you."

"You want to help me? You tell me what you mean about other kings and danger and then you leave so my face stops being blue, okay?" I sway a little and lean my hip against the sink for balance. "Tell me about the Valkyrie too."

He takes a step closer. "I think I make you dizzy, as well."

"I don't know. Maybe." My swimming head seems to agree.

His face softens. He lifts a hand up like he's going to touch my cheek.

"Don't," I insist. I feel like I'm cheating on Nick just by talking to him, which makes no sense since I talk to other guys all the time. "Please. Just tell me about the king."

His hand drops to his side. "He's here. He's vicious, a rogue, not supported by our federation."

"Federation?"

"The Pixie Federation." He brushes the thought aside. "It's complicated. Each kingdom is allied in a federation, which is ruled by a parliament of kings. We try to keep things in order, keep us safe from humans and humans safe from us, but sometimes things get messy, and not all of us are in favor of the federation. And some of us want more power—"

"Like this rogue guy?" I finish.

"He will battle me for your father's territory. It will hopefully be short-lived. It has already begun. I lost one of mine already. She was a physician." His eyes sadden.

"I'm not sure how I feel about this." The sink is cold against my hip. The coldness is so true it crosses the barrier of my pants and shudders into my skin.

"Zara, there is no choice. Your father was weak. You've imprisoned him. You've imprisoned some of my scouts with him. I have to free my people but I also need to control the territory. To do that I need to overthrow the king. It's already been sanctioned."

The room shakes because someone's flushed a toilet in the boys' restroom. The pipes must be connected. I ask my question slowly. "By overthrow, do you mean kill?"

He nods.

"I can't let you kill him." There's no emotion in my words. There's just truth.

"You can't stop it, Zara. If I don't, the other king will. It's just a matter of who gets there first. And honestly? Do you think killing is a worse fate than what's going on in that house right now?"

I don't answer.

"The other king has sent scouts too." His face hardens. "And Zara—he is not like me. He is not even like your father. He is much, much worse."

"Why don't you kill *him* then? Go after his territory?"

"I'm not strong enough to do that yet. I need your father's forces. I need numbers."

"Numbers," I mumble, trying to understand.

"He is strong. He is dark. That side"—his voice goes bitter—"always has an easy time gathering numbers, troops, whatever you want to call it."

"But you are the side of good?" I swallow, turn away from him, and turn the water on. It rushes out into my hands, my blue hands. "Don't you think everyone thinks they're on the side of good? Did that Valkyrie woman?"

"I'm sure she did." He touches my shoulder. I jump back. He turns me around to face him. The water still runs. It races out of the faucet. It races away.

"I am on the side of good, as are you. Your wolf will even be on the side of good. We all have roles to play," he says. "Your face reveals that destiny."

I blink hard a couple of times. His face distracts me. "I don't believe in destiny."

We stand like that for a second, then he drops his hand. I remember to breathe.

"So what should I do?" I ask, reaching behind me and shutting off the faucet.

He almost laughs. He goes back toward the stalls and leans against them like that's sexy or something. Note: leaning against public bathroom stalls? Never sexy. "Well, if it were up to me, you would show me where you are keeping the pixies, let me kiss you, and then you'd be under the protection of the federation and myself. We'd leave here and go to my home."

"You're crazy," I say. "I wouldn't go with you in a million years. Pixies can't be trusted."

"You keep saying that, but I don't think you believe it anymore." He smiles. "Let me explain. The five fae races of the Shining Ones all have differences and deviations. Some side with the dark, some with the light. That's what I meant when I said all pixies are not the same."

"You're saying my dad sides with the dark?" It makes sense. Pixies aren't just good or bad the same way people aren't just good or bad. That shouldn't be so hard to get my head around.

"I'm saying that your dad leans that way, but he is not committed. So many of us aren't committed. The weres especially lack any organization whatsoever. I doubt your wolf even knows of the federation." He's almost scoffing.

It hits me the wrong way. I pull my arm in close to my chest and hold it there with my other hand. "Well, it's not like anyone's gone out and told him."

"Listen, Zara. For me to stay here with you for too long?" He straightens himself up. "It would be dangerous. He'd track right to you."

He turns to leave via the window but I grab his sleeve. "Should my friends and I . . . should we leave?"

"He would find you eventually." He moves his face enough so I can see his profile: hard, determined, not human at all. "You could come with me. I could protect you."

All my breath sucks inside of me. I know he means only me going with him. "I couldn't."

"I thought that would be your answer. I have to go." His face saddens and then he bounds up the wall to the window, parkour-style, just a foot halfway up the wall and he shoots through the window and is gone.

I stand there.

My breath returns.

I pivot toward the mirrors.

I am still blue.

If I were capable of pulling a glamour I could hide it, but I'm not. The blue isn't my magic. It's his—the king's—one of them, anyway. I press my forehead against the cold, smudged glass of the mirror and try to calm down.

"Big breaths," I mumble. "Take big breaths."

It's not really working. The walls of the bathroom close in on me. The window hovers there, a big, dark square of danger. He got through. That means anything can. Anything. I shudder and look for weapons. I could attack with what? Paper towels? A toilet paper roll? It is pretty hard paper, but seriously? And I can't go out into the alley because *I am blue!*

A moan escapes my lips. I text Issie: `Come in Bathroom. ASAP.` I hit Send. Then I realize that's kind of bossy so I send her another text that says: `Please?`

She bounds into the restroom five seconds later. The door flies open into the concrete wall. Issie's mouth is all wide-open worried. "What is it? Do you need help? Did you get your—"

Her sentence breaks off as she slips on some water that's on the floor, arms windmilling as she tries to catch her balance. I lurch forward to try to keep her from falling into the sink. I grab her with my good arm.

"Oh!" she gasps. "You're blue again."

"Uh-huh." My voice is little-girl frightened tinged with a lot of big-girl frustrated.

"You can't go out there blue."

"I know."

Her eyes get a wicked light and she untangles herself from me. "Well, I have a great plan."

"You do?"

"Mm-hmm." She's smiling super big. "I know that I am the sidekick and I never get to actually have great plans or anything because that is not my role—"

"You are not a sidekick," I interrupt.

"Zara? Duh?" She pokes herself in the chest. "I'm the klutzy human in our gang of four. That's a lifetime sentence of sidekick, okay?"

"But—"

"No buts. I'm cool with that." She pulls out a package from her oversized purse, which is pink, polka-dotted, and totally cute. "The sidekicks normally get to survive, and don't have all those big moral dilemmas that the heroes always go through. I am so totally fine with that. Voilà!"

She whisks out a package with a Wal-Mart sticker.

"Crayons?" I ask.

"No, silly. These are too fat to be crayons. They're face paint." She waits. I stare.

"Get it?" She waves the package in front of me. She points to her own cheeks. "We'll make it like it's intentional. I'll paint my face too and then we'll paint everyone else's. It'll be part of the night's theme. I planned it ahead just in case this happened again!"

I jump up and down and then hug her. She is so tiny to hug. Not like Nick at all. Or like Astley.

"You're squeeing," she says as I let go. "I take it that means you like?"

"It's brilliant!"

She smiles even bigger and rips open the package. "See? Side-kicks? Brilliant." She examines the colors. "I think I would like to be green."

I grab the green. "Done."

Pixie Tip

Pixies can be annoyingly cryptic. Don't talk to them. They'll confuse you and laugh about it later like movie villains and physics teachers.

After bowling, the four of us (plus Gramma Betty) talk for-freaking-ever about whether Astley's warning is just a massive manipulation. Betty, Dev, and Nick vote yes. Is and I are undecided. Devyn does Internet research on Valkyries like that Thruth woman while simultaneously IM'ing Cassidy. Issie spends a lot of time acting fake happy. They go home and eventually Betty gives Nick the okay to sleep over since it's three a.m.

"Your grandmother," he mumbles into my hair as we cuddle on the couch, "is made of awesome."

We fall asleep there, curled up together, fully clothed obviously because we haven't actually had actual sex yet and, well, my grandmother is in the house. In the morning she's up and gone either out to breakfast at Sylvia's, this diner she likes, or to the ambulance, before we even move or yawn or stretch.

It's my shoulder that wakes me up. I've slept on it in some crumpling way and now my whole right hand and fingers are pinpricking and the shoulder itself is stiff and doesn't want to move. I groan and inch away from Nick. His body is so warm, were-warm, and I stretch my shoulder up.

He wakes immediately. His arm extends around me, nuzzles me closer. "It can't be time to get up already."

"Mm-hmm," I say, folding my legs up toward my chest.

He reaches out and his fingers graze the line of my ankle bracelet. I snuggle into his gray T-shirt. I rub the side of my face against his chest and for one second I feel safe, so utterly safe, like when I was a little girl and my stepdad would tuck me into bed. He'd put up a pillow barrier all around me because I was so afraid of monsters coming at night. Although I knew they wouldn't come, not if he was there. That's how I feel with Nick. Except really, it's a false sense of security. Because ultimately, we can only make ourselves safe. And Nick's attempts to keep me safe are only making him more vulnerable. Life is not all damsel-in-distress romance novels—my life is more of an everyone-in-distress horror movie.

"Amnesty, what you thinking?" he mumbles into my hair. His fingers flick the dolphin on my anklet back and forth.

"Nothing."

"Liar."

"I was thinking you're cute and all scruffy in the morning."

He smiles. "Even with my dog breath."

"Woof."

He covers his mouth with his hand and pulls himself up into sitting position. "What were you really thinking about?"

"I was thinking about when my father—"

"Which one?"

"The pixie one. When he broke in here. Remember? And he

flipped over the couch because he was so mad that I didn't let him in my room." I shudder. "That was awful."

"It was evil," he says. He stretches. "But you still feel guilty for locking him and the rest of the freaks up in that house, don't you?"

I don't answer.

"We didn't have any other choice, Zara. It was either that or try to kill them all."

"I don't believe in killing."

"Not even to keep someone else safe?"

"No. Not ever, and I'm not going to back down on this, Nick. I hate that you almost killed that pixie. I hate it."

"He would have killed me."

"You don't know that. You just assumed that because he was a pixie. Did you attack him first?"

He doesn't answer and his face shuts down, which means I'm right. Satisfied, I stand up and softly pad my way into the kitchen. "You want some breakfast?"

"Home fries?"

There are potatoes in a bag on the counter, the Yukon gold kind. "Check."

He smiles again. "Poached eggs?"

I open the fridge, stare inside it. A carton of eggs wait happily on the shelf, ready to be cracked. "Double check."

"Orange juice?"

I pull out the plastic container. "Apple cranberry."

He mock frowns, pulls himself off the couch, strides over. "Oh, I don't know. Apple cranberry is so . . . ."

"So what?"

"It's not really manly."

"What? There are manly juices? Orange is more manly than apple cranberry?"

He grabs the edge of the counter and leans back, stretching out his calves. I plop the juice container on the counter. He looks at me. His eyes are confused.

"Really, Nick. That is silly. You're already having poached eggs."

"So?"

"So how are poached eggs manly?"

He tilts his head. "They aren't manly? Quiche isn't manly, I know. But that's egg in pie form. Poached eggs should be fine. Although fried eggs are probably the manliest. Maybe we should fry them."

I put water in the egg poaching pan, pretending like I don't notice his still hands. I turn off the tap. I crack an egg into one of the poacher cups. It's dark plastic. It contains the egg, keeps it from running off everywhere. I do another one. "I'm thinking maybe we should run away."

"Seriously?" His tone is flat, awkward.

"I just have a bad feeling."

"Zara, you always have a feeling. We call it worry." He moves behind me. He puts his hands on my shoulders. His words whisper in my ear. "I can't run away, but you could go. I think it might be a good—"

"Not without you." A massive rock seems to form in my stomach. I pull him around, bring him toward me, hug him as tightly as I can, and say, "We'll fight them. We took down my dad. We've taken down so many since then. We'll take down these jokesters too."

"I will never let anything happen to you," Nick growls into my hair. "I will die before you get hurt again. So help me God, Zara. I will die."

"Me too."

"What?"

"I will die before I let anyone hurt you or Issie or Dev or Gram or . . ." I stop and pull my head away from his chest so I can look up at him. "This list is getting kind of long and melodramatic, isn't it?"

He laughs. His hand moves slowly up my spine. He starts leaning down for a kiss. "Yeah. It is."

We go feed them after breakfast, trying to make sure we aren't followed. I hate feeding them because I already know what I'll see, what I've seen a hundred million times: snarling teeth at the windows, eyes more feral than any weres watching us, movements that are sensuous and twisted, pupils that don't flash with kindness but with need—pure need, only need.

That is not what I want to become.

The entire way over I keep my seat belt on but lean so my head rests on Nick's shoulder. He keeps his arm around me, driving with one hand.

"The Astley pixie guy has me messed up," I say, touching the massive circular speedometer in the middle of the console with my pointer finger. I like how the line tells you exactly how fast you're going, all you have to do is look.

"How?" Nick says.

"He's just . . . he's made me question everything we're doing all over again, and he's—I don't know—I'm pretty sure he's the one turning me blue."

"Because he said he was."

"Yeah."

"And you just believe everything he says?"

I let my finger fall. "I know . . ."

"You trust too easily, Zara."

"And you patronize too easily, mister."

His shoulders relax. "Touché. I'm working on it, though."

We pass tree after tree. We pass a paint-peeling white house with lobster traps out in the front. We go deeper and deeper into the woods. Nick's fingers move along my arm. The fabric of my coat makes a soft brushing noise.

My cell rings. It's Devyn.

"I have news for you," he says.

The reception is pretty bad out here and the phone crackles. I cross my fingers. "What?"

"You have no pixie attributes in your blood."

"None?" I reach over and squeeze Nick's knee. The denim is rough and hard beneath my hand.

Devyn doesn't even pause. "No. None at all."

I squeal. Devyn laughs and complains that I've hurt his ears. I hang up and tell Nick the news.

His smile is larger than I've ever seen it before and he pumps his fist in the air. He kisses me even though he's driving. "That is so fantastic!"

"I know!" I'm bouncier than Issie. "I can't believe it."

"Well, I can." He looks at me proudly. His hand reaches up to the side of my face. His finger brushes against my cheek. "I am so happy for you, baby."

Happiness relaxes my muscles. I didn't know how stressed I was; how tense my shoulders were. It's like I've had a massively good massage. I grab Nick's hand in mine and squeeze his thick fingers. "I am so happy too."

We pull onto the side road and park. There is a snowmobile

hidden behind a bunch of trees. Nick and I get on, yanking our helmets over our heads. The engine roars to life. We zip across the woods.

I grab Nick's waist.

"Holding on?" he says.

I don't answer.

We zigzag through some trees, keeping to the trail. The woods are still and quiet, calm, filled with white light. When we break into a clearing Nick finally slows down and jerks the snowmobile to a halt and all my happiness about being totally human just flies away.

Nick's voice breaks through the silence. "Holy—"

I leap off the snowmobile. "It's torn down."

The metal barricade that we've built around the house looks like a very focused tornado came through. Sudden flashes of metal gleam through the snow. Broken railroad ties and rails scar the ground. Barbed wire twists around like the tails of snakes; they move in the wind like they are keeping time to some horrible silent song.

The house still stands there, tall and desperate. The silverware and wire we put over the windows has all been ripped apart, busted, tossed to the side. They are all just twisted metal skeletons, evidence that we were successful at keeping them here for a little while. Not anymore. I shiver. The wind whispers warnings into my ear. Is my father still here? Is he dead? Are there any pixies still inside?

Before I even know what I'm doing, I'm running across the snow toward our broken barricade. Nick catches up to me in two seconds, grabs me by the shoulder. "Zara, do not go in there."

"What? The battle is obviously over. It probably happened last night."

"It could be a trap."

"Nick, my father could be in there."

"You're the one always saying he's not your father." He glares at me.

"We can't just let him die in there."

"Of course we can." He stops and sniffs the air.

It feels like there are whispers in the big house, whispers that are just beyond our hearing. A shutter falls to the ground with a boom. I jump. Nick doesn't move.

"What?" I ask.

He doesn't answer.

"What is it?" I demand.

"I smell blood." He says the word slowly, quietly, like a curse.

"What kind of blood?"

"Pixie."

I don't know how I do it but I manage to pull myself away from him. I pivot and lunge for the front door of the big white Victorian house. The door hangs open, off its hinges. I lurch inside and stop. Nick is right behind me.

"Oh no . . . ," I whisper.

He pulls me into his chest, but I've already seen it. I've already seen and it's stuck inside my brain like panic and terror, like a bad horror movie image that won't let go: bodies twisted on the marble floor, blood splashed across walls like arteries have been cut, severed hands in the middle of the floor not connected to anything, eyes open, mouths stuck in screams. I yank away from Nick and stare. Then I start moving. I hold my breath as I go from one corpse to another.

"Zara, what are you doing?"

"Looking for my father."

I don't stop. I move past a woman in a torn pink dress. I move toward a man with dark hair, but it's not him. Blood leaks from his mouth. I close his eyes and start up the stairs. Nick catches my arm. "Zara . . ."

His eyes are pained but alive, hollow but still moving. I wonder if my eyes look that way too, or if they are like the eyes of the dead pixies, crumpled on the floor.

"I have to see if he's here, Nick."

His mouth tightens and releases. "I'll look with you."

"You don't have to." I walk up the big curving staircase, step past a blond pixie, male, young—not Astley. His throat has been slashed. Something in my stomach meets my tongue. I go to steady myself on the railing but there's blood there, too. There's blood everywhere. My hand presses against my lips.

Nick moves past me. "I'll go first. Take out your knife."

With the same hand that holds my knife, I grab on to the back of his jacket, follow him up the stairs. We get to the top. There aren't any lights on in the hallway that runs both directions.

"Can you smell anything?" I whisper.

"Death. I smell death." He takes my hand.

"Is anyone alive?" I whisper. "My skin feels spidery."

He breathes in. The heaters are on in here, but I still shudder. "Nick?"

He nods slowly, motions for me to move behind him a little more. I don't. I clutch on to his jacket, but I stay next to him as we make our way down the hall. My boots squish in something. I expect more blood, but it's water—spilled from a Poland Spring bottle that someone dropped by a bedroom door. It reminds me of when my stepdad died, right after we'd been running. He'd dropped a bottle just like it on our kitchen floor. Nick motions for me to be quiet, bringing a finger to his lips. He steps inside the bedroom.

I raise my eyebrows. The light is on in here, but nobody's in sight. There aren't even any bodies on the floor. The bed, full of satin and velvet sheets, isn't even ruffled. The hall is dark, scary, tinged with the smells of blood and old carnage. Nick scowls and makes a hand motion, telling me to stay. I shake my head no and follow him anyway.

His eyes meet my eyes. His eyes plead. My eyes must plead back, because he nods slowly and takes my hand in his. Our hands clutch around the knife. We take another step inside. There are two large wooden doors off of the room, beyond the bed. There's a dresser and a chair. There are shackles on the floor. I nod at the far doors and Nick's whole body gets caught in a shudder. His hand in mine spasms and relaxes and then holds tight. He is going to change. He lets go of my hand as he spasms again, but not before I feel, for just a second, finger digits shorten and morph into something alien, something shorter, something furrier. I am afraid to even whisper. I push myself back against the wall. The seams in Nick's pants rip. I won't look. I won't look. While he changes he is vulnerable. I'm vulnerable. I stare around the room, searching for threats, ready to protect him.

Nick snarls from somewhere down on the floor. Even though I know he won't hurt me, something inside my stomach flips upside down. Obviously, our cover is blown. I snap my fingers to get him to come closer to me, which I know I'll catch hell for later. He hates when I treat him like a dog. But he stands up and pushes himself against my side.

"What is it?" I whisper.

He answers with a low growl. His ears flatten against his head. His teeth bare. His eyes stare at the closest door.

I push my free hand down into the heavy fur on his back. Muscles ripple, ready. He's going to jump, to attack something. My fingers long for a collar, something to grab on to so I can hold him back, keep him safe.

The door flies open.

"Ah, Zara, or should I say 'princess'? Human still?" says the pixie standing there. He is tall, pale, dark-haired like me, older than we are. He licks his lips with a bloody tongue. He is not Astley. He is not my father. He is another one entirely and he exudes power. "Not for long, though. Look at that lovely blue tint. Getting close already."

I don't look at my arms or my hands. I stare into his eyes.

"You might want to check on Daddy." He smiles.

Nick's back muscles tense. My heart falls. The fur beneath my fingers is gone. "No, Nick! Stay."

Nick leaps over the bed and plows into the pixie man, who has jumped as well. They meet in midair. Fur mixes with flesh. Nick's jaws snap as the pixie opens his mouth to show teeth. They both move so quickly that they blur. The force of the jumps knock them sideways. They smash through a window and are gone.

"Nick!" My voice is a scream.

I stumble run to the window. They are on the ground, fighting. I can't jump. It's too far. I whip around. Something groans from the bathroom. "Zara."

My father stumbles to the door. His neck is gashed and bleeding. Blood clots his dark hair. I gasp, reach out my hand.

"Go. I'll be fine. Zara . . ." His voice cracks.

"What?" I reach out to him, pull him onto the bed even

though the whole time I want to go down, to help Nick, to do a million things all at once.

"Be careful. Warn your mother about me, if I—"

I nod. "Stay here. I'll be right back."

His eyes meet my eyes. He looks away.

I run down the stairs so fast it is like I am flying. I break out into the yard, where wolf and pixie stand off against each other. They are both bleeding and winded. Their eyes are wild and feral. The dark-haired pixie king smiles. Claws flash where fingernails should be. The wolf leaps.

"Nick!" The word escapes my mouth before I realize it, and he turns toward me for a second. It is all the king needs.

Crazy-sharp teeth slash into Nick's fur, ripping at his neck. Nick's teeth snap and close on the pixie's arm, but it isn't enough. The pixie claws hack into Nick's chest, throwing him to the ground. Nick's body spasms and he whimpers as blood gushes out of his neck. Fear overtakes me.

"No!" I run. I run over the snow, my feet crunching into it. I grab a railroad tie and put myself between the pixie and Nick.

The pixie lifts the corner of his mouth in a slow, degrading smile. "How fun. Iron in one hand. A knife in the other."

Nick's tail flops idly on the snow next to me. He makes a tiny wolf noise, then a large huffing of breath.

"You will not hurt him." I raise the tie higher. "Do you hear me? You will *not hurt him.*"

"Oh, scary human girl. I'm shivering." The pixie laughs and lunges toward us despite his bleeding arm.

I swing the tie. It clonks the pixie in the head and he backs away. A giant burn mark mars his pale, perfect skin. His hand reaches up to his head.

"I shall remember this," he says. He smiles—cocky—and reminds me, for a second, of my father. "Princess."

"Enough with the princess crap!" I lift the bar again, move in front of Nick's collapsed form. The bar is steady in my hands. My sprained wrist throbs but adrenaline is keeping me going. My voice is steady too, and for a second I don't recognize it even though it's coming out of my mouth. "I'll give you more to remember if you want."

His eyes widen, but so does his smile. He takes a step backward and lifts his arms to the sky. "I shall return for what is mine."

But I don't want him to go. I want to hurt him and this voice comes out of me, taunting, hard. "Why are you leaving now, huh? Why don't you just take me now?"

His head tilts slightly toward me, just on the right side. He's bleeding pretty badly from his ear and neck. "It pleases me more to leave you here watching your wolf die. I enjoy the melodrama. And I shall be back for you. Do not fret."

He flashes fast through the sky and is gone. Nick makes a soft aching noise that breaks my heart. I drop the bar, drop myself, heave Nick's heavy wolf body into my arms.

"I'm so sorry I didn't keep you safe," I whisper. "So sorry."

His chest moves up and down, ragged. I touch his ribs; at least one has to be broken. His eyes slowly open. They are big and brown and full of reproach. A tear falls onto his nose. It is my tear. His tongue reaches out and softly touches my cheek. I yank off my jacket, press it against his neck wound.

"I didn't mean to hurt you," I say. "I never wanted anything to hurt you."

He tries to lift his head up, but it falls back down. He closes his eyes again, letting unconsciousness take him in a way he would never let anything else. I settle him onto the snow, grab my new cell out of my pocket, and speed dial Issie, but of course there is no signal. Stupid granite mountains and bad cell phone towers.

I shift up, trying to pull Nick onto my lap and apply pressure to his wound. "I'm going to get you out of here," I whisper. "I promise."

When pixies die they lose their glamour. It's the glamour that makes them look like they have people skin. In death their skin is a light blue covered with tiny vines that seem like ivy crossed with darker veins that circle around their arms, across their faces. It is beautiful in a severe, alien way.

In order to get Nick out of here I have to walk past several bodies. In order to get Nick out of here I have to go back in the house and find something to drag him with, because I am not strong enough to carry him to the snowmobile, and the snowmobile can't cross the iron bars and broken wires.

I step inside the house and listen. There's no movement anywhere. No moans. Just death.

"Dad?" I yell up the stairs that are covered with an ornate red rug and dead pixies.

Nothing.

I have never called him Dad.

"Pixie king?" I yell again.

Nothing again.

I run up the stairs, trying to avoid bluish limbs, blood. I smash through the hallway and into the bedroom. He's gone.

"Great," I mutter. "Nice. Ditching me. Another nomination for Daddy of the Year right there."

I grab the comforter off the bed and drape it over my shoulder, barreling back down the hallway and the stairs and back outside. Nick is still collapsed on the snow in wolf form and he is still bleeding.

Placing the comforter down, I try to pull him onto it as gently as I can, but it's hard. He looks up at me with pained brown eyes. He squinches. His jowls flop and his eyes seem to ache with embarrassment as I move his hindquarters onto the blanket.

"I'm so sorry," I whisper. "I'm trying to be gentle. I swear."

He growls, just a tiny bit, and in a nice way.

I pull the comforter around him, grab on, and begin to drag.

Aristotle wrote, "We make war that we may live in peace."

I don't know what to think about that. I don't know at all. All the wars, all the dangers that have happened have always seemed far away. Still, I don't panic now that the dangers are here. I work methodically even though my face should be painted white with fear. My heart should be a drum machine, it thumps horribly hard. The entire time I work I scan the sky for predators, for pixies with sharp teeth, for women with black swan wings.

"You hold on," I tell Nick. "You hold on. I'll get you out of here."

I manage to make a kind of sled out of the comforter and railroad ties and fasten it to the snowmobile with chains. My fingers freeze and numb and make me clumsier than I normally am, but eventually it works.

"You okay?" I ask and he doesn't answer, barely whimpers. "You're okay," I tell him anyway. "This is the only life we have, so you have to be okay."

The surface of his body heaves out these bewildered breaths.

His eyes close and open. I reach my hand into his fur and watch as my fingers braid themselves deep. We are braided together. I know that. I know.

"I will not lose you," I whisper and it is an order, not just to him but to me.

Before I climb on the sled and go, I take a second and glance back at the pixie house. It's invisible again, protected by an old glamour that hides it from human eyes. But I know the middle of that field isn't some idyllic New England scene of softly fallen snow surrounded by pine trees that stand sentry and blah, blah, blah. No, I know that the middle of that field is blood and carnage. It is all that's left of the sentient beings that I trapped there.

This is my fault. It is at least partly my fault. And that knowledge presses against my ribs like some horrible, horrible weight that seems to suck all the hope out of me. And it's done. It's done. They are dead and Nick is hurt. There is nothing I can do to change it.

So I just rev up the snowmobile, check one more time to make sure Nick is secure, and try to move somewhere that my stupid cell phone will get reception and then I will call Issie and Betty and I will get help for Nick and I will try to figure out where my father is and how to stop the new pixie guy. Because it is obvious—really, really obvious—that he will be back, that he is not done, that the war has just begun.

Pixie Tip

Do not hesitate to kill a pixie. Just kill.

It takes about half a mile but I finally get reception. I stop the snowmobile, press speed dial, and rush back to Nick.

"Gram?" I blurt as soon as I hear a click.

"Nope. This is Officer Clark. This Zara?"

"Yeah. Yeah." I stare at the gray sky peeking above the trees like it's going to fix things. "Is Betty there?"

"Um." Officer Clark clears his throat. "Things are bad right now, Zara. We've got . . . Well, there's been an accident."

"What?" I whip around, almost drop the phone. "Is Gram okay?"

"She's fine. She's attending. It's just . . . it's bad. I've got to go. I'll have her call you."

"Wait. Tell her—"

He's hung up. A squirrel prances along a branch like a mad emperor. He chitters at me.

"I know, I know. Okay," I grunt back.

I check Nick. He is barely breathing. Blood covers the jacket I put on him, soaks his own clothes. I growl at him to fight and then I call Issie. It rings and rings.

"Hey, Zara." Her voice is dull but familiar.

I swallow hard, relieved. I go and squat by Nick, touch his sleeping form with the flat of my hand, scan the sky again for enemies.

"Zara?" Her voice wakes me up, solidifies me into something else.

"Issie. We have a problem. A big problem."

"What?"

My hand touching his fur starts to tremble, shake really. I can't control it. "It's Nick. He's hurt, really hurt. And the pixies— they're dead and some are gone."

"What do you mean? You weren't on the bus, were you?"

"What bus? Issie, listen! There were other pixies. They attacked Nick and—"

I stop because it sounds like Issie has dropped the phone.

"Issie? Issie?"

Nick's eyes flutter a little bit. His beautiful wolf lips move just the tiniest amount. Through my worry, through my fear, I can see him trying so desperately to hold on.

"Zara, this is Dev. Issie just passed out. Can I call you back?" Dev's voice is distracted, harried.

"No!" I yell into the phone. "You cannot call me back. Nick is—"

But he's gone. I call again but nobody answers.

"Crap!" The word frustrates out of me, loud, echoing.

I regret screaming it right away. There could be other pixies hanging out in the woods. They could have been watching me move the snowmobile slowly through the forest; watching Nick bump along behind me, watching and waiting for the perfect time to strike.

Attached to the side of the snowmobile is a fireplace poker. It's made of iron. It's not the best weapon, but it's something. I rip off the duct tape that keeps it in place and hold it in my good arm. Then I rush back to Nick. He's turned human.

"Nick?" My voice is tiny small. I drop the poker in the snow and fall to my knees, touch his face. His skin has lost all color. I move the blankets around so I can see his wounds. He's bleeding everywhere. And bruised. I cover him up again. "Baby?"

He moans.

"Nick?" Something wet falls from my face and hits his cheek. Tears. "I'm getting you help, okay?"

His eyes open. They aren't right. Pain clouds them. His lips move. I lean over him. "I can't hear you."

"I'm dying," he whispers.

"No, you are not," I insist. I kiss his forehead. It's a horrible fire. "You will not die."

His eyes close. He thrashes. I press my hand against his shoulder. It almost burns me. "You have to stay still, baby. You have to stay still. You'll make it worse."

His eyelids flutter and his body quiets. It seems like a monumental fight but he gets his eyes open again. I lean back down and press my lips against his. "You're going to be safe. I swear. I'll keep you safe."

His lips move beneath mine. "I love you." His eyes are strong for a second, intense Nick eyes. "I will always love you. No matter what."

"We'll always love each other," I say. "Okay? I've got to get you

back. We're going to get to the road and then I'll get an ambulance and you'll be just fine."

His eyes close. "Don't . . . worry . . . you . . . always . . ."

I grab his head in my hand and lift it. "Stay awake! Nick, baby,
you have to stay with me."

A woman's voice comes from behind me. "He can't."

My whole body shudders. I don't turn. I won't look at her. I
know who she is. The Valkyrie. Thruth. Something inside me goes
feral. "Get the hell away from us."

The air moves behind me. She vaults over us and lands on the
other side of Nick. Her wings are massive. She glows. But her face
is far from happy angel. It's more like a cold knife. It rips me apart.

"You cannot save this warrior," she says. Each word slices
into my stomach. Each word is a death sentence that I refuse to
hear.

I grab the poker and carefully step over Nick so I face her.
She'll have to go through me to get him. My fingers tighten
around the cold iron. "I won't let you take him."

"You have no choice."

"There's always a choice." I am not touching Nick. I want to
be touching him somehow, making sure he's there. I step back just
enough so the heel of my foot grazes his arm. He doesn't move.

Thruth's wings reminds me of a black, upside-down valentine
heart. She says, "No, you are incorrect. There is not always a
choice."

The wind shifts around us. Snow whisks into my eyes, brittle
and cold, and I wonder if she's doing that somehow.

"You will let him die here rather than continue his existence as
a warrior for good in the halls of Valhalla?" She sneers at me. "You
are both greedy and selfish, typical for a human."

"He is *not* going to die," I insist.

She nods. For a second a kinder emotion flicks over her features. "Yes, he is. Soon."

Something inside me crumples. Despair fills my head, my heart. My hands shake and my fingers loosen their grip on the metal. Nick is dying. He is dying and I can't save him. He is so pale and he is barely breathing. His body is like a shell, a coat hanging on a coatrack, lifeless and empty. My body scrunches up in half and then I manage to straighten back up again. I try to hand her the poker. "Then kill me. Take me too. Just—just don't . . . I can't lose him."

She shakes her head. Her hair flows out behind her, catching the wind. Her eyes harden. "You aren't a warrior. You're just a girl, a human girl."

Someone sobs. It's me. I beg. "Please."

She doesn't move. The wind stops. Everything is clear, unobstructed by flying snow crystals. I can see everything about Thruth; every hair, every feather. Still, I beg and refuse to accept it.

"Please . . . I'm half pixie. I'm not a human." I frantically push the poker her way. "I'm turning blue. That's pixie. Take me. If you have to take him, take me too!"

"No, your parent is pixie. *You* are still human, susceptible to pixie magic, destined perhaps to be a pixie, but you are a girl— just a girl." Her shoulders move a tiny bit and she steps forward. "You have not yet been a warrior. You have never killed."

Something steels inside of me. "Do. Not. Come. Closer." I flip the poker around and jab it toward her. "Or you'll be my first."

Her lips twitch almost like she's about to smile. She doesn't think I'm a threat at all. She sniffs the air. "Little one, there are pixies approaching."

She gestures behind me.

I do not turn. I won't fall for that. "You're not going to distract me."

She sighs. "Your warrior's time has come. I need to hurry before we both lose him."

Her posture changes. I steel myself for her and I jab the poker. She brushes past me as if I'm a puppy. Her arm knocks me to the side.

"No!" I scream the word like a curse, like a prayer, and twist myself toward her. Lunging, I grab at her ankle just as she pulls Nick into her arms. My nails break her skin. She bleeds red. I use my hurt hand to try to get a better grip. "You can't take him."

Her wings tense and tighten above us. They catch the wind and she lifts. She lifts straight up. She lifts straight up, pulling me with her.

"Let go," she says.

"No!" My feet leave the ground. "No!"

We are moving up. One foot. Another.

Her voice is frustrated. "Let go, girl! Humans can*not* enter Valhalla."

"You can't take him." My fingers slip. My hurt arm dangles uselessly. Damn. Damn. "I need him."

We move higher. We are six feet up now. I don't care. I am not afraid of heights; I am only afraid of losing Nick.

"Let him go," I plead. "I can take care of him. Please . . ."

She shakes her leg. "You are worse than a dog, begging. Where is your honor?"

"He is mine!" I yell. My fingers quiver from the stress of holding my weight. "I love him. Please."

"I am sorry," she whispers. She shakes her leg again. "We need the wolf for the battle. He is no use to anyone dead and rotting in the earth. Now get off me."

She kicks at me with her free foot. Her heel smashes into my fingers. They spasm. It's just for a second that I lose my grip but it's enough: I fall. My feet hit first. The shock of gravity and contact thuds all the way to the top of my head, but I almost don't topple over. My knees bend. I stand my ground, then a second later I plop backward on top of the poker. The hard cold line of it is just to the left of my spine. I look up.

They are gone.

I couldn't save him. I couldn't keep him.

"No." I don't yell the word. I whisper it. I whisper it over and over again until it becomes sort of crazy chant. "No. No. Nono. Nononononono . . ."

Everything inside of me empties like the sky. It's just this one massive hole that grows out of my stomach and keeps getting bigger and bigger, erasing all of me. Nick. Nick is gone.

Pixie Tip

Pixies don't care about your loss. They will not send you flowers or hold your hand. Forget about sympathy cards too. They'd rather bite you.

He's gone. His body bleeding and broken, his beautiful body, is somewhere I can't reach. His deep, growly voice will no longer speak. I'll never feel his lips press against mine. His fingers will never twine themselves into my hair. I'll never be able to tease him about Snausages or fire hydrants.

I spend a while on the ground, just staring into the white sky; staring, staring, and seeing nothing.

Something moves out of the woods. My hand reaches underneath my back, finds the iron shaft of the poker. It's cold from the snow. My fingers wrap around it, moved by an instinct that has nothing to do with my heart.

"She's wounded," something says.

I turn my head to the left but stay lying down. It's a female pixie. Her glamour is gone. She is all silver eyes, blue skin, and teeth. Her designer dress is tattered. She has no coat and no shoes. She's bleeding from the leg and arm.

Another one comes from the right. I have to turn my head to see him, too. He's taller, still capable of his glamour. He's wearing workout clothes, wind pants, a green and white hoodie. He has deep circles beneath his eyes. They both look . . . hungry.

"Wounded makes the kill easier," he says, "and we like easy right now."

I calculate my options. They think I'm wounded and I'm not. If I sit up they'll see the poker. I'll lose my only advantage, which is surprise. They slink toward me. I know how fast they can be, but they are slow. They act like cats, tormenting their prey.

"She lost her wolf boy," the woman says in a fake compassionate voice. Ice drips from her words. "Poor defenseless thing."

The hole in me gets bigger but the edges of it ripple with something dark and fierce. I think it's hate. It's their fault. I lost Nick because of them, because of pixies. The hate inside me is cold, but it pushes aside the sorrow just a tiny bit. It gives me purpose.

"It must be hard to lose something so smelly and furry and warm," the guy says. He leaps forward and lands by my head. His hand reaches out and wipes at my cheeks. His touch is hard. "Oh, she's crying . . . so sweet. Don't worry. The pain won't last too long. And anyway, we'll give you a whole new pain to think about."

A crow shrieks in a treetop. The male opens his mouth. His glamour is suddenly gone and his teeth are like nails, pointed and deadly.

"Oh, she's shuddering, poor baby," he mocks.

Nick is the only one allowed to call me baby.

I think. The woman is almost to us, slinking up but limping too. I'll have to take the man first.

"Did she land on her arm? Maybe it's broken. How fun." The woman giggles. "We could torture her."

"Falling from the sky as her wolf was taken from her wasn't torture enough?" he asks.

"She imprisoned us. Nothing is enough," the woman hisses.

He turns back to me. His eyes flash. "True."

He opens his mouth and leans forward. His hands come to both sides of my head. The drawstring from his hoodie dangles down, hits my cheek. He jerks my head back to expose my neck. "Maybe vampire style?"

For a second I don't react. For a second I think, "Maybe it'll be better this way. Maybe it'll just be better to give up." And yeah, maybe it would be. But not like this. I do not want this. My fingers tighten around the poker.

The pixie leans in. The woman leaps forward. She lands beside me and moans, obviously too injured for fast movement. Good.

"Just take her," she orders. "Hurry if you're going to go first."

"Shut up," he hisses back. His hands tighten on my face. His teeth come closer.

That's my cue. I buck my hips up. My legs kick and my arm whips out from behind my back. The poker smashes into his head. His eyes bulge and close. I roll away and spring up. The female pixie laughs. Rage fills me.

"Nice surprise, little *princess*." She spits out the word. "It will be so good to taste you."

"Right." Not a good comeback. I am beyond good comebacks. I am beyond pretty much anything. Nick's name echoes inside of me and that is all I hear right now, all I feel. I am on automatic.

A quick glance assures me that pixie man isn't moving. Pixie woman follows my gaze. "He's not dead, see? His chest rises. You're weak like your father. You don't have enough strength in you to kill us, do you? Just trap us, let us slowly go insane with need because you don't have the guts to do what you have to do. Do you know how many times I wanted to kill your father with his endless worries? But I couldn't—oh no—I couldn't because he was our king."

She would be beautiful if she weren't so pixie. Her long black hair flows out with the wind.

"I trapped you because you're monsters." I force out the words. "My father is a monster."

"Monsters? Why? Because we admit to the pain we cause? Admit we like it? Instead of pretending we're some sort of warrior hero like your wolf." She sneers. Her posture tightens. She's going to jump me.

"He is a hero. He protects people from things like you."

"And you." She sniffs. She smiles. "I can smell the pixie in you."

"I'm not like you," I growl.

"No. You're not. You cloak your evil, your violence, in the mask of good. I am just evil." She leaps.

I shift the poker so that the barb faces out and thrust it as hard as I can. It hits her in the chest. There's this sick sucking sound as it goes through skin. Her mouth forms an O. Her face smiles and then grimaces. Her hands reach for my neck. Long claws scrape toward me. I yank the poker out and step back. She falls.

We all fall today.

She doesn't breathe. I have killed something. I have killed. Moving in slow motion, I check out the other pixie—the man. He rolls over. His eyes aren't quite focused yet, but he'll be fine if I just leave him, just walk away. Instead, I raise the poker.

"This is for Nick." I jab it in, rip it out. Do it again. "And this is for me."

Pixie Tip
Pixies have this fear of metal. Metallophobia.

There is blood on my hands, blood on the wrap around my wrist, blood on my jeans. There is probably blood on my face. I don't care. I leave the blood smears there to rot and crust and cake on. I climb back on the snowmobile. I drive to the road, get to Nick's MINI. His key fob. It is always in his pocket.

"God!" I sob the word into my hands and it's not a swear, it's a plea, a real plea and then I lose it. I just lose it. I shut off the sled and sob and sob and sob on the silly snowmobile. I don't know how much time passes. I don't know anything. I just know that Nick is gone like my dad.

I'm alone.

The world is still. There's no sound of cars or wind or animals. Even the trees are still and lonely. I'm murmuring words softly to myself—or to this self that is me but not me, me without Nick.

Without Nick.

Without.

Nick.

I'm murmuring words to myself, to God, to Nick, but I don't think anyone hears.

"I can't do this," I whimper. I wipe at my face with my good hand, try to get rid of the tears. "I can't—I can't do this."

"Of course you can."

My head lifts up and I move my body just enough to see him. He stands there, snow billowing down all around him. His leather jacket isn't ripped or torn. His jeans aren't dirty. There are no wounds. He wasn't at the house at all. Flakes land in his hair and stick, morphing the blond to white. He tilts his head as we stare at each other, then he reaches out his hand. "Zara."

"I'm not coming to you."

He keeps his hand raised. "I didn't do this, Zara. You did. All this power trapped and contained, ready to be exploited. It had to explode."

He's right. Of course he's right but I can't bring myself to say anything to him. What's the point, really? I'm not even making my silence into something. I'm done looking for meaning, done worrying about what's going to happen to me, because the worst has happened already. People keep dying on me. First my step-dad, now . . .

The air stills. Far away in the distance something screams. I breathe in. Cold air pushes its way into my lungs. I breathe in again. My hand moves up to wipe at my face. The tears are icy against my cheeks. I breathe out.

Astley watches all this. His eyes glint with the reflection of snow. His nostrils flare.

"I can smell another king on you—not your father." He sounds like some sort of emotion. Worried? Yeah, I think that's it.

"He was there." I sway. "He hurt my father. He k-k-killed Nick. And that stupid Valkyrie took him."

I start to lose my balance. The world dizzies around me. Astley moves forward so fast that I barely notice and he catches me against him. The leather crinkles smooth against my face. It has no texture. It's just sleek and smells like dead cows.

"You are not well," he says.

"How can I be well?" I hiccup. I struggle against him. "I can stand up by myself, though."

He ignores me and sweeps me into his arms. "You should stop lying to yourself."

I struggle for a second and then give up. The snowflakes curl their paths to the ground, waiting for something to come, for explanations, for meanings. They land, one after another, piling up, covering things. They don't give me answers. Nobody just gives me answers. I always have to reach for them. "What do you mean, lying to myself?"

He sniffs the air. He cocks his head and listens to the wind and the woods the same way Nick used to. Astley's eyes shift.

"What is it?" I ask. "Do you smell something?"

He doesn't answer. Instead his arms tighten around me.

"Tell me. What is it?"

"Death," he says more softly. He jostles me against his chest. His fingers adjust to where they hold the side of my knee. His voice is heavy with sadness. "Oh, Zara. I can smell his death. You've had a shock, a tragedy. Come on. Let's go somewhere safe."

I don't answer. I can't answer. Having someone know about Nick makes it even more real and I don't want it to be more real. My throat closes up. He drops my knees and presses me against him, both arms around my waist, and we lift into the air. His words are soft in my ear. "Don't be scared."

The world beneath us blurs. Trees meld into each other, just a mass of white. We travel over the woods—so fast. The wind whips against my cheek. My eyes water from the cold force of it.

Finally I find my voice. "This isn't my first time flying."

"Your father?"

"Yeah. When he kidnapped me. He smelled like mushrooms when it happened. You do too. Why is that?"

"It's the earth calling us back. Won't be long," he says. "Close your eyes if you need to."

I don't. I want to see. In the distance, over on Route 3, I think, there are the flashing lights of rescue vehicles. Gram's there. That must be the accident. There's a big bus tilted on its side, but before I can focus we're past it.

Images of Nick and the other pixie force their way into my head. Blood. Teeth flashing. Skin ripping. The pixie's evil low voice and his smile. Shuddering, I ask Astley, "Are you stronger than the other one?"

His arms tighten. "I hope so. Someday I'll need to be. I can't believe he found the house first. I'll never forgive myself for that. I got too—distracted."

I swallow hard. A sob threatens to reach my throat. I push it back and say, "I think it's my fault too."

He doesn't answer for a minute and then says, "You know, that is what I thought too, when I first met you and when I found out about the—situation—but now . . . You didn't have many choices, did you? We haven't handled things well. Your father should have been dealt with by his own kind long ago."

I don't know how to answer. Even though the cold stings I tilt up my head and scan the sky looking for Nick as we start to get lower. We're by my house. The house where Nick and I slept and kissed and made breakfast. It wasn't long ago. It feels like forever.

Astley's hands shift. "Hold on, we are landing. I am not the best at landings."

He thuds to a landing and flops on his butt. I land half on top of him. He blushes and then smiles.

"Oh." I roll off of him. "You really aren't."

"We all have our weaknesses," he explains, hopping up to his feet. I stare at the house. It looks so calm and normal. It looks like nothing has happened. It looks good and fine and safe, but nothing is good and fine and safe.

I walk slowly up the porch stairs. Astley follows me to the door. He keeps his arms out around me, but not touching, ready to catch me if I fall, I guess. I fumble with the doorknob.

"Here, let me." He inserts my key and turns it for me. I step inside. He inclines his head.

"I can't let you in." My words come out slowly.

He closes his eyes for the briefest of seconds. "You don't trust me."

I don't answer. I am too tired, too sad to answer. The sun pokes out from behind a cloud. The light sparkles off the snow. I shield my eyes with my hand. It's too bright. Nothing should be bright. I start to step inside.

Astley's hand grabs my arm. "I can't just leave you like this. You're barely capable of communicating."

"You have to."

For a second neither of us moves. For a second the world seems to stop dead still. His hand slides up my arm and he holds me by my shoulders. I don't have the energy to shrug him off. "Do not let anyone in here. It's dangerous now."

I almost laugh, that's such an understatement. Behind him,

the MINI's tire tracks are gone, covered up by snow. He lets go of my shoulders and pulls a piece of paper out of his pocket. He writes a number on it and puts it in my hand. He closes my fingers around it.

"My cell. Call it if you need me," he says.

"I won't need you," I tell him, looking at the paper—a receipt from Holiday Inn—and stepping inside, "but thanks."

"Zara—" His voice stops me. I turn around. "You might."

I close the door behind me but don't lock it because there's no point. The only pixie who can get in here is the one that's already been invited and that's my father. It's a weird pixie rule, one of many. All of the pixies must be rampaging since they are finally free. They are probably searching for food, for revenge. The desire must be pounding through their weakened bodies. I know how that feels. It pounds through mine, too. Vengeance: that's the kind of feeling that belongs in a safe, shut off from the rest of the world, away from mothers cuddling babies, away from children on swings, away from humanity.

I fall on the couch, press my face against the red fabric, and breathe deeply, trying to catch the smell of Nick somewhere, something left over from last night, but I can't smell anything. My nose isn't that good. I smoosh a pillow into my face, but still nothing. There is no Nick: not on the couch I'm sitting on, not in his MINI still parked on the side of the road, not working at the hospital, not hunting in the woods, not anywhere at all. He's not here, even though I want to tangle my fingers into his dark hair, breathe into the depths of him, let him breathe into the depths of me, even though I want him here with me right now, all the time, forever. Even though he's not here.

I sit up and text Issie. `You  Must  Call.  Pixies Escaped.`

I can't tell her about Nick. Not in a text. I just can't. I send an identical text to Betty. My cell phone somehow falls out of my fingers and lands on the couch. I leave it there.

I wait.

Nothing happens.

I have no idea how much time passes. There is nothing to look forward to. Pixies killed Nick. There will be no flower beds and white picket fences for us. I will never kiss him again. I will never hug him again. I will never smell him again. It's the pixies' fault. It's my fault too.

Somehow, my body lifts up off of the couch where we slept. Somehow, my feet walk toward the kitchen and to the basement door. Fingers wrap around the knob and turn. I open it, go down the stairs. My feet make hollow noises as they hit the wood. We have a weapons locker down here. It is filled with things forged with iron. I've never been the best fighter. Nick says it's because I lack the urge to kill. My hands haul open the cover of the metal locker. My fingers grab a sword. I sheathe it and fix it to my belt with the big peace sign buckle. It is heavy against my leg.

I move through the house, silent as the dead. There is power in my choice. My story has lost its male protagonist, its romantic lead. I am just a shell. So my death won't be much of a loss and I will take down as many of those bastards as I possibly can, so there will be less to hurt Gram, and Issie, and my mom, and Devyn. That is my plan. I will avenge him and die doing it.

I step outside and head to the woods.

Pixie Tip
Pretending that they don't exist doesn't work.

The storm clouds have gone. Bright blue sky mocks down at me as I cross our lawn. I've still got my boots on somehow. I hadn't even noticed. There's blood crusted on one. I hadn't noticed that either. It doesn't matter. I pull my feet through the snow and ignore the blood, ignore the sky, and enter the trees. The snow is a little less deep here because of the canopy of pine needles above me. They catch some of the heaviness in their branches. It weighs them down. We are all weighed down.

I walk through the woods, listen to the winter sounds of crows cawing out the news to each other, harsh verbalizations of bird truths. Chipmunks squeal nervously when I pass. Theirs are the only tracks. There aren't any footprints except my own. Pixies don't always leave a trail. I don't know exactly how that happens. I don't care. The hows don't matter anymore, do they?

It takes ten minutes of walking before one calls my name.

"Zara . . ."

It's a woman's voice, low and raspy, like one of the jazz singers that Betty listens to on her iPod at night. I stop walking but don't grab my sword. Fear makes a tiny prickle along the back of my neck. This is what I wanted, though—what I want. I want a fight.

"Zara, come to me . . ." This time it's a male voice, high and clear, coming from the left, I think. They are trying to get me lost. Idiots.

"Zara . . ."

I shake my head. Haven't they noticed the sword hanging from my belt? Are they so cocky that they don't care? Am I that little of a threat? I follow the voices. They come from all around me now, above me, behind me, in front.

"Zara . . ."

"Princess . . ."

"Zara . . ."

The crows, the squirrels, the chipmunks have gone silent. My breath floats out of me, forms a cloud in the air. It's gotten colder. I don't feel it, though. I don't feel anything. I take another step forward and there she is—a pixie. I recognize her as one of my father's. Her hair is wild, red, out of control. Her mouth is a snarling trap. She's wearing a bathrobe over kitty pajamas, which is ridiculous but true.

"Princess." She smiles.

To my right, two more pixies appear, tall men, skinny with need. To my left, a branch snaps. Three more pixies appear: a woman, two men. More breathe behind me. One is in the limbs of a pine tree waiting to pounce. I say nothing, merely pull out my sword.

The red-haired pixie laughs. Someone behind me says, "Should we kill her now or make her watch us kill her friends?"

They seem to think about this for a moment. My sword waits heavy in my hand. For a moment nobody moves and then one of the guys on my right says, "I vote we almost kill her and then make her watch."

"A reasonable decision," she says.

I shake my head. "All you pixies ever do is talk. Blah. Blah. Blah. It's sooo boring."

Before they can do anything I lunge to my left, slashing the sword through the air. It's awkward but it works. The iron slices across one of the pixies' stomachs almost like soft butter. He falls forward. I twirl around, ready to strike again. They lunge all at once. I bring my sword up but I'm nowhere near fast enough and the red-haired one yanks it out of my hands, screaming in pain as she touches the blade. It burns her skin, giving off an awful acid smell. She yells a curse and one of them yanks my head back by the hair.

"Tie her up," she orders. "We'll do this slowly."

They have blue nylon rope. Something topples through the tree branches and lands in front of me, a pile of leather and denim and blond hair.

"Damn," Astley mumbles and he's on his feet before I can figure out what's happening. He pivots and rips me out of the arms of the two pixie guys who are holding me and yells, "Hold on!"

I do. He launches into the air. Pine needles scrape at our clothes. I duck my face into his chest. Pixies curse below us. I clutch on to him, trying to get a secure hold. He's got one arm wrapped around my waist. The other is trying to protect our heads from the branches. An arrow zips past us, missing us by inches, and then we are clear, above the tree line and into the sky.

"What the hell do you think you're doing?" he says the moment we're clear of the trees. His arm joins the other around my waist. "What is wrong with you? Are you trying to kill yourself?"

My hands pummel his chest. "I don't need to be rescued! Just give me a weapon and put me down, or fight with me! Let me go!"

"Zara. We all need to rescue and we all need to be rescued."

The world below us is distant and cold. We soar in the nothing space above the trees, below the true sky.

"I can't live without Nick," I say.

He groans. "Of course you can. We all live with our losses. We don't want to, but we can."

I blow off his little bit of moralizing and force myself to remember the events of the morning: the pixie house, the fight, the woman lifting Nick away. I need to get to Valhalla somehow, then maybe I can bring him back.

"Tell me about the Valkyrie," I insist.

He refuses to talk any more while we're flying and eventually we land awkwardly in the alley behind Martha's Café and the Riverside Dance Studio. A thin layer of snow covers the asphalt. The bricks that form the back wall of the building are crumbling. I touch them anyway, try to ground myself.

"Why are we here?" I ask.

He tucks in his shirt in quick immaculate gestures and explains, "I'm hungry. A restaurant should be safe."

He starts walking around the building. "It's too public. Although, they are so hungry they might be bold enough. I don't know. The hunger—the need—it can distort your judgment."

I run after him and grab him by the sleeve of his jacket. "Don't you have needs?"

"I do."

"How do you control them?"

"I'm a king, but I'm still young, Zara." Emotion clouds his face. "My father died recently and I'm new at this and the needs that overtake most kings won't take hold for another couple years at least." He gazes at me and squints. "Let me fix your hair. You have branches in it. And blood crusted on your face."

"My dad—my stepdad—he died recently too," I tell him.

"I know. I am so sorry." Two of his fingers softly touch my face.

I swallow. "I'm sorry too."

His hands move quickly, gently gathering my hair into a pony-tail. He picks some branches and leaves off of my hair and clothes and drops them onto the ground. He rubs at some blood on my cheek with snow and scratches the blood that's hardened onto my hands. He gives me his jacket to wear to hide some of the dirt and blood on my shirt. We start walking again and then I remember.

"I'm blue," I say.

"So?"

I wipe my hands on my jeans, fix my peace buckle. Reason sets in. "I can't go into a restaurant like this."

He takes me by the elbow. "Sure you can."

"No, people—people will—I'm wet from snow and scratched up and—"

"It'll be fine. I'll make up a story." He hustles me into the restaurant before I can object too much.

The big brown sign in the front says for us to seat ourselves. We walk over the black and white tiled floors, past the deep red booths and picture posters of old movie stars who were big-time a half century ago. He slides into a booth in the back wall beneath a picture of John Wayne in cowboy garb.

"I like this place," he says.

I put my elbow on the table and duck my head down, trying to shield my skin from the rest of the world.

"I love the pancakes." He hands me a paper napkin. "Try to talk, Zara. You really aren't communicating. It's worrisome."

I take the napkin, place it on my lap, stare at it for far too long, and give it a try. "It's hard to imagine pixies coming here and eating just like everyone else."

He smiles and hands me a menu. "Well, we do."

It seems like a silly concern but I say it. "I don't have any money."

"It will be my treat. It is the least I can do on a day like today."

I stare at him. "How come you aren't hunting down the bad pixies right now? That's what Nick would do."

"I am not Nick," he says so harshly that I startle.

"Obviously."

He lifts an eyebrow. "I was busy looking for you, Zara. You are the priority here for me."

I wait. Across the room a little girl finishes her pancake and climbs onto her dad's big lap. She whispers something in his ear. He wraps his arm around her waist and tucks her in close, safe. In another booth a twentysomething couple have hooked their legs together beneath the tabletop. Their fingers are entwined. It's all so fragile. I want to scream at them to enjoy it, to keep each other close, to love each other while they still can. I adjust the napkin in my lap. "Why am I your priority?"

"Because you are not safe." He grabs the sugar shaker and moves the crystals around, swirling them in a circular pattern. "And because I think you are meant to be my queen."

Pixies and their ridiculous queen obsession. I'm so tired of it.

I grab a sugar packet, try to ignore the people staring at us, and whisper, "I am *never* safe. What's so different now?"

He stops swirling the sugar. "What's so different now? Your father and his pixies are loose. Frank is here. That's what's different. Do you know what that means for you?"

"Unspeakable horror and evil?"

He sighs and before he can answer, and before I can ask him who Frank is, the waitress comes over with water. It's actually Martha, the owner. She has a sweet little gap between her two front teeth. I can see it now because her mouth is hanging open.

"Zara, you're blue, honey," she gasps.

I nod.

"Face paint," Astley explains. "It's not coming off. We've tried everything."

"Oh my!" Martha laughs and pulls out her pencil and order pad. "So now you're stuck looking like Cookie Monster?"

"It's not that bad," Astley says. "Much lighter hue."

"You poor honey." Martha giggles. "Let me go get you some paper towels and maybe some paint thinner."

She winks at Astley. He smiles back. I can't even speak. Everything inside of me is hollow. Wow. I miss Nick.

After she's gone for a moment he clears his throat and says, "Let me start off by telling you about the war, okay? The bigger war that's written about."

"I want to talk about the Valkyrie," I insist.

"The war is part of why she's here. The war is called Ragnarok or Gotterdammerung. It is legend but real, if you understand? During this time brother fights brother, son slays father. People start acting without morals." He starts swirling the big sugar container again. It reminds me of a snow globe. He puts the sugar container down. "I'm sorry. You are still in shock. Do you think you can focus?"

People are muttering at other tables, talking and whispering. I sip some water. "I'm trying."

"I know. Okay. I truly am sorry we don't have more time, but I think this is information you need to have."

"I don't mind. I'd rather know. I hate not knowing things."

"Me too. We are alike that way." He tips the end of his finger into his ice water. "The legend has it that Ragnarok, the war, happens after the worst of all winters, Fimbulvetr. The winter is three years long with no summer. And then the war—well, it will be the ultimate, most horrible war."

His voice trails off and then he takes a breath and continues, "It means that this place—Bedford, Maine—is like a homing beacon for fae, at least for pixies and weres. Think of how many there are here. They are here because this is the place of the final battle."

"No, it's not," I insist. "I won't let that happen."

"I am not sure if we can stop it."

My water glass is cold and smooth, slippery. I adjust my hold and say, "We'll stop it."

He brushes his fingertips against my hand, which is still wrapped around the glass.

I feel an electric warmth and lurch back. "What did you do that for?"

He blushes and looks away. "I couldn't help it. I apologize."

We are silent. The rest of the restaurant chatters on about a bus wreck somewhere. I keep catching words like "horrifying" and "band" and "Sumner," which is another regional high school up the coast about forty-five minutes away.

Clearing his throat he continues, "So, all the people, they will never survive. They are not strong enough, and there are sides. Even without knowing it, the fae are already choosing sides. Odin's sons—the forces of good, I guess you would call us—the heroes—"

"That's not egotistical at all."

"It is true. You don't think of your wolf as a hero?"

I close my eyes. Sorrow wraps its arms around my chest, squeezing it in tight. "Please don't talk about him."

"I apologize again, Zara, but I have to. He is part of the reason you are here."

I open my eyes and I know my gaze is fierce but I don't care. "He's the *only* reason I'm here."

He lets that sink in. He leans back in the booth, stretches his arms out in front of him, clasps his hands together, and cracks his knuckles. I've seen Nick do the same thing a million times. "The heroes are called to the battle. They come from all over the world to this place called Vigrid. It is prophesized that this is where the last battle will be fought. This is that place."

Bedford is that place.

I take in the booths, the chattering people, the smell of bacon, the way the lights hum and send down a soft yellow glow. This place seems so safe, so normal, so anything but a battlefield. It's hard to believe. I shift the topic back to what's immediately important and say, "The Valkyrie said she was taking Nick because he was a warrior."

"For Odin and Thor, yes. There needs to be eight hundred warriors."

"And they want Nick to be one of those warriors?"

"They will make him well and then yes, he will be kept at Valhalla until the battle."

I stand up and forget to whisper. "Then we have to go there! We have to go there and get him. He'll help us stop it before it starts."

"People are looking." He grabs my arm. "Sit down."

I don't want to, but I do.

"It is not easy," he says.

"She said humans can't go to Valhalla." He waits. He wants me to say it. So I do. I just blurt it out. "You'll kiss me, won't you? You'll turn me?"

"I would rather not do it because of this."

"Because I'm doing it for Nick?"

He nods. "I would rather do it because you want to be my queen."

"Saving Nick is the only reason I would ever do it," I say as his foot touches mine under the table. It happens again—the warm tingly feeling. I tuck my feet beneath the bench.

He appraises me. "I have not known you very long, Zara, but from what I know of you that is a lie."

"You're calling me a liar?"

"No. I'm saying *that* is a lie. You would do it for any of your friends, I think. You would turn to save your mother, your grandmother, maybe even a stranger, wouldn't you?" When I don't answer he continues. "You would turn because it is your destiny to turn," he says softly. "It is your destiny to be my queen."

"Destiny doesn't matter." I rip apart a fake-sugar packet and pour it in my water. The little grains swirl and spin, all caught up in the movement of the water. They bump into cubes and eventually settle to the bottom. "Let me talk to Issie and Devyn, tell them what happened, talk to Gram. Then we'll do it."

"We don't have much time." He almost smiles as I start stirring my water, trying to dissolve the fake sugar.

"I'll be quick." My mind races. "I have to call my mom, tell her that my dad is out again. She's in danger."

"She's not the only one."

"What do you mean?"

"Even without their needs—those pixies you imprisoned are going to want revenge."

"Nobody is hurting my friends." I rip open some real sugar and put that in this time. I clank it around with a spoon, watch it disappear, just get swallowed up, taken away.

I let that sink in for a minute and then I move on. "Okay. Fine. About the kissing?" I stare into his eyes. "Tell me what I have to do."

Pixie Tip

It is a myth that pixies glitter. Only the kings leave behind glitter trails. The rest don't sparkle or glitter or anything like that. Maybe they suffer from glitter envy.

After he eats, he won't let me walk back to my house. Instead we head out to the alley again. The pavement is cracked and desperate looking. Patches of ice cover pieces of the ugliness.

"I can run back," I say, even though I know it's dangerous and it'll take forever, but there's this tiny kernel of hope in me now and I feel energized, like I could do anything. I can get Nick back maybe. I could find him. That is, if Astley is telling the truth, if it's not all some massive, horrible trick.

"You have no idea how hungry and angry they are," he says disdainfully when I suggest running. "They will find you."

So he flies me home. I close my eyes the entire way and think about Nick, wonder what he'd feel about all this. He didn't make my choices for me when he was here and he's not going to start now. But still, I wonder. Will he still love me if I turn? My mood swings from hope to despair, back and forth with each gust of wind.

"Hold on, we're landing," Astley grunts. He flops into the snow. He tries to keep my arm from bumping into him too hard.

I hop up and start running for the house. He's still flat in the snow. One of his arms sank in up to his shoulder. The rest of him is all sprawled out and totally undignified looking.

"Thanks!" I dash up the steps.

"I'll see you at nightfall," he says, sitting up, brushing off his clothes.

My hand goes to the door.

"Be careful. Daylight will not keep them away when they are like this," he says.

I rush into the house and slam the door behind me. Leaning with my back against it, I try to take some deep breaths. My hands are shaking. They're still dirty. Everything about me feels dirty and contaminated.

"Nick," I whisper out his name. There's no answer. I close my eyes and try to feel him. I swear I almost can. I push away from the door and head to the bathroom. I will shower. I will shower and think. I will shower and think and not shake. I will shower and think and not shake and I will imagine what it'll be like to see Nick again. What it'll be like to hold him against me, to kiss his face.

It has to be possible. It has to.

It's in the shower that I really think about what it means to be pixie kissed. I won't be me anymore. I won't be human. My teeth, my skin, the way my mind works, will all probably change. I have to believe I'll still have my same old soul, right? I have to believe that.

The water chugs down, burning hot. The room smells sweet and clean. I grab the shower gel and squirt it onto a loofah, trying to scrub myself clean. There are so many variables. Astley might be lying. I might die if I get kissed. I might not find a way to Valhalla. Nick might not want to come back.

The weight of the water presses against my skin. I shut the faucet off and stand there, dripping. My stomach screams inside of me. I have to do this, really. There is no other choice. I eventually dry off and pull on some wind pants and my favorite pink hoodie that zips up and says CHARLESTON in big white letters across the front.

When I go into the living room I'm surprised to see that Issie and Devyn are on the couch. Issie's shaking. Devyn's got his arm around her. They both look up at me. Issie's eyes are haunted, filled with fear. Devyn looks like he's strung out on crack or something. They must've heard about Nick somehow.

"You're blue," they both say.

"I know." I brush their words away and sit on the couch next to Issie. "Did you hear?"

At the same time Issie says, "What happened to Nick? Oh man. He wasn't on the bus, was he? No, of course he wasn't on the bus. Those were band kids from Sumner. Nick is not a band kid from Sumner."

Frustrated, I kneel in front of her, try to put together her info with what I heard at Martha's, and about Betty being at an accident.

"There was an—at—" She breaks off. Her body leans forward. She hides her head in her hands.

Devyn rubs little circles on her back. "There was an attack. Issie saw it. There was a bus and pixies attacked it."

I try to put his words together with what I know about Gram and the lights I saw on the road when I flew by with Astley. It still doesn't make sense. "They attacked an entire bus?"

"It was an ambush. One stood in the middle of the road. Her clothes were dirty and ripped," Devyn explains.

"She looked like she'd been hurt," Issie whispers. "She was waving for help. The bus driver pulled over." She keeps her head in her hands. "I keep seeing it over and over again. I was coming from the other direction. It was on that long, straight part of Route 3."

Her voice shakes.

"Do you want some water? Let me get you some water." Devyn gets up and walks without canes to the kitchen.

"The bus stopped. The door opened. A couple of people came out to help the pixie. She had fallen to the pavement. And that's when— It just— It was bad. They came out of the woods. They came from everywhere. And the screaming . . . I could hear it even though I was in my car." She starts sobbing.

"Did you stop?" I ask.

"Of course she didn't stop!" Devyn yells. He calms down and says, "I have some water for you, Is."

She looks up and takes it. Issie's hand shakes so much that she might drop the glass. "I called 9-1-1 and said there was an accident and I called Betty, but . . . I kept driving. I kept driving."

Devyn takes the glass out of her hand and puts it on the floor.

"It was so bad," she whimpers.

"Shh . . ." He soothes her. "I know. I know."

She cries for a minute and then her sobs get a little quieter. Eventually, she hiccups. "I'm sorry."

"Nothing to be sorry about," Devyn says. He stares at me and pulls me aside. "One sec, Issie."

We stand by the kitchen sink. There are stains on the shiny metal.

"What is wrong with you?" he squawks. "You aren't even comforting her."

I swallow hard. "I'm sorry. I . . ."

Now it's my turn to lose it. I don't know what to say. My mouth moves. Nothing comes out.

Issie walks in and turns on the faucet to fill her glass up. "Wait. Where's Nick?"

"And why are you blue again?" Devyn's voice is an accusation.

I close my eyes for a second, pull in a breath, and tell them. It takes a while, but I do it. I tell them about Nick being taken away, about how I couldn't save him, not then.

Devyn's skin pales and he sways. He puts his hands through his hair, frantically, over and over again like a madman. His phone gives a text alert. He doesn't check it. Instead he just keeps at it with his hair. "You mean he died?"

"He was almost dead. I don't— She took him. She said there was no way to save him," I try to explain. Each word pains my mouth.

Issie shakes her head. "But Nick can't be dead. He's our hero. Our alpha male. Our—"

"Issie!" Devyn tries to interrupt her.

She glares at him. "What? He was! Am I not allowed to be upset?" She crumples, wraps her arms around herself. "I can't believe he's gone. Oh, Zara, I'm so sorry."

She tries to hug me but I don't want hugs right now. I want plans and action. "There's a chance to bring him back if I turn pixie."

"What?" Issie's mouth drops open and I begin the long explanation. As I'm talking, tears stream down Issie's and Devyn's faces. I just can't let myself go there now.

When I'm done, Devyn groans. "He'll hate that."

"I don't care," I insist. "I don't even care if he'll hate me, but I have to do it. I have to get him back here."

Issie brushes her hair off her face and wipes her eyes. "Oh, Zara, you'll be a pixie. That's what you've been so afraid of."

I nod so much that it's like my whole upper body is bobbing up and down. "I know."

They stare at me and give me all the objections I already know. I'm hurt. I could die if the kiss goes wrong. If it goes right I'll be forever changed.

"We don't know what it means, even," Devyn insists. "I've read you'll be beholden to the king."

"Like his slave?" Issie asks. "Creepy."

"He won't do that," I say. "Astley's not like that."

Devyn leans back into the couch. His voice fills with frustration. "You don't know him. He could be tricking you."

"He could," I agree. But my mind is already made up. They know that. "I have to try. You know I have to try."

"But—," Devyn starts.

"It's Nick." My voice breaks.

Issie's hands grab mine. "I know, but, Zara? How do you know you aren't fooling yourself that—that—it isn't impossible?"

"I don't." We meet eyes. Hers are full of so much worry, so much sorrow. "We'll have to call his parents," I say.

Devyn and Issie exchange a look.

"What?"

Issie gulps. She leans forward and says, "Zare, Nick's parents are dead."

"No they aren't. They're photographers. They're in Africa on some extended shoot for Animal Planet or something." I zip my hoodie all the way up to my neck. Nick would say I'm in "geek mode."

"No, sweetie. That's the lie." Is pats my leg. "The truth is that they're dead."

"But—but—" My brain can't wrap itself around what she's saying. "We've talked about them—talked about them coming home and how Nick feels with them being gone." I point at Devyn. "You've talked about it too."

Devyn cringes. "He wanted us to play along. So, we played along."

"But why? That makes no sense." I look from one to the other.

"Well, it's what he tells everyone," Issie starts to explain.

"I'm not everyone!" I pull my knees down, slam up off the couch. "I am the love of his life. I mean"—I totally lose my composure—"I'm supposed to be the love of his life."

"Aw, Zara, honey . . ." Issie comes after me, wraps her arms around me. "You totally are. You *are* the love of his life."

"Then why did he lie to me?" My words grump into the air, angry and hard and confused.

She looks to Devyn for help. "Because you weren't always the love of his life and he didn't trust you at first. So, he just gave you the same line he gave everyone else."

"And then he never trusted me enough to tell me?"

"People become trapped in their lies," Devyn explains. "He was trapped. I'm sure he wanted to tell you."

I let the words sink in for a second. They don't make me feel any better.

"So what happened to his parents?" I ask.

Issie twitters like a nervous bird. "They died at home. I think— Well, okay— The truth is that Nick's dad went crazy. He shifted and attacked his mom. Then Nick killed him."

That stops me. "Nick killed his father?"

"He shot him," Devyn explains. "He had no choice. His dad had turned feral. It"—he sneaks a look at Issie—"happens sometimes, not just to wolves but to all of us. It's like a virus, like the flu, but it hits shifters."

"But he . . . he murdered him? He murdered his father? And his father murdered his mother?" My hand covers my mouth and I stagger back. My shoulder bumps into the fireplace. I stay there and let it hold me up.

"He. Didn't. Murder. Him." Devyn's face turns red. "Nick had to do it."

"What do you mean, 'he had to'?" I move forward. "Because that's always the only option, right? It's all kill or be killed, right? To hell with science and medicine or even just regular old jail and police, right?"

"He had no choice," Devyn insists. "His father was wolf. He was feral. There is no cure. He'd have killed Nick next anyway. The rules are different for us, Zara."

"For 'shifters'?" I snark and make air quotes.

"Really, Zara," Devyn snaps back. "Stop being such an idiot."

Issie pops up. "Devyn! Don't call her an idiot!"

"She's being one," he says.

"It's mean." Issie's lip shakes. "You're acting cruel. We're supposed to be friends. We're supposed to band together."

"You're right." He makes a pretty obvious effort to control himself. "I'm sorry, Zara. I'm just so insane with worry. I'm sorry."

I wave his apology away. "It doesn't matter."

Issie shuts her eyes hard for a second the way she does when she's trying not to be upset and says, "We aren't sure why Nick didn't get the virus, but it's really really good that he didn't, and neither did Devyn or his parents and now his parents are trying to find a cure down there in their monster lab."

"They're trying to do a lot of things, Is." Devyn scratches at his reddish neck where his shirt collar meets his skin.

Issie comes over and puts her hand on my shoulder. "I am so sorry he's gone, Zara."

I whip away. "He's not gone. I'm getting him back, even if he did lie to me like a total jerk."

Her hand drops to her side. She shakes her head. "Zara—"

"I'm really mad, okay, Is? We're always going on about the pixies being liars, but look at us. Nick lied—a big one—Devyn never told me about his parents and his house. You and I lied by omission when we didn't tell them about talking to my father."

"We told them eventually," she protests.

"Not right away. They are lies by omission, but they're still lies and Nick's was pretty big." I blink hard a couple of times and take a deep breath. "Still, we need him to fight and you know I can do it," I insist. "I can go there and get him."

"That pixie could be tricking you," Devyn says. He stands and grabs his canes. "It's the most likely scenario, you know that. You can't trust pixies. Think of all the manipulation your father did to get your mother."

"Astley is not like my father."

"Oh man, Zara, are you trusting him?" Is says. "You aren't, are you? Please, please, please tell me you aren't."

"Zara, think." Devyn glares at me.

"Do not tell me to think. I am thinking! You are not the only one capable of thought, Devyn. I am *not* an idiot. My choices may not be yours. Our morals may not be the same, but I am not dumb." My voice is harsh. I try to calm it down. These are my friends. "I have a chance to get him."

"At best, if it isn't all some big farce, you will turn pixie!" Devyn says. "You won't be you and Nick hates pixies."

"I have to take that chance," I whisper. "I have to take that chance to save him."

Devyn shakes his head. "We need you here, fighting."

"I know you do, but . . ." I stumble for reasons. "Gram will be here. Mrs. Nix. And I will bring Nick back and we'll be stronger. I'll be stronger as a pixie, fight better."

"You could go all crazy like the ones who attacked the bus." Issie shudders. "Have you thought about that? You could hurt us or anybody."

"I've thought about that," I say.

Devyn lifts an eyebrow. "And . . ."

"And if that happens—at the slightest sign of that happening— you are going to kill me."

Pixie Tip

Pixies do not just live in England. That's a big lie. They are everywhere.

I call my mom to warn her. Because let's face it, my biological father is hungry and need-filled and when that happens he tends to want my very human, very vulnerable mother, the woman he's decided should be his queen.

It's like a miracle that I get through, because she's on the outer banks and the reception is horrible. Like here, there are not nearly enough cell phone towers. I hate that.

I tell her what happened but I leave out the parts about Nick and my plan. I already have to deal with Devyn and Issie not liking it. Instead I try to pump her for information about the bus accident and why that would happen.

She clears her throat. She always does that. "When the pixie king needs to feed he picks a young male and bleeds him. You saw that with Jay Dahlberg."

"Okay. Then explain to me what's going on with this accident."

"I guess this is what happens when the king is weak or uncaring and the pixies go wild. Say what you will about your father, Zara, but he had some control over himself and he had a lot of control over the pixies he ruled."

"You're talking as though you like him."

She sighs. "I don't. It's just . . . He tries very hard to be civil, to be kind, when it's not the easiest thing for his nature to let him be. I've got to credit him for trying."

"Yeah. That's like giving credit to a serial killer for only murdering people every other month."

"Zara, it's not the same thing."

"Isn't it?"

I know her so well that I can predict what she's doing. Right now she's crossed her legs at the ankles. She's running one of her small hands through her hair. "You are just like Daddy."

I know she means my stepdad, the one who raised me, the one who died. "I hope that's true."

"Why?"

"Because he was a hero." I let that settle in. I push my hand against my topsy-turvy stomach. Nothing will settle it down. I want to tell her what I'm going to do but I can't.

"Are you going to be safe up there?" she asks. "I know you're worried about me, but I—I'm worried about you, honey."

"I'll be fine." I am lying liar head. That's what Issie would say. I make eye contact with her across the room. She's in the kitchen putting water into a teakettle. Her face is red and puffy from crying. Devyn's got pokers and iron swords strewn across the kitchen table. He looks like he's in shock, moving on automatic. Those weapons won't help him fight when he's in eagle form, but they could help Issie and me. Although, honestly? I wasn't all that hot with the fighting a little while ago, was I? Devyn lifts up a sword, weighs it in his hand. His eyes are so different from the Devyn I know. His eyes are piercing and angry and hollow all at once.

He turns to Issie. "We're going to make them pay."

She doesn't say anything.

"I'm going to make them pay, Issie, for what you saw . . . for Nick."

She responds with a quote, " 'People sleep peacefully in their bed at night only because rough men stand ready to do violence on their behalf.' That guy who wrote *Animal Farm* said that, I think. The Orwell guy."

"Zara?" My mom's voice refocuses my attention to the phone.

"Sorry. Sorry. Got distracted," I say. "We need to think of a way to keep you safe, Mom. Okay?"

Her voice comes back all fake strong. "You take care of yourself. I'll handle me. How's Nick?"

"Nick is good." I choke the lie out as Issie puts the kettle on the burner. She makes a sobbing noise. I walk out of the room and back into the living room so my mom won't hear. I think about Astley and how I have to trust him. "Do you think all pixies are bad?"

"Yes, Zara," my mom says. "Yes, I do. I don't just think it. I know it."

"And you'd never trust one?"

"Honey, no—never. I trusted your father and look what he did. He came after me the moment your stepfather died and he didn't just do it in a nice way. He kidnapped you." Her voice becomes strong now. It's not fake at all. It's real. "You can never trust a pixie."

But I have to trust one. I have no choice. If I don't it means I've given up on Nick, and I can't do that—not ever.

After I've hung up, we call Mrs. Nix and tell her what's happened. She chitters and worries and exclaims, "We have to close ranks!" Her voice turns into her bearlike growl. "I'll be right there."

I click the phone off and announce, "Mrs. Nix is coming."

"Good!" Issie almost sounds perky but can't quite make it. She puts tea bags into cups. "That's good."

"And Betty called and she should be clear of the hospital soon and then she's on her way home. And my mom is staying hidden."

Devyn leans against the counter. His face seems a lot more pale than normal. It must be hard for him to move around without his canes. He's got Gram's laptop behind him and he's been researching. "Did you tell them about Nick? Or what you're going to do?"

"No." My voice breaks. "I can't tell them about it because then—"

He stares at me with his eagle-eye look. I stare back and try to gather up my strength. I don't know where it went for a second. I press my lips together, try to push my shoulders back.

His voice goes all teacher/uptight father. "Are you sure about this?"

"No."

"Oh, Zara." Issie stops dunking the tea bag in hot water and comes over to grab my hands. "You don't have to go pixie. There could be another way."

"*I* could go," Devyn says.

"No," I insist. "They might keep you."

"Why would they keep me and not you?"

"Because you're a warrior."

"Wounded warrior," he scoffs.

"Don't be ridiculous." Issie abandons me for him. "Of course they'd want to keep you." The horror of the realization pales her face. "You are *not* going!"

"*I* am the one going," I say as calmly as I can. "I am the worst fighter. I can't help much here."

"Actually, I think I'm the worst fighter," Issie says.

I don't tell her that I've just killed. Instead I lie and say, "Okay. We are tied for worst fighter, but I have pixie in me. I can survive the change better and he's—he's *my* boyfriend."

Devyn nods as though he is starting to come around to my plan.

I grab a mug that has a picture of a horse on the side. I pull the tea bag out and set it on a paper towel. The brown liquid stain of it spreads and spreads across the white absorbent paper like some kind of plague.

"But, okay . . . Let's just say he really is there. What if he likes it better there?" I ask. "What if he's mad at me for bringing him back?"

"Oh . . . like in *Buffy*? When Willow brought her back from the other dimension when she died and then Buffy was all sad and empty inside because she hadn't been in a hell dimension at all, she'd been in heaven? Like that?" Is pauses for a second. "I felt really bad for Willow then . . . I mean like major bad. She was playing with the powers of the universe and everything, but to have ripped your best friend out of some nice happy heaven dimension especially after the giant snake thing comes out of your mouth and everything. I'd do that for you guys. Totally. Don't think that's what I'm saying."

I poke at the paper towel. "Is, I have no idea what you're talking about."

"It's a TV show," Devyn explains. "Cult classic. From the 1990s."

"Oh."

"But you get what I mean? Like you're afraid you'll take him from heaven?" Is asks.

I wipe my hands on my pants. "Yeah."

Devyn's eyes meet mine. "Zara, I've been researching, and everything that pixie"—he spits out the word like a curse—"told you seems to be true. If Valhalla exists it exists because Odin and Thor are collecting warriors for the fight of all fights. I can't believe they'd just let Nick go. I'm not even sure you can find your way there."

"Why not?"

"Well, the only information I can find says that Valkyries take warriors there."

"There's got to be another way," I say.

"There always is." Mrs. Nix appears in our kitchen. "I let myself in. Now why don't you tell me why you even want to go to Valhalla?" She looks around the kitchen, mentally calculating the situation. "Where's Nick?"

Nobody says anything.

Mrs. Nix pushes her glasses up her nose. She repeats her question, "Where's Nick?"

This time her voice gets a little bit more growly.

"You know about Valhalla?" I hedge. "So it's real? How come you've never told us about it before?"

"I only know about it because my mother told me, and when she did . . ." She pauses. Her hands go into the air like she's trying to grab the right words. "It was more like a fairy tale. I haven't told you about it because there was no need, and you, Zara White, are trying to change the subject. Where is Nick?"

Something outside screams. It's shrill and loud. Issie jumps into Mrs. Nix's arms. Devyn moves toward her protectively. I race to the window, pull back the curtain, and peer out into our front yard.

"What is it?" Mrs. Nix asks. Her voice fills with alarm.

"Pixies," I answer. "A lot of pixies. They must've just missed you."

They are twirling around in some sort of weird dance. Their feet twist over the snow in fancy, wild footfalls. Their arms reach up toward the sky. They are circling figures in the approaching dark, dancing around something.

"What if they try to get inside?" Issie asks.

I try to make out what's going on. "The only one who can come in here is my father."

"And what if he does?" Devyn asks.

I don't hesitate. "Then I'll kill him." As I search for him in the dancing forms, I notice it. How did I not notice right away? I leap back from the window. "Give me a weapon."

"What?"

"Give me a weapon," I insist. My good hand is out. "A poker, I guess. No—a sword."

Mrs. Nix slams the hilt into my hand. I rush toward the front door. "Stay here. Except Mrs. Nix. You might want to change."

"Uh-oh. She's entered military commander mode. Zara? Why are you in military commander mode?" Issie's wringing her hands but I don't have time to talk anymore.

Devyn goes to the window. "Holy—"

"What is it?" Issie shrieks but I'm already at the door, throwing it open and charging outside.

"It's Betty," Devyn answers. "They've ambushed her. She's surrounded."

Definition

Hero: you might want to be a hero if and when you and your friends are attacked by pixies. Remember, though, that heroes often die.

The wind hits me first, bringing waves of snow that obscures my vision with pure white. It only lasts a second. The snow slaps my skin and melts. I blink the water away from my eyes and charge, just rush headfirst into the pixies. My sword guides the way.

They howl. One turns, it's a man. Betty takes the opportunity and strikes. She leaps on his back. He staggers forward just one step, trying to stay balanced. Her tiger teeth sink into his neck. Even with all the shrieking I can hear her fangs drop through flesh, hear flesh rip, hear bones break as she shakes the pixie's body. He falls to the ground, limp, twitching in his Wal-Mart jeans.

"Betty!" I scream a warning.

Three more are closing in on her. She leaps from the dead pixie and growls. Her large paws leave the snow again as she turns, snapping. I can't believe this is my grandmother. She doesn't change often, but when she does it's stunning.

Something has smashed me from behind. I am falling. My trunk twists as I do. I pull my sword around and slash the air before I even see what's got me. It's pixie. It's female.

She smiles. Snow melts into her red hair, splatters over her cat pajamas and bathrobe. "Princess . . . we have you to thank."

I thrust out with my sword. She dodges it and one of her hands pins my neck. The other pins my arm. Damn, she's strong.

"How does it feel to be the one who is trapped?" she whispers. "How does it feel to be the one who is weak? The one who is about to die?"

"I don't know," I grunt. Her hand on my neck is cutting off my air. The world spins. I choke out, "You tell me."

My feet kick out in this total ninja move Nick taught us. The force of it heaves my chest up and breaks her hold. It's not much but it's enough to allow me to roll out of the way.

She falls sideways. Pixies shriek around us. Betty growls, low and menacing. The pixie lunges back toward me. My sword is slashing through the air before I think of it. The weight strains my shoulder. The blade hits. It goes through the cotton of her bathrobe. Her stomach bleeds out. It stains reddish blue. The color spreads onto the cats on her pjs. She just laughs. Blood spreads and spreads.

Someone is screaming. Someone is lifting a sword through the air and slashing it down into a neck. That someone is me. I wrench it back out.

I stand.

A life flows away below me. My third. I have killed three times. I turn away, raise my sword, and keep screaming. Things move in slow motion. Everything but me.

Devyn flies out of the house and swoops down, attacking a

pixie man with wild blue hair and some nose bling. His talons zoom in for the eyes.

My sword slashes through another pixie's stomach. He's bigger, built like a lumberjack. He staggers but doesn't fall. His eyes go wilder, even more silver. He smiles and lunges for me again.

I raise my sword but I don't bring it down. Instead, a large bear crashes into him. Mrs. Nix. They fall to the snow, twisting. Mrs. Nix makes no noise. She grabs his head in her mouth.

I turn away.

There are so many. They swarm toward us. Betty is trying to fight four at once. Her long torso shakes with rage. She's bleeding from her shoulder. I stomp my way toward her. I'm still wearing my slippers. My feet will regret that later. Right now, I feel nothing—just anger and this wild, wild need to protect and avenge.

An arrow zips through the air and stabs into Betty's side. She bucks from the impact and pain. A roar fills the air.

"Zara . . . ," one of them whispers behind me, from the woods. "Come to me . . ."

I ignore it. It's an old trick and I am so past it now. Another arrow flashes through the air. Devyn dives and grabs it in his beak. He drops it to the ground. I rush toward Betty. The pixies are closing in. I hack at the one closest to me and miss. He backs away. His long black leather jacket flaps in the wind.

"Fashion faux pax right there, buddy," I sneer. I lunge forward and yank the arrow out of Betty's fur. She howls and turns on me. Our eyes meet. Fear stills my breath. I back away one step. Something hits the wrap around my wrist. Betty's muscles tense and she leaps over my head. All I see is the white fur of her belly, giant claws, and she's gone.

Turning, I watch her land—claws out—on another pixie.

Mrs. Nix has barreled back toward the house, swatting a path clear of pixies. She leaves them writhing and bleeding in her wake. Issie stands at the door holding a crossbow. She's not saying anything, just squinting, focused. She pulls back an arrow. I don't get a chance to see where it goes. A pixie on my right has yanked back my arm. Another one bites my wrist. Pain spirals through my arm. I drop my sword. I kick back and make contact. The hold doesn't loosen.

"Fall back!" Issie yells. "Fall back! There's more! Get inside!"

Mrs. Nix lumbers up the stairs of the porch. Devyn swoops down after the pixie attacking me. His talons rip into skin. The flapping of wings smash the air around us. The pixie loosens his grip to swat Devyn off. But the other one is still sucking on my wrist. I don't have anything to hit her with. My knees. I pull one up and smash it into her chest. Nothing. I scream, still trying to reach my sword, which has sunk in the snow.

"It's got Zara!" Issie yells. "Damn you, evil pixie jerk!"

Someone yells. I can't tell if it's me or Is. "Betty!"

One of Issie's arrows zings through the air but goes wide. I kick at the pixie. She doesn't let go. Her fingers turn into claws. And she grabs for my waist, pushing me down. The pain is crazy. I'm trying to cause some serious pixie pain, but I'm failing big-time.

"Zara!" It's a male voice.

Nick? No, not Nick. It's a little lower. It's a little more husky. Something wild and blue yanks the woman pixie off of me. It's a man. A male pixie. He's howling, ferocious. His forearm smashes the woman pixie in the face. Bones break. He smiles, satisfied, and turns for me. There is blood in his mouth. It stains his teeth. He lunges for me.

"No!" I scream.

He yanks me into him. I smash my arm against his chest. Pain shudders through me. I don't care. I haul back again.

"Zara, don't." His voice is deep and familiar. His eyes, his silver eyes, meet my own. "You were supposed to call."

I recognize him even without the glamour. "Astley?"

"Hold on." He's insisting. I'm clutching at him as best I can, but my wrist wound is making it hard. He's shoving me into his chest. Pain makes me whimper. Every part of my being feels painful, sharper, while the craziness all around me dulls into a haze. It's just me and him.

"Zara, hold on!" he orders.

My face smushes into his chest. His chest is smaller than Nick's. He doesn't smell like Nick either. He is not Nick. He is Astley. My slippers aren't touching the ground anymore. He's taking me out of here, taking me somewhere safe? But just rescuing me is not good enough.

I struggle against him, try to push away. "What about Issie and Gram? I have to help."

"They're going inside. Look." He angles his body so I can see down. "They'll be okay."

Betty and Mrs. Nix can't be seen. Only Devyn is circling around the pixies, back outside again.

"He's searching for me."

"He cannot see you. Glamour. I couldn't fly anywhere without it." Astley smiles. "Do you want him to see you? I can make it so."

I think about it for a second and shake my head. "No. Then he'd come after us."

I imagine Devyn arguing with me, his eyes dark and condescending. His long fingers pointing and gesticulating. It would just slow the process down.

Astley's rib cage moves as he takes in a large breath and then he starts flying faster, rushing over treetops. I hide my face in his chest so I don't have to deal with the cold. My toes ache with the chill. I must have lost my left slipper somewhere. My wrist still bleeds but the sharp stabbing pain has morphed into a dullish throb. When he tells me that he's taking me to his hotel room, it does not make that throb any better.

He tightens his arms around me. "Something in your pocket is buzzing."

"My cell phone. I don't think I can get it now."

"Don't try, I might drop you."

I sneak a peek down at the earth below us. We're a good twenty feet above the tiny pointed spears of the treetops. "I don't want to be dropped."

"I shall not let you fall, Zara. I promise." His muscles shift. "Hold on. We're landing."

"Can you do me a favor?" I ask. My phone starts buzzing again.

"Saving you doesn't count?"

"Do not tease. We don't know each other well enough for you to tease."

"I am the king. I should be allowed to tease."

"A king. Not *the* king. Right?"

"Right." He pauses. "Is not teasing you the favor?"

"No. The favor is—can you not call me Princess?"

"But you are."

I shudder. His arms tighten around me and I say, "I know, but—my father calls me that and you know I . . ."

He finishes for me. "You do not wish for me to remind you of your father?"

"Yeah."

He nods. "Good idea. Brace yourself, we are landing now. Hold on."

I do.

Pixie Tip

Pixies can out-nasty the nastiest, even on a good day.

Astley leans forward to touch my face, maybe to apologize for the hideously bad landing, I'm not sure. I pull away a little bit. His hand falls. The motion is slow, as if we're both accident survivors, badly dazed, looking to each other for comfort but afraid to move, afraid to even exist. For a minute we don't say anything. Then my cell phone buzzes again. I can't quite get it out of my pocket because my arm is so bloody. Astley reaches down and pulls it out for me.

"You're blushing," he says.

"You just reached in my pocket. It's kind of intimate."

He smiles a wicked smile and hands me the phone. "There is candy in here as well."

"Skittles," I explain. "I like them."

We're still all tangled up. I check the monitor. I have five missed messages, all from Issie's phone. They all say the same thing. R U Ok? Where R U? When I ask him to, he texts back that I am fine. His fingers seem so mammoth on the phone's tiny keyboard. It buzzes again right away. Small Injuries. Where R U?

That one I am not going to answer because then I'd have to deal with a rescue. Still, I look around me, take in the Dumpster, the big blank two-story wall, the snow, the heating unit. Astley leans back on his heels and waits.

I wait too. I'm not sure what to do. I check out the scene a little more. He's staying at the Holiday Inn, which is kind of funny. You never expect pixies to do normal things, but I guess they do . . . or at least some of them. Megan and Ian went to high school. I'm sure some must have jobs, or else how do they get clothes? I don't know. There's so much I don't know about them.

"You're staying here?" I ask as we disentangle ourselves from behind the Dumpster.

"I admit it is not the snazziest of hotels, but there are not a lot of choices in your town," he says, snapping my phone closed. "I can fly us somewhere better if you would like."

"No." I shake my head. I brush snow off my arms, and that just makes my wrist bleed more. "I'm good."

"You are far from good." His hand clamps around my wrist, pressing against the wound, trying to stop the blood. "You are shaking. You have lost blood. It is dangerous to even attempt to kiss you now."

My heart stops. "You have to. We have to hurry."

"There are no certainties here, Zara," he says as he ushers me toward the hotel lobby door, past all the cars in the parking lot that are covered with snow. I'm a little slow because of the whole one naked foot on the snow thing. He notices. "You want me to carry you?"

"No!" Flying was enough contact.

"You are going to get frostbite on your toes."

"No, I'm not."

He stops and starts yanking off his shoes. "Take these."

My mouth drops open. He's squatting down and pushing my naked foot into his leather shoe.

"You are freezing," he scolds.

"I'm fine. Your shoes are too big anyway."

He tugs off my slipper and puts my foot in the other shoe like I'm a baby. "Then shuffle."

I protest, because truthfully I feel badly about it, even though I know that pixies can handle the cold really well. I shuffle forward. With his feet all shoeless and vulnerable, he walks next to me past a big old Chevy Suburban and some other cars. Someone's key fob clicks a car unlocked. The little beeping noises echo in the parking lot. He holds the door open for me.

As we enter the lobby, the woman at the front desk looks at us and staggers backward. She puts a shaking hand over her mouth. Her eyes are scared deer-in-the-headlights big and kind of match her over-the-top hair. Her other hand reaches out and points at us. Her bracelets jangle against each other because her hands are quaking so much.

"You're—y-y-you're—," she stutters. She shifts positions and knocks something heavy to the floor with her hips.

Astley leans into me and whispers, "I forgot to reassert my glamour and you are blue."

"Plus, I'm bleeding and you're barefoot. It looks weird," I agree as we shuffle past the rose-covered hotel lounge couches. "Poor lady."

The woman's hand, the one that's been pointing at us, drops to her side. She makes a tiny whimpering noise.

"Hey!" I scan the name tag as I approach the desk in my bizarro weird shuffly step. "Deidre. It's okay. We just came back from the freaking wildest party ever. It was so insane. Check out my skin. To die for, right? I hope the freaking dye washes off."

"Oh . . . ," she sputters, trying to recover. "Wow. Wow. Those teeth . . ."

"I know. His outfit is way better than mine. Totally unfair." I nod and use my arm to nudge Astley past the desk. Then I throw over my shoulder a little bad-girl-to-bad-girl banter. "He is so going to freaking pay for that."

"That's right, honey," she shouts to me. "Make him pay real good."

We hurry down the carpeted hall and a couple steps to where the rooms start on both sides. Astley looks at me with a completely amused expression. "Why are you saying all those freakings?"

I let out my breath. I'd been holding it, I guess. "That's what adults expect teens to sound like. The whole dumbing-down thing."

He smiles. There's a lot of teeth in there.

"Your teeth *are* scary," I say. "I do not want teeth like that."

"So . . . you are saying you do not want to do this?" He stops me with a little extra pressure on my wrist. We are in the hallway by rooms 125 and 127, according to the brass number plates on the doors. "This is your choice, Zara."

My legs don't feel steady at all. I silently start reciting phobias, trying to get a handle on things, on my fear, but it's not doing any good. I lean against the wall. "Give me a second."

He blinks and turns so I can see his face better, then seems to change his mind. His voice is calm but his eyes are super focused and hard looking. "It is an enormous decision."

Swallowing hard, I get my cell phone back and call my grandmother. The phone barely rings before she picks it up. Her voice is like a pitchfork jabbing through the air. "Zara! Where the hell are you? Are you okay?"

"Yeah. I'm okay. Are you?"

"Fine. Fine. I can take more than that crap they dished out. But where are you?"

"I'm with Astley."

"She's with Astley," she says. It's muffled. She must have turned away from the phone. "He's the king? You are with the *king*? Has he kidnapped you?"

"He saved me," I whisper.

"Zara White, you are far too smart a girl to believe that a pixie king would ever save you. You are not, I repeat, not to let him kiss you," she orders. "I will go to Valhalla to get Nick. I understand what you're thinking but this is all a manipulation. You are not strong enough to do this. Think of the long-term repercussions."

I interrupt. "I love you, Gram. You know that, right?"

"Zara!"

"I love Issie and Dev and Mrs. Nix too, and Mom, okay?" My heart lumps into my chest. It's like a hand stuck in a snowbank— raw cold pain. "I love you!"

I click the phone off before I can understand what she's yelling into it.

His voice comes from behind me. "You okay?"

Am I okay? Blood from my wrist seeps through his fingers and drips on the floor. I have no choice but to be okay: I have to be the one to do this because I am the one responsible. I went inside the house. Nick followed me there *and then he died.* And if I don't get him back, then everything inside of me will be dumped into that cold snowbank and nothing could ever pluck me out. Yeah, I am okay. I am peachy. I push the thoughts aside, stare at the ground as we shuffle walk down the hallway a little more and say, "I feel bad about the blood I'm dripping. It's on the carpet."

He laughs. "You are kidding, right? You are about to turn and you are worried about bloodstains?" He cocks his head and studies me, which makes me feel super self-conscious, and he says, "Aren't you worried about being my queen?"

I pull in a deep breath. "Look. I am scared to freaking death about all of this, okay? I am terrified about what it means to be a pixie, about being your queen and the long-term repercussions of what I'm doing. I am scared about Valhalla, that I might fail to get Nick, that he won't love me once I've turned anyway. I am scared about all the pixies running loose. I am scared that you're lying to me. I am so freaking scared. But I just have to do this. I have to do it one step at a time and if I think too much, then I won't be able to do anything. The fear will paralyze me, you know?"

He chuckles and pulls open a stairway door. "You said 'freaking' twice."

"I'm upset."

"Most people swear when they are upset."

"I'm not most people."

He takes my elbow. "I know."

He tilts his head and stares at me. I stare at him too, take in the silver eyes, the blue skin, the thick hair, the scary-sharp teeth. He brings my wrist up between us and holds the door open with his foot. "Are you sure about this?"

"Do you think I'll survive?" I whisper.

"The kiss?" he whispers back.

I don't pull my eyes from his gaze. "Yeah. The kiss. All of it."

"I shall make sure you survive, Zara. I promise." His pupils don't flicker. There are no obvious movements that show he's lying. "I need you to be fine. If you are to be my queen, then I shall need you to survive, to be strong, to help me fight."

"For the good guys, right?" I say all jokey loud.

"Right."

From behind us a woman's voice shouts, "There they are!"

We both whirl around. Deidre, the woman from the front desk, is standing with a tall, thin hotel security guard in a gray uniform and she's pointing at us, which is ridiculous because we are the only other people in the hallway.

"Pointing is rude," I whisper to Astley. "We should run."

He shakes his head. "Hold steady. Maybe I can handle this."

The security guard thunders down the hall toward us, his cheeks flapping like dog jowls, and I gasp/groan, "Maybe? What do you mean, maybe?"

Astley grabs my hand and takes a step in front of me. "Sir? May I help you?"

The security guard's pupils flare. "You hold it right there."

"Hold what?" Astley asks, and I swear I think he really means it.

"It's an expression," I hiss. "It means 'stay still.'"

"Don't get sarcastic with me, punk." The security guard stands up straighter. He surveys us. "What kind of freak are you, dressed like that?" He gestures for me to step forward. "Are you okay, miss? Has he hurt you?"

The hall seems suddenly miniscule and filled with the security guard's cologne. It's claustrophobic. Claustrophobia is the fear of—

"Miss?" his voice barks out. "Are you listening? I need you to step forward."

"She's in shock," Deidre says. For a second I wonder if there's anyone out front. I glance around while Astley starts talking again.

"Really, sir. We're quite fine. We were at a masquerade party. My girlfriend became a bit carried away and—"

"Kid! I told you to let go of the girl." Security Guy turns to Deidre. "Go call the police. I'll hold him here."

My fingers tighten around Astley. He squeezes back. "Sir, I can assure you—"

"Go now!" The guard's mouth opens wide as he shouts at Deidre. She rushes off. He steps toward us and whips out his radio.

"Glamour him; he's going for backup," I hiss at Astley.

"I'm trying," he hisses back. "I'm not the best at that kind of glamour."

The guard stops right before he raises his radio to his mouth and stares at us hard. Well, stares at Astley, really. "You match the description of those freaks who went after the Summer bus. You one of them? Don't answer. You go up against the wall."

Astley starts to move forward but I yank him back.

"Run!" I yell and throw the Skittles in my pocket at the guard's face.

Astley actually listens. He turns and I yank him toward the exit sign behind us as the security guard keys up his radio, frantically calls for backup, and begins pursuit.

Definition

Pixie kiss: the pivotal act of changing from human to pixie. It is often deadly, rarely sexy.

We rush up a flight of stairs and into another hall with the boring hotel carpet and beige wallpaper. We race past door after door until we stop outside room 259. He slides the key card in and yanks me through the door, slamming it shut behind me. We flatten ourselves against the wallpapered wall, motionless. I hold my breath. Thirty seconds later the sound of running feet fills the hallway.

"They didn't see which room we went into," he says. "We should be safe."

I swallow hard, take in the two double beds with matching brownish comforter, identical twin pillows on each, the short pile beige carpeting. There's a brass light. There are curtains, an air-conditioning unit. It looks so normal. It's just a hotel room. It's just any ordinary hotel room, but it's where I am going to lose my humanity and become . . . become something else.

"What if I am?" I blurt.

He grabs a white towel out of the bathroom and wraps it around my wrist. "What if you are what?"

"Like my father?"

"He is not the worst of us. Not by a long stretch." He ties the towel ends together.

"I know." I remember the king that almost killed Nick today. There was nothing human in him at all. "What if I become like that?"

He touches my chin. "You will not, Zara."

"You sure?"

"I shall not allow it."

He won't allow it.

Eremophobia, fear of who you are.

Ereuthrophobia, fear of blushing.

Ergophobia, fear of work.

Eremophobia, fear of who you are.

"What are you chanting?" he asks. He sits me on the floor. He stretches his legs out so they touch the bed duvet thing that drapes between the mattress and the box spring.

"Phobias. I do it when I'm scared." I cross my legs and then jerk away because my knee is touching his leg. Nick would hate this. A lump forms in my throat.

"I'm sorry you're scared."

"Yeah. Well, it'd be weird if I wasn't, wouldn't it?"

"It would."

Felinophobia, fear of cats.

Francophobia, fear of France.

Frigophobia, fear of the cold, or of things that are cold.

Eremophobia, fear of who you are.

What is the name of the phobia for being afraid of becoming

a monster? What is the name of losing who you are forever? Of your body changing so completely that you no longer recognize your former self? Because that is the phobia that is tweezing through me, plucking out all rational thought, all hope. Who am I going to be if I do this? Will I be cruel? Stronger? Will I still be me? If my body changes will I still be Zara White?

"I've been writing a book called *How to Survive a Pixie Attack*," I say. I lean my head backward to rest against the wall. "Funny, huh?"

"Funny why?" His voice is hard and clear despite how close we are, despite the bitterness that's in my own voice.

"Because it turns out I'll be telling people how to survive me."

When he doesn't respond I lift up my head so I can stare at his face. He's flushed.

"What is it?" I ask.

"You are so scared that you are shaking."

"I think we should just do it," I blurt. "Just kiss me before it's too late to do any good."

"You sure?"

I think about it, about what will happen to me. My humanity gone. My teeth no longer the same. My skin no longer the same. My blood no longer the same.

Genuphobia, fear of knees.

Gephyrophobia or gephydrophobia or gephysrophobia, fear of crossing bridges.

Eremophobia, fear of who you are.

"You'll help me?" I ask frantically. "When I come back? You'll help me so I'm not a monster like the ones who . . . like the ones that . . . I love Nick," I insist. My heart flutters hopelessly in my chest. Tears threaten my eyes.

"Of course you do," he says softly, not quite a whisper really.

I say it again. "I'm doing this because I love Nick."

"I know."

I bare my neck. "Okay, do it."

He laughs. He actually laughs. "That is not how it works. We are not vampires."

"So, where do you kiss me? This jerk pixie tried once. I can't remember what happened really well, though."

"It is your lips. Not your neck."

I remember it now. Ian's face coming closer and closer. The evil in him was like this gaseous substance in the air. He'd broken my arm. He wanted to break me. I push the memory out of my head and ask, "Will it hurt?"

"Probably. You are meant—"

Someone pounds on the door. "Security."

Astley springs up, muttering a curse. "We have to hide."

He motions for me to roll under the bed. He does too. His eyes are wide and haunted. Above us dust bunnies mingle with metal springs.

The pounding comes again. "Security."

Astley holds a finger to his lips and then grabs my hand. We are terribly close under here and I am super allergic to dust. My nose twitches. His eyes widen. A key card slides through the lock mechanism.

"Glamour us," I whisper frantically, "like when we're flying, so he doesn't see."

He cringes as if he can't believe he didn't think of it himself and then squeezes his eyes shut for a second. I cross my fingers that it works.

Heavy shoes thud into the room. A security radio crackles. The closet door slides open. The foot thuds become harder as the guard steps onto the bathroom's linoleum floor. My nose explodes. I can't help it. I start to sneeze. Astley grabs my nose hard in his hands. My ears pop. Pain ripples through my eyeballs, but there is no sound as the sneeze shudders out of me.

Still, fingers appear at the end of the bed and the dust ruffle lifts. Two brown eyes and a thin nose appear. If he reaches in he could touch our feet. I try to send the security guard telepathic messages: *Do not reach in. Do not reach in.*

The ruffle drops back into place. The feet retreat into the hallway. The door slams shut. I yank my head back to get my nose free.

"That was so close," I whisper.

His hands grab both sides of my face. "Are you sure you want to do this?"

Nodding, I make the words come out. "I'm sure."

"There is no going back, Zara." His fingers run down my cheeks, twining into my hair.

"I know."

His silver eyes are so close to mine. His breath touches the skin by my lips, just above my lips, really. "Is your wolf worth this, Zara? Worth losing your humanity for?"

"Yes, he is." I close my eyes, picture Nick and then Is, Gram, and Devyn. I even imagine Cassidy and Callie and Giselle. "They all are."

My words rest in the air for a minute. We scramble out from beneath the bed and sit there. My hands wait in my lap. My wrist is still bleeding. All that matters is that I buck up enough to do this, and that I survive; survive to get Nick back, survive and maintain my humanity too.

There is no failure allowed here.

And my fears? I've just got to push them away. Astley smells like mushrooms and man. He smells like the earth and the cold wind. I open my eyes for a second, but his face is so close that it just kind of blurs.

"I'm going to do it now." His lips are so near mine that they touch when he says the words "going" and "do."

My hand clenches into a fist. The blood seems to drip faster out of my wrist.

"Relax, Zara. It is far less dangerous if you relax. I promise." He backs away a half inch or so. I can feel it. The air shifts. I swear I can feel his longing, feel him trying to wait, to be strong.

"I feel like I'm cheating on Nick," I blurt.

"By kissing me?"

I open my eyes. "Yes."

He has put his glamour back on. He's a handsome guy again. His nose crinkles a little bit as he stares at me, trying to figure me out. "Do you think he's even going to love you after this? Your wolf's a bit of a bigot."

"I was a bigot too."

"Not anymore."

I shrug. "I don't know. Bigotry isn't that straight and easy. It isn't there and then suddenly gone. It's like a bad germ waiting to pounce and infect you even when you think an antibiotic has eradicated it from your system. But that's not the point. What the point is—is— Oh! Can we just do this?"

Without thinking about it, I reach up and grab his face with my hands. I'm not super powerful because let's face it, one arm is hurt, the other arm is bleeding, but I manage to yank his head an inch toward mine. Our lips meet. Nothing happens. It is just lips touching lips. My eyes stare into his grass green ones. He isn't too blurry now. I don't know why. I start to pull away. I am going to ask him why nothing is happening.

I don't get the chance. His hands, his uninjured hands, wrap around the back and side of my head. He pulls my face closer to him. Our lips press against each other. The world goes weightless. There is only our lips, just our lips touching each other. It is smoke. It is dust. It is light and earth and wind. The world spins away, losing itself layer by layer. I know this. I know it, but I can't stop it. I can't stop anything about it. All I know is the kiss.

Need.

That is all there is. If I could move, I would press his lips closer to mine. If I could move, I would beg him to never stop.

Words.

His lips move against mine, still kissing, but murmuring words in a language of wings and gods; the language of pixies. It has to be. His fingers spread across my hair. My whole brain throbs with words that I can't give meaning to.

Pain.

And then it all changes. The words become fire stabbing into my head. My skin burns with some sort of flame that seems to shoot right out of my neurons. His lips leave my lips and I am alone. I am consumed. I am pain. I am lost, lost, lost.

"Astley!" I gasp his name.

His hands reach underneath me, lift me to the bed. I twitch. I know I'm twitching. He smooths the hair off my forehead. "It has started. It will be okay, Zara. I will be here the whole time."

"Make it stop," I moan.

"I can't. I can only share my strength, help it go more easily for you."

"This. Is. More. Easily?"

He laughs. It's a sad sound. I try to open my eyes to see him, but I can't quite. It's like someone is rubbing red dirt into a million little cuts all over my skin. I pant out the words. The cuts spiral deeper than my skin. They twist down to my veins, my muscles, my bones.

"The process is going quickly," he reassures me. His hand rests on my forehead. "I promise you. You will survive this. Feel my hand. Feel my strength. It is yours now, my queen. I promise you. I am yours."

My head swims. Images flash in front of my eyes. Issie hopping up and down in the hallway because she managed to get a C on her physics test. My stepdad opening his arms for a big hug after I broke the five-minute-mile mark for the first time. My mom brushing my hair with my Barbie princess brush. My mom swimming with me in the pool shouting "Marco" with her eyes closed, laughing, looking for me. Betty burning spaghetti and somehow crusting it to the bottom of the pan. Nick. Nick's beautiful brown eyes. Nick writing Amnesty International letters with me, his super-big hand making the pen disappear beneath his fingers. Nick's lips, warm and wild and real. Nick lifted up into the sky.

I scream.

Astley's hand comes over my mouth. "I am going to make you pass out now, Zara. You cannot scream. We are in a hotel and people will notice. It is better this way."

The last thing that I hear is him promising that everything will be okay. The last thing I think is Nick's name, one syllable that means everything in the world to me. Nick. I hold on to that name, hold on to him, as my body spirals downward and away. But then I lose that too and the final thing I think is about me,

Zara. What will I be when I wake up? I don't know if I'll survive and if I do—I might be so awful, so horrible, that Devyn will have to kill me, or I will have to kill myself. A giant whimper fills up my soul. I may have just made the biggest, most awful mistake. I may have just given myself away.

Pixie Tip

Many pixies hide their true appearance through use of magic called a glamour. This is a good thing.

I have absolutely no idea how much time has passed but when I wake up, the hotel room looks exactly like a hotel room, only the sheets on the bed are ripped to shreds, there's blood splattered on the white telephone on the bedside table, and there's a tired-looking blond guy gripping my hand. These are pretty significant differences.

Someone moans. It takes me a second to realize that someone is me and that I'm moaning because my skin feels like it's been shrink-wrapped and ironed. My mouth aches and everything tastes coppery, like blood. My stomach groans and clenches. That's a familiar feeling—hunger.

Astley leans up on his elbow but doesn't let go of my hand. "Hello, beautiful."

"Don't 'hello beautiful' me," I whisper. My voice is so hoarse. I clear my throat but my voice still comes out weak. "I know I'm not beautiful."

He smirks. "Believe what you have to believe."

"Did it work?"

He nods. His eyes shift. "We were successful."

"You look sad."

He's still nodding, just the tiniest of movements. "I suppose I am."

The whole hotel room seems stale and dirty now. The drapes are shut over the window. The heater rumbles on, blasting out moderately hot air. Astley is in human form and wearing a gray T-shirt and jeans like any normal non-pixie person. His face is rigid. I'd say he looks sad *and* frightened. My heart softens.

"I thought you wanted this. I thought I made you more—powerful, made you more—stable or something?" I clear my throat again. "Wow, I sound like I've been smoking for fifty years."

"I am a pixie king. It is what I have to want." He gets up and goes into the bathroom.

He must turn a faucet on, because I can hear water running. My tongue sneaks out of my lips. It brushes against my teeth—my very sharp teeth. Panic hits me. I have to see. I sit up. All my muscles protest. Things pop in my shoulders and stretch along my spine. My fingers seem to all suddenly have arthritis. I reach down my leg. The anklet Nick gave me is still there. The fragile chain hasn't broken. The dolphin and the heart still hang against my skin. I start to swing my legs over the side of the bed.

"What are you doing? Lie down! Stay still!" Astley rushes back in with a glass of water. His hair is all askew and his eyes are wide. He pushes me toward the head of the bed, grabs some pillows off the floor, and says, "I saved these. I couldn't allow you to destroy good pillows."

As he puts them behind my back I ask, "I did this to the sheets?"

"You certainly did. You scratched me as well." He shows me long marks down his forearms. They are starting to heal already but it's obvious that they were deep and painful.

My stomach threatens to explode. "Oh . . . man . . . I am so sorry."

"It is normal." He grabs the glass and puts it to my lips. "What is not normal is that you are capable of sitting up already. That is extremely quick. Less than thirty hours. Most people are out for fifty at least. Not my queen."

His queen?

What have I done? I sip the water and eye him. He actually looks proud of me. Glancing down at my blue skin, I notice that the wound on my wrist is gone. Wait! My wounds are gone. I put the glass on the nightstand and start waving my arm around in the air. "It's not sprained."

"An extra benefit when you are turned by a king. I heal you. If"—he gets all sheepish sounding—"I don't kill you."

I shift my weight, swing my legs over the bed. I croak out, "I need to go save Nick."

"Not yet," he insists. His hands go to my shoulders. I know he'll push down if I try to stand up. "You aren't strong enough yet. We aren't even sure how to get to Valhalla. Rest for a minute, at least."

The world stops. Anger pulses through me, cold, blue, and icy. I can hear it in my voice. "What?"

He doesn't move his hands. "I'm asking you to rest for a moment. You've just gone through a significant change and—"

"No! What do you mean you don't know how to get to

Valhalla?" I jerk sideways to get away from his hands. "You let me change and you don't even know how to freaking get there!"

He chuckles. He chuckles! "You said 'freaking' again."

"Do not tease me." I start sputtering, I'm so upset. I roll away from him and to the other side of the bed. "I can't believe you tricked me! You're just like all the other pixies. I never should have trusted you."

"I am not like your father." His mouth hardens.

"Liar!" I start to get up but he's there before I can get my feet touching the ground. I put them down anyway and stare up at him. He's all golden and handsome with his glamour on, but it's not real. He's not human. He's pixie. And he's tricked me.

"I haven't tricked you, Zara. I just haven't told you the entire truth." His hand moves out like he's going to touch my hair, but I swat it away. His face shuts down. "We will find a way to get to Valhalla."

"I can't believe I turned into *this* for nothing." I lift up my hands. The nails are different, longer, stronger, more like claws. I repulse myself.

"It's not for nothing. We will find your wolf." I listen to his assurances and try to believe. Try to find faith in what I've done.

"And even if we don't, you're meant to turn, Zara. You are stronger now. You will be safer." He taps my fingernails. "They extend when you fight. Your sense of smell will be enhanced. You won't want to eat meat at all. My people don't get the bloodlust, because I don't really get the bloodlust."

" 'Don't really'?" I quote him.

"Not important." He eyes me. "You know, you do not ever have to see your pixie self. You could just put on a glamour right now. It will hold awhile. Then you will have to reassert it again."

I perk up a little, I think, but I'm still simmering over the Valhalla thing. Maybe I won't need him to get there, maybe Devyn and Issie can help me figure it out, so right now I have to be calm, force the ice out of my veins, my strange pixie veins, and get information out of Astley. "I don't ever have to see myself as pixie?"

"You will still be pixie. You just will not have to see it. And the world will not either, which is a good thing. The world is not quite ready for us." He jumps away and hustles over to the closet with its sliding mirrored doors. He rustles around in there for a moment and comes back with a branch from some sort of tree. He is suddenly standing much taller. "Hold this."

I take it in my hands. I can feel the life energy it used to have. It's like a sound, a resonation. It's amazingly beautiful.

"Each of us has a tree that represents our line. Your tree is now birch. It represents a purging or a rebirth, which is appropriate given that you are who you are."

I get what he means, but I don't push it. I make him work for it. My stomach growls.

He clears his throat, runs his hand through his hair, and journeys on. "You are the daughter of a pixie who has lost the way of truth. You are now the queen of a pixie who believes in honor. That is a sign of hope, of renewal for all our people. The birch represents that."

"But the birch is your tree already?"

He nods. "It is my line's heritage. We have always been the hope of the race."

"Pretty lofty there," I tease. Wait. I tease? Why am I teasing? I'm angry. I am so angry but at the same time I feel comfortable, like I finally belong somewhere.

He blushes. "I know. Just hold it, Zara. There is a ceremony I must do."

A ceremony. I don't know what to think about that. I hold my breath. I was born holding my breath. That's what my mom said. She said they had to encourage me to breathe. It was just like I was trying to kill myself as a baby, but when I finally took in air I gasped it in deep and hard like I was suddenly hungry to live, to breathe, to just be. That's how I feel now. Part of me wants to hold my breath and not let this pixie self be real. That part is repulsed, clinging to my humanity. The other part is breathing in big breaths of air, filling my new lungs with it, feeling ready to save Nick, ready to face anything.

I blink hard, try to settle down my thoughts, and ask, "Is the ceremony thing going to hurt?"

"No. The hurting is over, I swear to you. This is important though." He brushes a long dark hair off his T-shirt sleeve and drops it on the ground. "I am not yet exactly sure how to get to Valhalla, but I am positive that you have to do this and I am positive that I shall find a way to get you there, so help me, Zara. I shall not let you down."

I believe him. I think it's the way his eyes peer into mine or the way his lips move so confidently as he says the words, but I believe him. I don't 100 percent trust him. I only trust Nick and Issie and Devyn and Betty that way, but I believe that he wants to help me.

"Okay." I clench the branch so hard it makes a cracking noise. Before he can answer, my whole body twists in pain. I gasp. "I thought you said the hurting was over."

"It is!" He gently loosens my fingers from around the slender branch. "But this branch is you now. You have to keep it safe. If it burns, you burn. If it breaks, you break."

The branch suddenly seems very delicate, very precious. I can't believe he's serious.

"So all of us have a branch? All us pixies?" I spit out the word. When he nods I continue with my thought. "So if I wanted to kill that king who hurt Nick all I'd have to do—"

"Is find his branch and destroy it," he finishes for me. "But it is not that easy. Most of us have pretty elaborate safeguards."

My head jerks up. Our eyes meet. "I don't."

"I know. The tradition is that the king and queen keep theirs together." His gaze doesn't falter.

"You're asking me to trust you with my life." I swallow hard. The vertebrae in my neck crack and stretch, trying to get used to the movement.

He gestures at me. "You already have, Zara."

"True."

I flop back on the bed and close my eyes. The world spins. All the smells of the room are way more intense than they used to be. The faux-lemon chemicals from the comforters, the smell of bleach and toilet, old cigarette smoke, Astley's mix of mushroom and wind. There needs to be a turn-off button for noses. This is too much. My hands twitch against the smoothness of wood. I have to decide what to do with my branch, maybe trust Astley with my life again. It feels like every choice I make takes me farther and farther away from Nick. I groan.

"Are you in pain?" Astley's voice tells me he's hovering right over me. His smell is so intense.

I must keep from breaking apart. I must keep from breaking into myth and fable and stay Zara. I must stay Zara. Or else these new teeth of mine will rip the world apart. Or else this blue skin will glow with need and evil. "Do pixies have souls?" I whisper. I swear I can smell my words as they float out into the world. They smell like sorrow staggering into a lonely street.

The bed shifts as Astley sits beside me. "I believe we do."

"So I don't have to be evil."

His laugh is forced, strained. "Nobody has to be evil. Not any pixies or any weres."

"All the weres are nice," I protest. These words? They smell yellow like old grief.

"Not all of them. Just like not all humans are good. You know that, Zara."

I think about all the Amnesty letters I write, trying to save people, trying to convince leaders and dictators to do the right thing. Then I think about how I've killed. I've killed at least three pixies. I am both a murderer and a savior.

"What is good?" I ask.

"Acting with honor. Trying to keep others from being hurt. Trying to protect your family and friends and other people from harm."

"Even if it means hurting others."

"Sometimes we must."

I moan again, pull my branch up toward my heart, and keep my eyes closed. "The words wound. They slam into my head and they smell. The words smell like things."

His hand brushes some hair away from my face. I don't cringe. I don't have the energy. "Do you still want to see yourself?"

I shake my head hard like a three-year-old.

"Okay. Would you at least like to learn how to assert the glamour?"

"Yes." That is an easy choice. "I'd be good with never seeing myself like this."

The blue of my skin seems to shout at me. It seems so ugly now and I know that's because Nick will think it's ugly. I stare at my fingers with their fingernails that are ready to lengthen into claws and everything inside of me shudders with what I've become.

Astley's hand touches my shoulder lightly for a second. "Zara, you are going to have to deal with who you are."

"One step at a time. First you show me how to do the glamour thing. Then we figure out how I get to Valhalla. Tell me what to do."

"It is rather simple." He smiles a calm, sweet smile and his face transforms into something beautiful. He touches the side of my face with his finger. "When you were human did you ever change the pressure in your ear by moving your jaw a bit, just tightening the muscles?"

"Um . . . let me think about it. Yeah? I guess so. It made a clicking noise, right?"

"Exactly!" His voice gets the tone of a happy teacher. He presses a little on my skin. "So what I want you to do is—"

I've already done it.

"Amazing," he says, clapping his hands together, "you are stunningly impatient but a fast learner."

I open my eyes and look at my hands. They are human hands. "My teeth feel normal."

"They should. Your glamour affects you as well. You can look through your glamour and the glamours of other pixies, see us for what we really are if you want to."

He stands up and stretches, surveys the disaster that is his hotel room. I make the decision then. "Take my branch."

"Are you sure?" His eyes widen.

"I'm sure." I hold it out to him. He takes it reverently, carries it like it's a brand-new baby, and places it in the closet. He slides the mirrored doors shut. He murmurs some words in a language I don't understand and his hands seem to glow. The room becomes warmer. The smell of honey and mushrooms becomes thicker. The glow fades.

"Is that it?" I whisper, afraid to disturb anything.

"That is the first part. I have bound our branches. Our fates are now joined," he says solemnly.

"Joined." I stand up. My body protests. He rushes over, arms outstretched. He's ready to catch me, I guess.

"How are you feeling? Are you dizzy?" he blurts.

"A little." I adjust to standing up. "But good. So let's get going."

"Get going?"

"I have to save Nick." I walk across the room, grab my cell phone off the top of the television storage unit, check for texts and missed calls. There are about a thousand. The world comes crashing in. I start scrolling through the texts. It's all about me coming back, me telling them where I am, me not doing anything stupid until Betty talks to me, and so on and so on. My head spins a little more and it's not from the whole pixie transition. It's from stress. "Let's go."

My clothing situation, however, is not the best. I realize this suddenly and blush. He catches on and shows me a bag from Cadillac Mountain Sports and pulls out some green socks with smiley faces on them and a pair of running shoes. One of his people got them while I was "transforming." Thanking him, I take the socks and sneakers and start putting them on.

"Can I have a minute by myself?" I ask and then I realize what I'm doing—I'm asking him, like he controls me. He *can* control me, though. He showed me that. I don't want that. So before he can answer my wimpy question I head to the bathroom like it doesn't matter that he's the pixie king, that my needs, my emotions, are linked to his needs and his emotions.

Plus, if I am going to panic I am going to panic in private, damn it.

I shut the door behind me. The goldish handle is cold and shaking. No, it's my hand that's shaking. I haul in some deep breaths, lean against the door, grab a towel rack for balance. It stings. I jerk my hand away. It must have a little iron in it. Man . . . can I not touch anything? The towel racks are a silvery metal. The sink faucet is metal.

The entire freaking world has metal in it and a lot of that metal contains iron and steel.

I take another big breath.

Another.

I can't calm down.

The bathroom is standard hotel issue. A mirror covers the entire wall. It's positioned above the sink. There's a toilet and a shower that are beige and boring. Not everything is like that, though. The white towels on the floor are streaked red with blood. Tissues in the trash can are clumped up and crimson. There's even a streak of blood across the mirror, dried now, but still disgusting. All this blood must be mine, I guess. Astley had scratches but . . . Shuddering, I grab a disgustingly red washcloth and use it to turn on the faucet. I stick my hands under the warm running water and start scrubbing at the skin. Is it even my skin? The water only makes me feel a tiny bit better because underneath that skin is pixie. I may look human but I'm not human anymore. I am something completely different.

"What have I done?" I whisper the sentence to myself and each word takes weight, and takes hold, pushing me into something angry. I say it again, "What have I done?"

Anger slashes through me. My fist slams down into the granite sink counter. Dust flies up from the impact. I move my hand. There's a dent. I've dented the stone. How could I have? Because I'm a pixie, that's how. Wow. Just . . . wow!

I inspect my hand. Nothing is broken. If I were human things would be broken.

"I am not human," I tell myself. I don't look in the mirror. I don't want to stare and mope and question.

Well, part of me really wants to stare and mope and question, but another part really just wants to celebrate. I am strong. No. I am incredibly strong. If I'd been like this before I could have helped Nick fight that pixie; I could have protected Issie and Betty and Dev a lot more.

Gingerly, I touch the gold-colored doorknob. It doesn't hurt. I open the door and peek out. Astley's at the far end of the room, staring out the window, but he turns when I clear my throat.

"I'm really strong," I say.

"Yes, you are."

"No, I mean really strong. I dented the sink."

"Don't worry about it, Zara." His face barely moves and his tone of voice doesn't change. "It is not a problem."

Not a problem? Okay . . . I start shutting the door. "I'm going to shower."

There, I told him. I didn't ask him. I lock the door behind me, but I know he could rip it off its hinges. I could rip it off its hinges. I check out my arms, use my left hand to touch my right bicep and triceps muscles. They are granite hard. It's cool, but it feels dangerous. My happy fizzles right out because I know that I could hurt the bad guys, but I could hurt the good guys too. I hit the counter without even thinking about it. What if I get angry at Devyn and hurt him? Or anyone? What if I can't control myself, like the Incredible Hulk or something?

Astley seems very much in control of himself, but those other pixies, my father . . . Shuddering again, I take off my clothes, grab a disgusting and bloodied cloth and use it to turn on the faucet. Stepping into the shower, I start praying for the warm water to wash all my doubts and fears away. It feels good but it doesn't quite work. I rest my forehead against the cold shower wall.

"I will still be me," I tell myself, the water, the air, God. "I will still be good."

I cross my fingers. I have to.

Pixie Tip
Fact—pixies can control their needs. Fingers crossed on
that one.

After my shower I dress and head back into the bedroom part of
the hotel room. I can't believe how long I've been here alone with
him. My stomach flip-flops. He's run a comb through his blond
hair. It looks nice, calm. A muscle by his left eye twitches.

"Are my moods linked to yours?" I ask, twisting my hair up
into a ponytail like I'm all casual when really my heart is beating
eight hundred beats a minute because I'm so nervous scared. Or
maybe that's just how pixies' hearts beat.

"Not really," he says. "If we mated they would be."

I raise my eyebrows to tell him that's not going to happen and
follow up with the more important question. "Am I going to hurt
anyone? I mean, am I going to be able to control myself?"

"Not all pixies are blood-lusting monsters."

" 'Not all' isn't good enough." I start grabbing ripped up sheets
off the floor and try to stuff them into the tiny plastic waste baskets
they have in hotel rooms. "I want to know if I am going to be evil."

He crosses the room toward me, his face twisted with concern, I think. "Zara—"

"Look at this." I shove a torn up sheet in his face. "I did this, didn't I? I just dented a sink in there. I am ridiculously strong and I've seen what pixies can do, Astley. They killed Nick. They kidnap boys. They—I can't be like that!"

His hands grab me by the shoulders. "You won't be."

"How do you know?"

"I shall not let you." His fingers move slightly but he keeps a grip on me. His eyes soften. "And, more importantly, you will not let yourself be like that. That is not who you are, Zara."

For a minute we just stand there, not moving, not saying anything. "You don't think so?"

He lets go of one of my shoulders and moves some of my wet hair behind my ear. It's intimate, but I don't move away. "I promise you, Zara. You will have needs, but you can control them."

"So would my friends be safe if I were near them?"

"Of course."

It makes sense. When Megan and Ian were in high school with us they didn't just go around constantly killing. I explain this to Astley and he sits down on the bed, crossing his ankle over his knee.

"That's because their ruler had some control over his needs. There are occasional rogues who are unattached and they become . . . relentless in their desires, but we usually catch them very quickly. It is when a king such as your father loses his control that things become deadly." He seems to be choosing his words carefully. "That will not happen with me."

I eye him. "You promise?"

He nods. "I give you my oath."

The sheets in my hands seem so heavy. I try to fold them but they are unruly, too slashed and blood-hardened to obey my wants. "You have to kill me if I'm evil. That's what I told Devyn and Issie too. I'd rather die than hurt people."

"I do not know if I am capable of killing you, Zara," he whispers. He stands up and takes the sheet from me. "I do know that you are not going to hurt people. You can use your pixie strength, your reflexes, for good."

The sheets are evidence of my change. The way my brain buzzes with strength and my overloaded senses are more evidence. What do I know? I know that up until a few days ago I had never killed, but then I did—and I was human. Now that I am a pixie it is so much easier. I know things that regular people only imagine: that there are pixies and weres and even Valkyries that exist in our world; there is evil that is so thick and real that it chills your skin just to think about it. I know that needs can be controlled for years and years inside the hearts of living things; that they can bide their time as we go to school or work, snuggle in our warm beds, run with our dads on warm southern streets. They bide their time and then they strike. I hope that maybe there will be a time when those needs are controlled completely and people won't be in danger, but that time is not now, that time is not yet.

"We'll fight them, won't we? After I get Nick back, we'll get the pixies under control," I say.

"Once we determine how to get the wolf back exactly, yes." He fingers the cuff of his sweater, and even though he always meets my eyes when he talks, he doesn't this time.

I glare at him. "I am still angry at you about that."

He runs his palm across his eyes. He must be tired because even his voice is weary when he says, "I know."

There's a rap at the door. Astley looks up and glides past me. "One moment."

He moves in catlike strides to the door and opens it. There's a beautiful, tall woman, maybe in her forties, with long black dreadlocked hair. I catch the smell of her, woodsy and mushrooms, just like Astley. She murmurs in a low voice, "Did she survive?"

"She did," Astley answers.

"Remarkable. I have the information you requested."

He steps into the hall and closes the door behind him. I hurry to get my shoes on. I've been faking how good I feel. Truth is, it's like my skin has fractured and been put back on again—crooked. It doesn't matter. What matters is that I'm one step closer to saving Nick. Standing up again, I look around the room, trying to find some kind of clue—something that will help me figure out the next step. I walk to the door and pull it open. Astley's still out there talking to the woman.

She starts to go down on one knee, bending her elegant, long legs. "My queen."

"Oh! Don't do that!" I grip her shoulders with my hands and pull her back up.

Her eyes shine with tears that haven't quite made it out onto her cheeks, but she stands up. She's a good half foot taller than I am. I have no choice but to let go of her shoulders. I stick out my hand instead. "Zara. It's nice to meet you."

"Amelie." She takes my hand in hers. Something electric passes between us—a shock almost. She looks like she's about to kiss my hand instead of shake it, but Astley clears his throat and diverts her attention. Instead, she just says, "It's an honor to meet you. You look remarkably well. Usually, the change is not so"— she searches for a word and finds it, I guess—"easy."

I let go of her hand. A look passes between them as we all stand in the overlit brightness of the hotel hallway. They're hiding something. I know because the air practically shimmers with them keeping something from me.

"So, what are you talking about?" I ask.

Astley studies me. He finally breathes in and says, "She was giving me an update on the situation."

"With the pixies?" I correct myself. "The bad pixies?"

He nods.

"And . . . ," I prod.

"They seem to be calming down a little after the school bus incident." His voice and eyes are hard. "Your father, however, is missing. The other king was last spotted at Wal-Mart."

I almost choke. "Wal-Mart?"

"I know." His eyes get a mischievous look that vanishes quickly. "He is an incredible threat, Zara. If he keeps taking your father's people as he has been doing, he will be stronger."

"Which is why we have you," Amelie says.

"Because I make Astley stronger." I push my hair behind my ears. I catch myself at the movement. That's familiar. That's something I've always done. I want to reassure myself that I am still me. But I'm not, am I?

Astley clears his throat. "You will. You already do, but you will more when you come back from Valhalla, which is why we need to make sure you do come back."

At the end of the hall, one of the room-cleaning women rolls her cart to a door. The cart overflows with paper towels and toilet paper and clean glasses and regular bath towels. The piles seem pretty uneven and ready to topple over. I want to go help her. She looks up at us and raises an eyebrow. I wonder who will help her.

If all the danger that's supposed to happen really happens, if there's some sort of massive war, who will help the humans? Who will help the ones in the crossfire? Who will keep Issie and my mom and people in Spanish class and this cleaning lady and everyone else safe?

Pixie Tip

If you suspect someone is an evil pixie do *not* invite them into your house to hang. Cool pixies? Totally different. Remember: a pixie can't come in your house unless invited.

There is no way I can do this without Devyn and Issie. I need them. Due to his super-fierce researching skills, Dev might already know how to get to Valhalla. And Issie? Issie might be able to reassure me that I didn't do this all for nothing, that Nick is still alive, that I haven't been totally duped by Astley. So, I make this king—my king—take me to Issie's. We fly there again. I am almost used to being in the air. One bonus about being pixie is that the cold doesn't matter as much. It's amazing.

There is something so comforting about Issie's home. It's two stories and all-American looking. The garage is right next to the house and there are these sweet green shutters. I've never seen it in springtime but I bet there are tons of flowers planted along the stone walk. I bet there are daffodils and tulips and daisies. It warms me up just thinking about it, even though I'm so scared to see Issie, so scared of what she'll say once she knows that I've really done it. She's my best friend. I can't lose her *and* Nick. It would be too much.

And I am also scared of me. Even though I feel in control, I am terrified that some sort of crazy need will take over, and I'll just . . .

"You will be fine, Zara," Astley says.

"Are you reading my mind again?" I ask as he pulls my hat down over my ears. His hands linger there a little too long before he takes them away. This guy has kissed me. I know what that meant on a transformational level, but I don't know what or if it means anything on a regular guy/girl level — not that I really have time to think about that right now.

He brushes some lint off of his dark green corduroy jacket. "No. Just your emotions."

I make Astley stay outside. He stands on the driveway, wrapping his arms around his chest, which makes his jacket gape at the neck a little bit.

"This is going to take a few minutes at least," I tell him. I stare up at Issie's bedroom. It glows yellow from the light. I can smell Issie and Devyn in there. Issie smells like butterflies and vanilla and yellow daffodils. Devyn smells like feathers and wind and some sort of musk. Devyn. A guy. Will I want to bleed him? No. No. I refuse to let myself even think about it. It's so disgusting. I refocus. There's another smell I can't quite recognize — lavender, I think. I don't know who that is. The front door waits for me. I don't want to knock. I don't want to wake up Issie's parents.

"Can I fly?" I ask Astley, who seems to be waiting for me to go before he leaves, which is polite.

"Probably not. Maybe. Don't try yet." He stumbles over his sentences. "Usually, it's only kings who can fly. It's part of what makes us different. You can jump, though."

"Jump?"

"Jump. Big jumps. Really long or really high depending on

your need. Try that." He motions for me to jump, using his hands and lifting them into the air.

I bend my knees and focus on getting some momentum. I leave the air and thud onto the windowsill. My feet turn sideways for balance and I grip the molding. I'm too scared to rejoice in the fact that I've just jumped ten feet, but honestly? Wow.

"Excellent!" he yells. "I'm going to fly off for a bit. There are a lot of pixies in the woods. I might try to convince some to pledge to me."

"Good. Great. Uh-huh." I don't know what to say so I try, "Be careful."

My fingers are turning white from the gripping. There are some paint chips on the window casing. I wonder if they're lead. Does lead hurt pixies? I turn my attention to inside Issie's. Her room is entirely green and she has a lot of stuffed bunnies on her bed and lining the floor. That's enough to make me gasp normally, but that's not why I'm gasping now. I'm gasping because Issie is in there with Devyn. They are all spiffed up, which must mean it's the night of the dance, and they are holding hands. *Holding hands!* I want to do a happy dance right there, hanging on to the windowsill, but then I look farther into the room. Cassidy's in there too. She looks deep in thought and she's studying a bunch of crystals like they are cheat sheets for the SATs or something. This makes no sense. Why is Cassidy there? When did Issie and Devyn start holding hands? I have got to find out, but first I test myself: Am I craving anything? Do I feel out of control? Wild? Do I have needs? No. No. No and no. I bang on the window with my knee because I'm too afraid to let go.

Issie turns around and her mouth drops into a big O. She rushes over and her sweet round face shows up at the window. "Zara!"

She throws the window open, pops off the screen.

Devyn grabs her shoulder. "Wait. Don't let her in."

"What?"

Devyn scrunches his nose in a totally uncute way. His eyes cloud over. "She's turned. I smell it. Plus, look, there's dust all over the sill."

I check it out. I wonder if that's my dust or if it's from Astley. Do queens make dust?

"So?" Issie's brow furrows.

"So, she's pixie. She could hurt you," he insists, looking at me warily.

His hand moves to grab Issie's arm. It's the arm she used to open the window. Cassidy backs up against the wall. She's gripping a black crystal really tightly in her hand.

Issie's face goes cranky. "Man, you're a dork sometimes, Devyn. I mean, I love you, but you are a dork and you are way not trusting."

"You're *too* trusting," he argues.

"It's Zara!" Issie exclaims.

"She could attack us," Cassidy says. Her eyes narrow as she looks me over. "She's pixie. We don't know—"

"You told her about pixies!" I sway on the windowsill and try to give them begging eyes. "Guys? Please! I'm going to fall."

Devyn reaches under the bed and grabs two knives and a sword. He gives both the knives to Cassidy and Issie. He takes the sword himself. He and Cassidy point the weapons at me. Issie's points toward the carpet.

"Okay! Come in." Issie gestures for me to hop into her bedroom. Devyn starts to protest again and she wipes her free hand on the shiny fabric of her black cut-out dress. "My house. I get to decide. Don't eat me though, Zara. Promise!"

"Never." I slide in through the window. I want to hug Issie but I can tell she's still nervous by the way she's hopping up and down so instead I just say, "Thanks."

Devyn gets in between us, probably to protect Issie or something. He levels the sword at me. "How are you feeling?"

"Achy. Strong. Fine."

"Do you feel compelled to hurt us?" His hand holding the sword doesn't shake. His voice is all strength.

"No." I want to tell him to calm down but Cassidy is still brooding against the back wall, staring at me like she can actually see my pixie self, and Issie's getting all talky again.

"Wow. Is that all it takes? I was hoping I had to mumble some ancient Latin words or recite something in Celtic or maybe, you know, do a special dance or something in order to let a pixie inside. It seems so anticlimactic. What am I babbling about?" She shakes her head, drops her knife on the bed, and lunges forward, hugging me.

"Issie, don't!" Devyn yells.

"Devy, shut up." She is thin boned and fragile, but hugging her is still warm-good. It feels like home. She smiles super big when she lets go. "I am so glad you're back!"

"I'm glad to be back," I tell her and then I ask, "So you trust me still?"

"Of course!" Issie exclaims while Devyn says flatly, "No."

Cassidy has moved closer, her knife ready. "Issie, you should grab your knife again."

"Why? She's not going to hurt me," Issie answers. "It's Zara."

"Pixie Zara," Devyn corrects. "Not our Zara."

Not their Zara. I close my eyes for a second, trying to not let my frustration overwhelm me. Emotions are so much stronger now they are almost solid. I open my eyes and pull myself together enough to say, "I don't know what to do to convince you that I'm not going to hurt you."

Cassidy steps forward and slips in between Devyn and Issie until she gets to me. She's wearing a long beaded skirt and a couple of thin spaghetti-strap tops layered in black and purple. Her bracelets jangle on her wrist and she lifts up her hand toward my face.

Devyn starts to grab at her arm. "Be careful—"

She waves him off. "I'll be able to tell."

I have no idea what's she's going to do or even why she's doing it but I choose to stand perfectly still and let whatever happens happen. Her eyes are brown and deep. They remind me of Nick's and that's reassuring somehow. She reaches up and gives Issie her knife. Both her hands and her fingertips touch my forehead. For a second nothing happens and then I feel like I've stepped into a spa. The world is humid warm and my blood pressure drops about forty points.

She smiles. "No evil intentions. Her soul is pure."

She drops her fingers and smiles triumphantly while I stutter, "W-w-what? How would *you* know?"

Issie lifts her eyebrows. "Turns out Cassidy is part elf. Her great-great-grandfather was fae. It makes her be able to do certain things."

"Elf? Seriously?" I shake my head and then I start laughing because it's just so wild and cool and not what I was expecting at all.

"Not that much," Cassidy explains, "but enough that I can read people, tell if they are good or not, do a little magic to see what people are doing, see the future sometimes."

"That's why she was itching all the time. Elves have reactions to synthetic fibers in human clothes. It's also why she's hanging around Devyn all the time," Issie explains, flopping on her bed. She motions for me to join her and I do. "She could sense that he and Nick were different too."

"I wanted to figure it out," Cassidy explains. She goes back and sits on the floor, surrounded by stuffed bunnies and crystals.

"But I thought . . ." I don't finish my sentence because it's too embarrassing.

Issie finishes it for me, "That she liked Devyn. Yeah. That's what I thought too, obviously, and I thought Devyn liked her, but that's not what was going on at all."

"Oh," I say because I can't think of anything else to say. I want to ask about Devyn and Issie holding hands. I want to ask about it so badly but I don't know how.

"Devyn and I are a couple now," Issie blurts out.

Devyn nods. He's still got a death clutch on the sword, but at least it's not pointing at me.

"Really? That. Is. So. Cool!" I squee and launch toward Is. We hug hard and she laughs. I turn to Devyn. "It's about time."

"I know," Devyn groans and flops himself into Issie's green beanbag chair. "I was just so afraid to ruin our friendship, and I was worried about the were/human interaction, and then when we lost Nick—"

Sorrow crashes back into my chest, hard and fast. Something goes *ping* in my heart.

"He realized that life is too short and too precious, yada, yada, yada," Cassidy says. "That's not important. What's important is our next step and catching up. Right?"

I almost smile. I like Cassidy.

"Everything has gone all to hell," Devyn says. His hand scruffs up the top of his hair. There's actually product in it. He went all out for Issie.

"It's nice that you aren't zombie/uncommunicative Zara now. It's weird that being a pixie is an improvement, but I guess it's because you're hoping you can get Nick back and . . . Sorry!" Issie takes a big breath. "We've all been a little stressed since you disappeared."

"Yeah," I say, "me too."

Then they catch me up. They tell me that the pixies have been wild. There are two eighth graders missing. The pixies have surrounded Betty's house pretty much all the time. She has to make up excuses and carpool with a cop in order to come and go.

"I'm worried this was all a trick, Zara." Devyn leans forward on the beanbag. "I mean, there may be good pixies, Zara, but we don't know for sure. We don't know if we can trust them. We don't know anything. Honestly, I'm still having a difficult time trusting you and your transition despite Cassidy's reassurance. Our lack of knowledge is ridiculous. You'd think that, being weres, we'd have a clue, but we don't. We're finding new things out all the time."

"Like?" I prod.

"Like . . ." He stops for a second, thinking. "Like that Cassidy is part elf."

I grab one of Issie's pillows and hug it to my chest. It smells so human, so Issie. For a second I just want to wait here forever and let whatever happens happen, you know? But that wouldn't bring Nick back. That would just be wasting all this pixie pain, and I so want it to mean something.

Issie and Devyn have been doing this little telepathic/psychic message eye-contact thing and Devyn finally loses his aggressive posturing and returns to his normal dorky self.

"So I was doing some research—," he starts.

Issie interrupts him, all proud. "He found a professor who specializes in Norse mythology, which is just so brilliant cool. He found his number and Skyped him in Sweden and everything."

"Cool." I nod. I'm impatient to hear more.

He continues, "And I was asking him all these vague questions until he finally just blurts out, 'Are you seeing pixies? Or shifters?' And I was really hesitant about it, but I told him the truth."

"And he didn't think Devyn was nuts!" Issie covers her mouth with her hand. "Oops. Interrupting. Sorry."

"Well, from what I gathered, the professor is not fae, but he believes, which is rare," Devyn starts.

Is clears her throat.

"With our lovely Is as the exception," he adds and pets her head. She sort of wiggles. "Anyway, he referenced this ancient book, *The Vercelli Homilies*, which talks about Satan being the mouth of this goliath dragon reaching up to swallow the world. It was first referenced in 800 BC as the Crack of Doom. Fenrir was this ancient wolf monster who will be killed by Vidar. That's the myth that happened first. The Christians adopted the image."

"I have no clue what you're talking about," I tell him.

"It's the myth. It's the myth behind what's happening now. You know, with the Valhalla stuff. The myth says there will be a massive battle. Fenrir will try to swallow the world." Devyn looks to Is for help.

"It's also in *Buffy!*" Issie pipes up. "The high school was right on a hell mouth and every season Buffy had to stop the apocalypse and stuff so Sunnydale didn't get all sucked in with the rest of the earth following."

"What?" I don't get it.

"Why don't you watch *Buffy?*" Issie pouts. "I have all of them downloaded. I'm always begging you. You'd totally get this if you did."

"I don't—I—um, because I was always making out with Nick?" I say.

She presses her lips together, smiling, and then says, "Good answer."

Cassidy agrees but Devyn gets impatient. "But we don't think that's exactly what's happening here."

"No giant wolves waiting under the high school to swallow us up?" I snark.

Issie elbows Devyn. "Look! Even turning pixie has not made our Zara into a true believer. Her level of skepticism continues. Yay!"

I point at her. "No teasing. It just sounds ridiculous."

"It *is* ridiculous. The fact that I'm an eagle is ridiculous, but it is, Zara. It just is." Devyn runs his hands through his hair, frustrated. "Anyway, all of this is in the Poetic Edda. You can look it up. However, it might just be a massive metaphor for evil taking over the world and not a literal mouth of a wolf that will eat us all. I know this is hard for you. It's hard for all of us without Nick. And we thought we lost you too."

His voice breaks. Issie and I both jump up and hug him. Cassidy rubs his back. We all stand there for a second.

He breaks away first and continues. "This relates to us because

Nick was taken to Valhalla to be a warrior for when Ragnarok happens."

"That's the big end of the world fight where everything is destroyed, including heaven and hell," Cassidy interrupts, pulling her sweater around her.

"Astley told me this. I got it." I pull away from Issie and go to the window and look outside. The world is cold and quiet. I can't see Astley. I can't see the other pixies hiding in the woods waiting to pounce since it's so dark, but I can smell them. "And this big fight—you think it's going to happen soon?"

Devyn blows hair off his forehead. "I hope not."

"You've always got to root against the apocalypse," Issie says. "You know?"

"I know." I sigh. "So all we have to do is get Nick and then, you know, save the world."

Even though Cassidy is there I blurt it all out: I tell them about Astley, and how mad I am that I don't even know if Nick is alive; how freaky it was turning pixie; how I was so afraid I'd hurt them but how it's cool being so strong, and not being quite so cold. I don't tell them all the crazy mixed-up feelings I have about kissing Astley; about how I miss Nick.

"We can find out if he's alive, I think," Cassidy says when I'm done.

"Cassidy did that for us before, with you," Devyn explains. He looks at her like a proud dad or something. "She showed us you in the hotel room—"

"You were screaming," Issie says, "and shaking. It was scary because you were so pixie, you know? No offense."

"None taken," I say, but I'm not even really paying attention. I'm totally focused on Cassidy. "Can you do this?"

She nods and starts fiddling with her crystals, running a small one back and forth between her fingers. "I can try. You guys talk. I need a minute to prepare."

"I hate when she does this, actually," Issie says, and her skin pales like she's going to pass out or something. She starts hard hugging one of her stuffed bunnies, a Peter Rabbit in a blue coat. "The pixies have been tracking us. There are probably some in the woods right now. Every time we go out, we have to be careful. One grabbed Mrs. Nix."

"She got away," Devyn says.

"It's been horrible," Issie continues, "these last couple of days and we were so worried about you. Worried that you might have died—that you might have—"

"Gone all evil?" I suggest.

She nods. "Yeah."

I swallow hard. The silence in the room is unbearable. I think about the ceremony I just went through. I think about the plan, what needs to happen next. I clear my throat. My breath scissors through my chest. I press my hand into my stomach and accept what I've done. I've done it for a reason. I've abandoned my former self to save Nick, and that's worth it. It's worth it. No regrets. Issie hiccups the way she does when she's trying not to cry.

"So," I say, trying to get them to move on, to get rid of the funeral feeling, "the other anagram . . . did you figure it out?"

"No."

"Sore spot for Mr. Genius."

Devyn comes to where I'm sitting on the bed and grabs my hand. "You think he's dead, don't you? You think you've been tricked."

It's all I can do to nod my head a little up and down. "Yes." My voice is tiny again, just a frantic, desperate whisper. "And hoping that—no, believing that—he's alive is the only thing holding me together, you know? Because I just don't want to—I just can't imagine existing without him. I know that I *can* exist without him, but it would be so hard."

I lean into Issie. She wraps her arms around my shoulders and pats my head.

"I'm ready," Cassidy says.

"Maybe we shouldn't—," Devyn starts.

"We have to," I interrupt, sitting up straight again but still holding on to his hand.

Cassidy has cleaned out a corner of the bedroom floor so there are no bunnies or clothes. She's placed crystals in a circle around her and it looks like she's put some water into a salad bowl in front of her. She sprinkles water around the circle and then she reaches out her long arms and closes her eyes, mumbling something. The air suddenly feels different, charged, the way it is before a thunderstorm. Her hair begins to move around her face like there's a wind there, centered just on her.

Devyn's hand tightens around mine. A tiny whimpering noise escapes Issie's mouth and then it's like the wind that's been centered on Cassidy moves out and hits us, only it's not just wind. It's more like an electrical current, charged and seeking power. All my atoms seem to buzz and drain and shimmer somehow.

"It's draining us," I gasp.

"It will be okay," Devyn reassures me.

Cassidy no longer seems aware of anything. Her body trembles like she's overwhelmed with electricity. The lights in the room snap off without anyone touching them and there's a ghostly glow right where Cassidy is. I start off the bed. "I can't see her."

Devyn holds me back. "It's part of the process."

And then suddenly the glow changes. Gray lines shift within, turning into shapes. There's an image of a bed, and something is in the bed. For a second, I think it must be me in the hotel room again, but the bed is all wrong. This one looks like it's made out of tree trunks. The bedspread isn't standard hotel issue. It's made of fur. I squint at the image. My heart stops. There's a familiar guy in that bed. His eyebrows are a little too big on his perfect face. His cheeks are sunken in like he's lost weight but his mouth is moving. His mouth is moving.

"He's alive." I sob out the words and every single organ inside of me seems to slam into one another in some sort of crazy happy dance. The hole that dread made just fills up with hope. "Issie. Look! He's alive."

She's crying too. Devyn's hand releases mine and he pulls in a huge, heartrending breath.

Nick's mouth keeps moving.

"What's he saying?" I ask and lean closer. The image isn't perfect. It's foggy and not even in color, but I don't care because it's Nick, my Nick, and he's alive. I stare at his lips. Those lips I've kissed and lost myself in a hundred million times. They move and shape a word: Zara.

"I'm coming, baby. I'll come find you, I swear." I step toward him.

He doesn't hear me. He moans in pain and the image shivers. I grab for him, but I'm zapped back, shocked away by whatever magic Cassidy is making, and then the whole thing is gone. In just a second it blinks away and the lights turn back on. The computer hums to life. Our cell phones beep. In that same instant, Cassidy starts to fall forward but I get there and grab her before she can hit the floor. I bundle her into my arms, stand up, and carry her to the bed, trying to lay her on it as gently as I can.

Issie gasps. "You're so strong."

"I know! There are pixie advantages. I smell everything too and I can jump." I put a pillow under Cassidy's head and smooth out her hair. She looks like she's suddenly lost ten pounds. Nick looked like that too. I turn around and wipe at the tears that are still trucking down my cheeks. "He's alive, guys. Nick's alive. Do you know what this means?"

Devyn's eyes are watering too and he starts to answer but he seems too choked up to be able to speak for once and Issie just motions for me to go on, for me to say it, probably because she knows I want to say it so badly. I want to scream it from the mountaintops and every other single miserable cliché in the universe.

"It means that I'm a pixie for a reason. It means that I'm going to find Nick and bring him home," I say.

Devyn and Issie grab hands. Their fingers twine together. I notice it. I think Cassidy notices it too, because she murmurs from the bed, "So cute."

"You forgot a part," Issie says to me.

I don't know what she's talking about. My fingers flex, long for Nick's fingers, and I say, "Which is?"

Devyn finishes for her. "That we're going to help."

"All of us," Cassidy insists.

"All of us." I repeat her words and let myself smile for the first time in days. I touch the anklet Nick gave me. It's still there. It hasn't broken. We haven't broken. "Cool."

Issie checks her watch. "We are totally late for the dance."

Cassidy gasps. "True."

Devyn kind of rolls his eyes.

"I better get going," I say, but Issie's grabbed me by the arm. Anger floods through me, irrational and hard. I could totally rip free from her. I could strangle her. I could kill her. I shudder. That's what I can do—this new me. I can kill easily. But I won't. Breathing out, the anger dissipates.

"You are coming with us," Issie insists.

"I don't think so." I flash Devyn panic eyes but he just lifts his hands into the air. "Dude, I am looking for help here."

"Nick would want you to go," Cassidy says, standing up. "You need a dress. Do you have a dress? Or is it all old band T-shirts all the time?"

"Not nice," Issie says, wiping at her eyes, "but true. And we have no time for Zara to go home to get a dress. There'd be a big scene with Betty. You aren't up for that right now, are you?" Before I can answer she says, "No, I didn't think so."

I flop down on the bed. Devyn says, "I don't think Nick would want her to go without him."

"Thank you." I smile at him.

"No problem," he answers.

"Well, Nick isn't the boss of her and he isn't here and I want her to go." Issie has gone over to her closet. "Now, what you may not know about me, Zara, is that when I was a freshman I had a thing for dresses."

"She only wore dresses," Cassidy agrees. She goes to the closet with Issie. They start murmuring about colors and sizes.

"There's no fighting this, is there?" I ask Devyn.

He plops onto the bed next to me, leans back, and puts his hands under his head. "Nope. It'd be harder than killing a pixie. No offense."

"None taken." I poke him in the side. Then all the air rushes out of me. I'm a pixie. Everyone is acting like that's okay and maybe it is, but things—things are different. I am different.

Cassidy turns around holding up a deep green dress with a plunging sweetheart neckline that has all these ornate circles around the empire waist. "How about this one?"

"It's fine." I try to smile.

I must fail, because Issie goes, "What's wrong? Do you not like the dress? It's beautiful."

"No. That's not it . . . It is super nice, Issie . . ." I struggle to find the words. I sit up. So does Devyn. "I—I just don't know how this is all going to work. I'm different now . . ."

Cassidy drapes the dress over the chair at Issie's desk. She comes over and squats in front of me. Her hands grab mine. "You said it before: you are a pixie for a reason."

"How do you know?"

She tilts her head. "The elf in me."

"That's her excuse for everything now that she's out," Issie explains, "but she's almost always right."

"You must feel different, Zara," Cassidy says, ignoring her. "I know you think this is all about Nick, but it isn't. It's about you too. You changed for *him*, but *you're* the one who changed. You were brave and crazy and proactive, and Betty and Devyn have been monumentally ticked off at you this entire time, but Zara, *you* did it and it was meant to be."

Her words echo around in my head. I always think of Nick as the brave one, but I am too.

"I want you to be right," I finally say.

"Well, good." She lets go of my hands. "Because I am. Devyn, please move your guy self out of the room so we can get Zara dressed."

"Done." He skedaddles through the door, closing it behind him.

Issie claps her hands. "Good. Let's make you presentable, pixie princess."

My heart hiccups as I hear her say that word—princess—and it's like all the truth in the universe is falling down, like the descent of snowflakes taking one last trip from sky to earth before settling on the reality of what they really are.

I whisper my question, stare at myself in the mirror on her wall. "You think you can?"

"Anything is possible. Right?" Issie pauses and answers her own question, grabbing a hairbrush. "Right."

And the thing is? She *is* right. Anything is possible. I am a pixie for a reason. I am Zara—a different Zara, but still Zara. What happens to us all is partially up to me and it is my job, my duty, to protect my friends. So that's what I will do. That's what the pixie in me makes me capable of.

"Make me presentable, guys," I say, standing up. "Make me look like a queen."

Acknowledgments

Every once in a while a woman is lucky enough to meet her own John Wayne, a cowboy who knows how to love and be loved, who knows how to treat her and be treated, who knows what it is to be a hero kind of man and who occasionally rides off with a writer into the sunset after he's carried her over far too many swamps and rivers and fended off the rattlesnakes and bears. I am so lucky to have you. I love you. Thank you. This one is for you.

Thanks to Emily Ciciotte for being made of awesome even though the phrase makes her cringe. Every day you teach me what brave is, Em.

Thanks to Betty Morse, Bruce Barnard, Lew Barnard, Debbie Gelinas, and Rena Morse for being such a great family.

Thanks to Bruce especially for teaching me what it's like to face your own pixie.

Thanks to the Bar Harbor and Mount Desert Police Departments (with a special thanks to Sgt. Shaun Farrar, Marie Overlock, and Chief Jim Willis) for giving me the tools to help me understand their world and for being SO patient with me—especially you, Marie. You are all heroes every day.

Thanks to Michelle Nagler, Caroline Abbey, Deb Shapiro, and the crew at Bloomsbury. You all are so patient and work so hard. This would not be a story without you, especially you, Michelle. Seriously, you make me wonder how a human being can be so smart and talented and amazing and have such a great gift for story (and um . . . gift of patience too).

Thanks to Edward Necarsulmer IV. You are way more than a fantastic agent; you are the best kind of human and philosopher and friend. I do not know how I would survive without you. You say I give you faith? You give me strength and wisdom and kindness every single day. And that goes for the beautiful and brilliant Erica too! Thank you for keeping me sane and strong and for showing Em the best of New York and the best of people.

Thanks to Jennifer Osborn, William Rice, Steve Wedel, Devyn Burton, Chris Maselli, Laura Hamor, Tamra Wight, Renee Sweet, Emily Wing Smith, Evelyn Foster, Melodye Shore, Jacob Day, Dorothy Vachon, Kelly Fineman, and my friends on Facebook, LJ, MySpace, and who have emailed me. You make the world and my life so much better! Thank you so much for helping me through a tough kind of year. Strudel for everyone!